W9-CFG-703

THE SORCERER'S HOUSE

THE
SORCERER'S
HOUSE

GENE WOLFE

A TOM DOHERTY ASSOCIATES BOOK
NEW YORK

This is a work of fiction. All of the characters, organizations, and events portrayed in this novel are either products of the author's imagination or are used fictitiously.

THE SORCERER'S HOUSE

Copyright © 2010 by Gene Wolfe

A Tor Book
Published by Tom Doherty Associates, LLC
175 Fifth Avenue
New York, NY 10010

www.tor-forge.com

Tor® is a registered trademark of Tom Doherty Associates, LLC.

Library of Congress Cataloging-in-Publication Data

Wolfe, Gene.
The sorcerer's house / Gene Wolfe. — 1st ed.
p. cm.
"A Tom Doherty Associates book."
ISBN 978-0-7653-2458-0
1. Ex-convicts—Fiction.   2. Abandoned houses—Fiction.
3. Supernatural—Fiction.   4. Magic—Fiction.   I. Title.
PS3573.O52S67 2010
813'.54—dc22
2009040726

First Edition: March 2010

Printed in the United States of America

0 9 8 7 6 5 4 3 2 1

To Neil Gaiman,
the best of writers and the best of friends

ACKNOWLEDGMENTS

I would like to express my gratitude to David G. Hartwell, Stacy Hague-Hill, Vaughne Lee Hansen, and Christine Cohen.

Dear Shell:

I promised I would write you after I got out, and I like to keep my word. I am in Medicine Man, at a motel too cheap to supply stationery. Envelopes and this notebook filler from Wal-Mart will have to do. God knows I do not miss the screws or Building 19, but I do miss my friends. You most of all. You and Lou.

No job yet and none in sight. I would try somewhere else, but I cannot afford a bus ticket until my allowance comes. Not that I am flat. Not yet. I am going to try to get my brother to front me some money if I can. He owes me not one damned thing, but he has plenty, and three or four hundred right now would mean the world to me.

Still, I may be able to score some cigarettes if you need them. Anything like that. Let me know. Riverman Inn, 15 Riverpath Road— Room 12. I do not know the zip.

———

Yours,
Bax

Dear George:

This letter will surprise you, I know. You and I have been e-mailing since my conviction. Twice a year, perhaps, if not less. And sending Christmas cards; or rather, I have sent them. I hear from Millie by phone when somebody dies. Why a letter now?

I know, but I doubt that I can explain in a way you will accept as sense; you have always been the hardheaded practical one, and I have admired you for it much, much more than you can ever have realized.

Yet I, too, can be practical at times. As you shall see. Practical and, in a perverse way, fortunate.

I am living now in my new house, which is in fact a rather old one. It is not large as such houses go, I suppose. Five rooms downstairs, plus bath. Four bedrooms upstairs, plus bath. I got it by being practical, George, and it is quite a story.

I had been staying in an exceedingly run-down motel, the Riverman. There I had only one room, although it had a hotplate and a tiny refrigerator. (A room that was always more or less dirty, I might add.) The manager's name was Mutazz something, and he cannot possibly have disliked me half as much as I disliked him. I know he cannot have, because he would infallibly have poisoned or strangled me if he had. He was quite definitely (indeed, definitively) of the poisoning or strangling type. "A thief by instinct, a murderer by heredity and training, and frankly and bestially immoral by all three."

Now you see, I hope, why I chose to write a letter. If I had e-mailed you, you would never have read this far. As it is, you will have already thrown down my poor little missive in disgust at least once. I am not asking, George, because I know it. I understand your character, which is choleric to say the least. If I have been fortunate just this once, you have picked it up again.

Or perhaps your sainted Millie will have fished it out of your wastebasket and read it. Perhaps she is telling you about it now as the two of you lie abed. Like that poor girl in the Arabian Nights, she hopes to keep talking until you fall asleep.

Do you think any of that matters to me? I am tempted to post this to myself.

Now about the house. Please pay attention. It is important to me at least.

It stands half a mile, perhaps, from the Riverman. I had noticed it more than once, a white house in good repair but a house that had clearly been vacant for some time. A few windows were boarded up, and the lawn was full of weeds; a few days ago, I investigated further.

The front door was locked, as I expected. The back door was locked also; but a small side door had been broken open. I went in. A vagrant had certainly camped in the house at one time. He had built a fire in one of the fireplaces, had cooked on it, and had slept, apparently, on a thin pad of newspapers laid before it. The papers were more than a year old.

It occurred to me, George, that I might do the same. There were disadvantages, true. There was no running water, and no electricity.

Ah, but consider the advantages! No rent to pay. None at all. Several rooms at my disposal instead of one small bedchamber. No sinister landlord lurking over my shoulder. I moved in the next day.

Long before I had gotten settled, it had occurred to me that I should make the place as respectable as possible. Thus I would be seen by my few neighbors as the legitimate occupant of the house. No one calls the police because a householder is living in a house.

It had been the lawn—or rather, the lack of one—that had called my attention to the house. The same would be true of others, beyond all doubt.

I called upon my nearest neighbor, an elderly widow whose own lawn was considerably overgrown. "Do you have a lawn mower, madam?"

Well, yes, she did. But she was too old and ill to mow. A man was supposed to have come to mow it, but . . . She hoped the town was not too offended. Would there be a fine? She didn't know. . . .

And so on.

I explained that I had moved into the house down the road. Most of my household goods, I said, were still in storage. If she would lend me her lawn mower, I would be happy to mow both lawns.

She was delighted, and invited me to dinner.

Knowing you as I do, George, I anticipate that you will accuse me of welshing on my promise. With a dinner and the old lady's friendship in sight, I did no such thing. I mowed both lawns, and trimmed them the next day.

The windows were next, obviously, and presented several difficulties. I would have to knock the boards off, cut glass to fit, and putty it.

Think of me as you will, George, I am nothing if not resourceful. Old Mrs. Naber's garage, where her lawn mower was kept, supplied a rusty hammer. New houses were being built at a location I sometimes passed on the bus. Though I usually keep very regular hours, I boarded the bus late one evening and got off at a stop near the construction site. It supplied glass, and—ah, miracle of miracles!—a half-filled can of putty. I put the latter in my coat pocket, tucked some glass under my arm (it was still paper-wrapped, and might have been anything), and walked home.

Next day, the hardware store supplied a glass cutter at a very reasonable price. I used a plastic knife from Wendy's for a putty knife and, after wasting one sheet of glass, did a very creditable job on the most visible of the broken windows.

Now occurred events so strange that you are quite certain to dismiss my recitation of them as lies. You will say, "a pack of lies," if I know you. And I do.

As I was repairing the window, it had struck me that it might be possible to negotiate an agreement with the owner of the house—assuming that someone owned it. I would maintain the house, as I had been doing already. The owner or owners would pay for more glass, paint, and so on. They would also pay the utilities; and I, in recompense for my work, would live in the house rent-free.

It seemed to me a reasonable arrangement, and one to which they might very well agree. I called upon a real-estate agency. They made inquiries for me, and were able to direct me to the correct one. In fact, the nice young woman there who assisted me even set up an appointment for me.

"His name"—I recall her exact words, I believe—"is Baxter Dunn. Oh? Yes, I see." She covered the mouthpiece with her hand. "Tomorrow, Mr. Dunn?"

"Certainly," I said.

"At eight?"

I nodded.

She smiled as she hung up her telephone. "She was expecting you." It seemed oddly phrased, but I did not question her about it. She gave me her card—Doris Rose Griffin, R.E.C.—and expressed her entire willingness to assist me in any matter concerned with houses, properties, or undeveloped land, and shook my hand heartily.

Her smile, if you will pardon a bachelor's weakness, made me wish that I had some such matter to lay before her.

That night I slept well, foreseeing a comfortable future. With no rent to pay, I might buy small comforts with which to furnish the house: a gas ring, a cot, and an inexpensive but comfortable chair. Even a table, I felt, was not beyond the realm of possibility. Soon I would be vastly more comfortable than I had been at the Riverman.

I was in for a rude shock, George. I will not conceal it. I had, all unknowing, underreached myself.

But first . . .

Not long before dawn I was awakened by stealthy footsteps. Throwing aside the blankets I had taken from the Riverman, I rose and found my flashlight. The tread was light, but very real. Several persons were walking about upstairs.

There is only one stair in the house, or so I believed at the time. I mounted it step by slow step, making no more noise than absolutely necessary. With every step a new question occurred to me.

Who were the intruders?

What did they want?

Were they armed?

How might I expel them without making enemies?

None of which were in the least relevant. I saw the glow of a candle and directed the beam of my flashlight toward it. The intruder who held it dropped the candleholder with a bang (at which the candle went out), and fled toward a window, dashing through it as though it had been an open door.

I ran after him, having seen enough to know that he was a boy of thirteen or fourteen. I cannot tell you, George, how vividly I pictured him lying on the ground fifteen feet below that window with a broken leg.

Or a broken neck.

Raising the window, I looked out. He was not there. My light probed every shadow, but he was not to be seen. At last I went back downstairs and circled the house. No boy. No loose white shirt. No dark breeches. No shoes. No anything.

At which point I concluded, as anyone would, that the fall had not injured him seriously and he had made off. In the morning—but it was almost morning already, and I had an appointment at eight at

Murrey & Associates. It is late in the month, and the state of my finances dictated foot transport.

For some reason I had anticipated that the office would be small and old, I suppose because the agency in which Doris Griffin worked had been of medium size and fairly modern.

I had been wrong on all counts. It was not an office at all (in the sense I had intended) but a private house, large and well kept. Martha Murrey greeted me at the door. Since I shall be saying a good deal about her, I had better describe her. At a guess she is in her late forties. She is tall rather than short (by which I mean a few inches above average height), and has a good, slender figure. I found her sparkling blue eyes and rich brown hair quite attractive.

"Good morning, Mr. Dunn! Good morning!" She shook my hand. Women in real estate have developed their own style of handshaking, I find: firm, brief, and vigorous.

I apologized for my appearance.

"Travel! Believe me, I understand. I've done a great deal of it. Once, believe it or not, I caught the shuttle from here to Chicago, waited a couple of hours in O'Hare, had a one-hour layover in Denver, laid over at LAX, and arrived in Honolulu a complete scarecrow. I was stopped by a policeman who thought I might be deranged, and to tell the truth by that time I was. Have you had breakfast?"

"To confess the guilty truth, Mrs. Murrey, I rarely eat it. It's a bad habit, I know. But I like to rise at dawn like the Greeks of the classical period, spit on my hands, and get right to work."

"You'll work much better after scrambled eggs, toast, and—do you eat pork?"

"I'm a stray dog, I fear." I sought to soften it with a smile. "I eat whatever I can find."

"Then you'll find bacon in my breakfast nook. Do you have any objection to cheese?"

"None, I assure you."

"Scrambled eggs with a little sharp Cheddar. Perhaps some chopped onions and bell peppers?"

She waited for me to object, so I said it sounded delicious.

"It will be, Mr. Dunn. I'm no great cook. I've been much too busy making money all my life to learn it. But I can do a few simple things well. Follow me. Have you seen your house?" She was already hurrying down a bright and gracious hall toward her kitchen.

I said I had.

"It's in poor repair, I'm afraid."

"It is," I said, "but there's nothing I can't take care of. That's what I wanted to talk to you about."

"I quite understand. We've two good plumbers in town, Mr. Dunn. I recommend them both, and I'll give you names and address." Mrs. Murrey was breaking eggs. "The only electrician you should even consider is KJ&A. They charge—is that a joke?" Her cheese grater spun.

"It is, and a good one."

"They charge, but you get quality work. The others are cheaper and give you a free fire. Now for plastering—"

I fear I interrupted. You, dear brother, are forever interrupting me. Or at least you were, in the old unhappy days when we still met face to face. You accused me of being long-winded, an accusation that often droned on for five or ten minutes at a stretch. You, therefore, are not to fault me for interrupting Mrs. Murrey; this although I fault myself.

My interruption: "Might I speak about the electricity before we go further? It's shut off."

She stopped her pepper chopping long enough to admit that it was.

"I would like to use power tools." I forbore saying that I hoped to persuade her to pay for them. "A quarter-inch drill and a little sander at the very least. Without electricity that will be impossible."

"Don't worry about a thing, Mr. Dunn. Are you of Irish descent, by the way?"

"Scottish by adoption, and believe me I am as close-fisted as any Highlander."

"Scots together then!" This was accompanied by a bright smile and a second handshake. "I'll phone today, but the power company may take a week to turn it on. Will that bother you?"

"Yes," I said, and made it fairly forceful. "I don't mean to give you trouble, Mrs. Murrey, but it seems certain to make things more difficult."

"Then I'll keep after them. You keep after them, too. Will you want a phone? Landline?"

"You spoke of plastering. Quite frankly, I wouldn't do it without heat. Getting the gas turned on would be more advantageous than a telephone."

"I'll do it. That won't be any trouble." She looked down at the eggs she had been whisking. "Time to start the bacon."

It lay sizzling in the pan in less time than it has taken me to write about it.

"See this? It's clean, I promise you. I'm going to put it on top. That's the secret to cooking bacon right, Mr. Dunn."

I admitted I had not known it.

"You're married, I take it?" She was looking at my hands.

"Why no," I said.

"Now the eggs in this pan, and only a little cooking is plenty. Scrambled eggs cook after they leave the pan." The whisk kept busy. "The main thing now is not to leave them in too long and to make certain that everything cooks equally."

"I see."

"I got so busy talking I forgot about the toast." She smiled, begging pardon. "There's the bread. Would you pop four slices into that toaster for us?"

I did.

"Are you divorced, Mr. Dunn? I am."

I shook my head.

"A widower, then. I'm terribly sorry!" Out came the eggs and into a willow-pattern bowl.

"No," I said. "I'm afraid I'm just an old bachelor, Mrs. Murrey."

"You're not old!" Plates, silverware and glasses, all very swiftly indeed. "Orange juice? Milk? I never drink coffee until I've eaten. Making good coffee requires too much attention."

"Might I have both?"

"Oh, absolutely. You must be thirsty."

"I am. I've been working in your house, you see, and there's no water."

(A man came to turn on the water, while I was writing about Doris Griffin. It would have been pointless to write it then, George, as I'm sure you'll agree.)

The eggs were delicious, and I told Mrs. Murrey so. I could easily have eaten all the bacon; but my self-control, which invariably fails to keep me at a desk for more than an hour or two, was steely now. I ate two luscious strips and left her four.

"I'm sure you're anxious to get the deed, Mr. Dunn, but I wanted to explain about the money first."

It seemed possible, even if it was not probable, that I might be paid. I told her, "Very little has always been enough for me."

"There isn't any. It's all gone. The original fund was twenty thousand. Perhaps you know?"

Busily chewing toast, I shook my head.

"Presumably Mr. Black was thinking only of the taxes, which at that time were less than two thousand a year. They've gone up, however."

"I understand."

"There have been maintenance costs, too. Maintenance can be quite costly."

"It need not be," I told her. "Not if I do it."

"Are you a do-it-yourselfer, Mr. Dunn?"

"A jack-of-all-trades, and good at some." I am not skillful in modesty, George. You are surely aware of it. Even so, I made the attempt.

She smiled. "Just the sort of owner the old Black place needs. It was originally painted black. Did you know?"

"Why, no. I had no idea."

"A&I Properties had it painted white the first time it needed paint, and I don't blame Mr. Isaacs a bit. I'd have done the same thing."

"So would I!"

"Thank you. Five years ago, it needed repainting again. Needed it very badly. So I had it done."

She waited, seeming to feel that I would berate her for it.

"White, naturally."

"Yes, white. I could've had it dun, of course." She laughed nervously. "I thought of it, but it wouldn't have been very attractive."

I nodded. "A yellowish gray, isn't it? With darker mane and tail. Horses are that color sometimes. Do you play the races, Mrs. Murrey?"

The question surprised her. "Why, no."

(This is getting lengthy, I find. I shall switch to the other hand.)

"I did for a while," I said. "It cost me quite a bit of money in the long run, though I enjoyed it at the time. I've always liked horses." I was struck by a thought, George; no doubt the same one has occurred to you. "You know, I was about to say that our family name is taken from the town of Dunmore in Scotland, and had no connection with the color; but I suppose the town's name may very well refer to it. I can easily imagine a yellowish-gray moor."

Mrs. Murrey chewed, swallowed, and looked baffled. "It would have cost extra to have it painted that color, I'm sure. Do you think it would be attractive?"

"Not really."

"Anyway, painting it used up the rest of the money. I haven't been able to do much of anything since. Frankly, Mr. Dunn, it's a wonderful relief to me to be able to turn it over to the new owner." Mrs. Murrey reached across the breakfast table, and we shook hands again. I have found that real-estate people are great handshakers, George. Excuse me if I have said that already.

I intended to explain that I was not a buyer, but she had gone before I could get out the first word. There was just time enough for me to borrow a bite of scrambled eggs from her plate before she returned, and I made the most of it.

"Here's the deed, Mr. Dunn. As you can see," she pointed, "your name is already on it. You don't have to register it again. A&I, and I subsequently, have managed the property on your behalf. That was in accordance with instructions left by Mr. Black. Would you like to see them?"

I shook my head, which was an error. I admit it, George, although you always say I will not own to having made a mistake. I ought to have read them and asked for a copy. I suggested coffee instead.

After two cups of her truly excellent coffee, I left Martha Murrey & Associates with the deed in my pocket—left hoisted very high indeed upon the horns of a dilemma. I find myself the owner of a valuable piece of property; but the taxes are in arrears, the utilities will doubtless bill me at the end of this month, and I lack the pecuniary means to restore it to salable condition.

I will not ask you for a loan, George, having sworn that I would never do any such thing again. But if you were to send a few hundred dollars to me at the address above, I would undertake upon my honor to repay three for two as soon as the house sold.

Please consider it. Look upon it as an investment rather than a loan to your brother.

Yours sincerely,
Bax

Dear Shell:

I have a house now. It is a little run-down and there is no furniture yet, but I seem to own it (I have the deed) and I am living in it. That is why I am writing you. It is a big place, and if you needed a place to crash, you would be more than welcome anytime.

The side door is a problem. Somebody broke in a while back, and now kids come in at night—or that is how it seems. There are funny noises and so forth. I am going to nail it shut.

As I said in my last, I have not found work; and to tell you the truth, Shell, for the last month I had pretty much stopped looking. I came to Medicine Man to get away from my brother George and his friends (the people whose money I took) and the university. Fine,

I did. Nobody knows me or knows I have been in prison. But there are no jobs worth having. I even tried to get on as a substitute teacher at the high school. Their list is full. Young people leave this town to find work.

Now I might start looking again. Meantime, I am trying to fix up this house. (I keep finding more rooms and more broken windows.) I learned quite a bit in the woodshop and on the maintenance crew, and I have always been handy. When I get it fixed up, I will probably sell it or at least put it on the market. Meanwhile, I have this big house with running water, and I am doing all I can to get the electricity turned back on. It is hard with no money—I am sure you must know all about that. But my allowance will be along soon.

You will be welcome anytime you get out.

Yours sincerely,
Bax

Dear George:

This is written largely to clear my mind, but it gives me an opportunity to mention an unfortunate deficiency that I should have brought up in my previous letter.

You may have been trying to reach me by e-mail, no doubt because you want certain points clarified before you undertake the highly profitable investment I recommended. I no longer have my trusty laptop, George. I was compelled to put it in pawn to pay my rent at the Riverman. Thus far—I am not complaining—no means has appeared by which I might reclaim it. Soon, I hope.

Meanwhile, you may reach me via snail mail. Within the week, perhaps, I will have a telephone; but of what use is that to us when you will no longer speak to me? (Should you abrogate your boorish resolution, allow me to recommend Directory Assistance. At present, I do not know my number.)

Now to the principal business at hand.

George, I find myself in possession of a fascinating apparatus. I do not know what it is or what purpose it may serve, and yet it must *have* a purpose—someone went to great deal of trouble to make it.

You may recall the young prowler I surprised in this house. Yesterday it occurred to me that the candleholder and candle he had dropped might be of use, and I went to find them. As I was looking (it was already dark, so that I had to search by flashlight), I recalled that he had been carrying something else as well. Then that he had appeared empty-handed when he fled to the window. Had he dropped that, too? As it transpired, he had.

It is of some yellow-brown metal I believe must be tarnished brass or bronze. Its frame (as I style it to myself) is perhaps ten inches by ten. (The width of my thumb, George, is my measure for one inch. I measured it in that fashion just now, having it before me as I write.)

Within this frame are three concentric rings. In the center is a disk graved with a sort of arrow or pointer. One may move the rings independently for the most part, though at times the movement of one occasions the movement of another. At first I thought they were merely catching or sticking, but the movement is sometime retrograde. The pointer can be moved independently of all three, but at times moves of itself. If I were forced to guess—and I am—I would guess that the rings contain hidden magnets to which the pointer responds when they are aligned. This seems anything but likely, I confess; but I can think of nothing better.

On both sides, the frame, rings, and pointer are scribed with strange glyphs. There are stars of various kinds, shaded circles that may represent the phases of the moon, a horned skull, and a great many more that I could scarcely sketch, far less describe. Some may be indecent. Some appear menacing.

Today I carried it to the pawnshop on Broad Street, that being the only establishment in town that might, I thought, be interested in such a thing. The graybeard who operates the shop examined it carefully, as I wished, and at last made an offer which I declined.

It was not because the paltry price he suggested meant nothing to me; on the contrary, those meager dollars would have bought beans and bananas enough to keep me fed until my allowance arrived. Two considerations moved me, both strongly. The first was that I feel quite confident the apparatus I have described is worth thousands. And the second (which you will already have anticipated) was that the apparatus is not mine. What if the boy were to come to my door and request its return? What if his mother or father came?

I returned home, as I have indicated, disappointed and hungry, but still in possession. I was toying with it when I observed that all three rings bore glyphs suggestive of fish. I lined them up and directed the arrow toward them, then went a-fishing.

Here, George, I must describe my grounds, which I have scarcely mentioned to this point. My house has its back to the river. Behind the house is a considerable lawn. (I know, for I have mowed it.) Behind that is a patch of wooded wild ground that slopes fifty feet or more to the water. It is from this wooded patch that I obtain fuel for my fire.

It will not surprise you to learn that I possess no fishing gear; I was forced to improvise. String became my line, a safety pin my hook, and so forth. Bait offered no difficulty, since this soil shelters a plethora of worms. I fished, as I said; but I caught nothing. My lucky charm (as I had hopefully thought of it) had brought not a single bite.

Day ended. I gathered wood, returned to this house, built up a small and somewhat smoky fire, lit the boy's candle, and immersed myself in Thucydides.

My reading had just reached the bit about the Spartan army besieging Oenoe when it was interrupted by a loud and persistent pounding at the door. I opened it, expecting the boy's parents, or—just possibly—the boy himself.

In that I was wholly wrong. The middle-aged man who had knocked smiled broadly, introduced himself, and shook my hand when I responded.

"I was getting worried about you," he said. "At first I thought you'd gone to bed, because the house is so dark. Then I saw your fire through the window, and for a minute I thought the house might be on fire. Power failure?"

"No power yet, I'm afraid. The company's supposed to hook it up, but they haven't done it. I'm camping in the house for the present. No power and hardly any furniture." (That last was a lie, George. It slipped out of itself, and I sincerely regret it. The truth was, and is, that I have no furniture at all.)

"I see! I see! Say, neighbor, do you know about oil lamps?"

No doubt I smiled. "Only in old books, I'm afraid. Have you got one?"

"Sure do, and I'll lend it to you. Gives a hell of a lot more light than that candle. Just give me a minute."

He hurried off to his truck, which was parked in my driveway, and returned a few seconds later with a tall lamp and a bottle of what proved to be lamp oil. Inside, he showed me how to fill the reservoir and manage the wick. "This right here will give you as much light as a good reading light, and it'll burn just about any kind of vegetable oil. Believe that? I'll burn olive oil. Burn lard, too, or kerosene."

He lit it from my candle and blew the candle out. As he had promised, its clear, bright light was amazing.

"Now what I came about was fish. I been fishing up to Brompton Lake and caught a lot, so I've been giving some to the neighbors. Like a couple? They'll be good eating."

"I certainly would. And thank you."

"How 'bout three? Give you three easy as two."

I admired his fish, listened with proper appreciation to a (thankfully) brief synopsis of his adventures that day, graciously accepted three fish of medium size, thanked him, and promised faithfully to return his lamp as soon as my electricity was on.

His fish—when I had leisure to examine them—proved to be a catfish, and two others that may perhaps have been bass. My lengthy sojourn at the Riverman had left me with a small frying pan, salt, and pepper. I filleted one of the bass in record time and cooked it over the fire.

I was desperately hungry by then, George. I know my plight will not move you, but I was. I do not know when I have eaten anything better than that fish.

The second bass was filleted, cooked, and eaten only slightly more slowly.

Had the catfish retained a spark of life, I think I might have carried it down to the river and released it. It did not, and I knew that it would spoil unless I cooked it at once. My faithful paring knife opened it as it had the others, and I gutted it, as I had the others, on a sheet of newspaper.

A gleam caught my eye. I shall always remember that moment.

It was—and is—a ring. I extracted it and washed it at the old sink in the kitchen. The setting is simple in the extreme, though somewhat massive: a ring of gold rising to grasp a gem that winks and glows in the lamplight like nothing I have ever seen, now a reddish green and soon a greenish red, both touched with yellow and black.

I ate my catfish slowly, enjoying it but full of fish already, and more full of thoughts. Finished it, cleaned up, and began this letter.

Something has changed, George. I feel it, although I cannot put my finger on it. My luck? That is what I would like to think. If I had funds, I would lay a bet.

But I have been down that road before. No doubt I would go down it again, though the very thought sickens me.

I have been given three fish. Three fish, I feel, ought to signify something; but I have no idea what. I have been given—no, loaned—a lamp. Rubbing the lamp (yes, I tried it) avails nothing. And yet . . .

I found a ring in a fish's belly, like a boy in a fairy tale.

Suppose that all this had happened when we were boys, George. What fun we would have had! Now I am only a man, alone in a dark house and a little frightened.

———————————

Yours sincerely,
Bax

Dear George:

My first thought upon awakening was to take the ring to the pawn-shop on Broad Street—the place that has my laptop. I recalled the very low price I had been offered for the apparatus the boy had left behind, however, and thought better of it. A little farther along there are several jewelers. I took it to the nearest.

He looked at it and shook his head, looked at the stone through his loupe and shook his head again. "Just costume jewelry, sir. I don't want it, and I doubt that anybody does. A glass jewel and what looks to me like a brass mounting. It's old, but it never was valuable and never will be."

And in all honesty, George, it looked very ordinary and cheap indeed as long as it was in his hands. When he laid it on his counter, the jewel began to glow again. I slipped it back on, and when I saw it in the sunlight I seemed to have a fortune on my finger.

"To you, Bax." Isn't that what you will say? "Just to you."

Well, no doubt you are right.

Home again and wishing for breakfast, I found mail. The return address (I have it here) reads Country Hill Real Estate. I confess it took me a moment to place the name. Let me transcribe the entire letter:

Dear Mr. Dunn,

May I ask a favor?

Our management here has instituted a new policy. Once per week we must lunch with a prospective client. (And write a one-page report when we return to the office.) I need a *prospective* client for this week and thought of you. You don't have to buy or sell anything, you understand. How are you making out with your new house? Tell me that, and we're (I'm) in.

Lunch will be on me. I'll put it on my expense account, and Mr. Hardaway will see it there and pat my pretty little head.

Anywhere you want to go. Order whatever you want.

BUT let me know right away so I can relax. Just phone and ask for Doris.

Hopefully,
Doris Griffin

I have no telephone as yet, and could not afford a pay phone—assuming I could find one. Neither stopped me for a moment. I walked to Mrs. Naber's, returned her mower, thanked her, and asked to use her telephone.

Doris would certainly expect me to have a car, but there was nothing I could do about that short of stealing one. I explained that my license had expired—I did not say why—and asked her to pick me up. She agreed readily.

To say that I became thoughtful would be an egregious understatement. I took the apparatus out of the closet and examined it more carefully than ever. The three rings were still aligned to fish, as I had left them, although the pointer had wandered away.

And here, George, I made a discovery, one I ought to have anticipated. You will laugh, but it shocked me at the time. When the rings were aligned to fish, several other things fell into line as well.

You may call it superstition, but I laid the apparatus flat and returned the pointer to the three fish.

Doris's little sedan purred into my driveway not long after that. I had feared that she would want to look at the house, but she blew the horn and I hurried to join her.

She shook my hand. "Good to see you again, Mr. Dunn! Thanks ever so much for helping me out."

I insisted that the pleasure was all mine.

"Do you like the house? I take it you're going to live there?"

I said that I liked it a great deal—only a slight exaggeration—and that I was certainly going to live there for a while.

"What about your wife?" Doris was backing out of my driveway. "What does she think?"

I explained that I was unmarried and asked where we were going.

"Anyplace you want." She smiled warmly. "Do you know the restaurants in this area?"

"Not at all," I said. "I haven't been here long, and I live very simply for the most part."

"What would you like? What about steak? Men always want steak."

I find it difficult to decide what I want for lunch when I have missed breakfast, George. Everything sounds good.

"Mexican? Chinese? There's no decent sushi to be had here, I'm sorry to say. We've a good German place, though, and I like the Lakeshore Inn . . ."

I fear I licked my lips. "Does it have good seafood?"

"Absolutely! Super-duper seafood." Doris pressed the accelerator. "It's out in the country and will give us a beautiful drive and a chance to talk. So the Lakeshore Inn it is. You'll love it!"

I did. The building is old and rambling, and must have been built as a summer resort; the restaurant simple, old-fashioned, and unpretentious.

"You'll think I'm mad," I told Doris, "but I had fish for supper last night, and now I find I crave fish again. Are you sure you like it?"

"I love it." She gave me a sly grin. "Besides, this is outside town and that gives us a wonderful excuse for a long lunch. I'll make up all sort of real-estatey things for us to have talked about. Would you like an appetizer?"

I had been looking at them, and I said so.

"There's a shrimp pizza. What about clams cardinal?"

"What would you like?" I asked.

"Well, to tell you the truth, I usually order the fish chowder. The chowder here is superb."

I signed a waitress and said, "We'd both like the fish chowder."

Doris added, "With a long spoon for me, please." The waitress eyed her strangely, George, as may be imagined.

"What was that about?" I asked when the waitress had gone. "I know, 'Who sups with the devil need have a long spoon.' But am I that bad?"

She smiled. "It's just a joke. Have you spent much time in the house, Mr. Dunn?"

"Quite a bit. I'm living there."

"Really?"

"Yes, certainly. Why should I pay rent at a hotel when I own a house? If you think I'm wealthy, I'm sorry for having deceived you. I'm not."

Doris looked around as if she feared someone might be listening. "When we talked in the office, I was sure you weren't. Today—well, I've been looking at your ring."

"I'm not. Your initial impression was quite correct. No church has mice poorer than I."

"I understand." She nodded. "That's a cat's-eye opal, isn't it? I've heard of them."

"If you say so." I held out my hand. "Do you mind if I don't remove it? It's hard to get off."

George, the truth is that I was terrified she would see it for what it actually is: an imitation stone in a brass mounting.

"Besides," she took my hand, "I've got to hold your hand this way."

"There is that."

"Have you seen many ghosts?"

"If I had known you wanted me to see them, I would have made every effort."

She released my hand. "The Black House is supposed to be the most haunted house in this part of the state. You know: Moans. Rattling chains. Unearthly noises. Ghostly lights flickering in the windows."

"Oh. Those."

"Yes. Your everynight supernatural manifestations. The kids call it the Devil's House. . . ."

"Ah! The long spoon."

"Exactly. Since you own it."

"I don't have a tail."

She giggled and covered her mouth. "Prove it!"

"Or horns." I pointed to my head.

"I'll acknowledge that you have no horns if you can tell me about one tiny little ghost you saw."

"Well, there was a boy. Do boys count?"

"They might. Go on."

"The house has three doors," I explained. "Front, back, and side. Someone had broken in through the side door, so I've nailed it shut."

"The pot thickens."

"That's 'plot.' "

"You say it your way and I'll say it my way."

Our chowder arrived; it was indeed thick, I suppose with roux.

"I only got a glimpse, you understand. But he seemed a perfectly ordinary boy." Honesty made me add, "Although he was oddly dressed."

"Ah, ha!"

"I assume he came in through that side door. There's a narrow flight of stairs leading to the second floor, and that was where I found him. I'd heard him walking around over my head."

"Ghostly noises! Tell me about his clothes."

I sipped chowder, which gave me a few seconds in which to recall them. "A white shirt with wide sleeves and tight cuffs. I remember that." I paused to stir my chowder. "It's rather odd, really. I remember the whiteness of it. As though it were new and he had just put it on. I had a flashlight, and when the beam hit him he ran to a window and jumped out."

"Really?"

"Yes. I was afraid he'd broken a leg, but when I raised the window and looked out he wasn't there."

"He jumped out of the window and closed it behind him?"

I shrugged. "That's how it seemed."

"I—when I asked about ghosts, I didn't mean you had to make something up, Mr. Dunn."

"I didn't make it up, and he wasn't a ghost. I know he wasn't because he dropped things. Real things. I still have them."

Doris hesitated, sipping chowder with what seemed her whole attention. At last she said, "Was one of them that ring you're wearing?"

I shook my head. "There was a candle in a candleholder and a sort of . . . old-fashioned children's game. I believe that's what it must be. With a spinner, you know."

"You're not married." I don't think she had heard me.

"Neither are you," I said. "I've noticed you don't have a ring."

"Actually, I do. I have three. To begin with, I have my wedding ring and my engagement ring. I just don't wear them anymore, Mr. Dunn. I'm a widow."

I said I was sorry to hear it.

"Not a grass widow. Ted died two years ago. He had—let's not go into the medical details. They get messy."

"I understand."

"And I've got Ted's ring." She sighed. "I have it, and I never wanted it. I wanted it buried with him. They don't let you watch them close the casket."

I nodded.

"After everything else was over, after he was buried and all that, the undertaker gave me Ted's ring. He'd taken it off his finger before they shut the lid. Would you do me a big, big favor, Mr. Dunn?"

I smiled, though I was very much afraid that she was going to cry. "If I can, yes."

"You can." She opened her purse. "I want you to take Ted's ring. I want you to wear it. You don't have to wear it all the time, just now and then when I can see it. Do I have to explain?"

"You don't," I told her, "but I think it would be better if you did. It would give me some guidance."

"All right. As long as I have it, it's Ted's ring and it breaks my heart every time I see it. If you wear it, it will become Mr. Dunn's ring. For me. So, please?"

I nodded, and she got it out. It is a broad band of gold with a basket-weave design, a little worn.

"Third finger left hand is out." She handed it to me. "Anyplace else. Where will you wear it?"

"Wherever it will fit," I said, and put it on.

"That's fine. I'm really very grateful." She smiled, although her eyes were ready to weep. "What would you like for lunch?"

"I haven't decided. What are you having?"

"I haven't, either." She buried her face in the menu, I suppose to hide her tears.

Overhearing us, the waitress said, "Did you see the special, sir? On the chalkboard as you came in?"

I shook my head.

"We call it the Lakeshore Hat Trick. Three kinds of fish, all cooked different. There's pike blackened with Cajun spices, a blackfish cake—that's a Chinese delicacy, sir—with a sweet Oriental glaze, and white-fish in black butter. Three small portions, sir, but taken together they make a big meal, and it's only nine ninety-five. I've been serving a lot of them today, and everybody likes it."

"Fine," I said. "I'll have that."

From behind her menu, Doris murmured, "So many shades of black."

In the interests of veracity, George, I must interrupt to tell you that while the pike was indeed black, thanks to black pepper, the blackfish cake was not. I would assume that the living fish are black. The black butter was in sober fact brown. It had been mixed with what I took to be vinegar and poured over capers.

I asked Doris to tell me something about Mr. Black. Can you understand how utterly at sea I feel? A man I never heard of signed his house over to me and left the deed with a real-estate agency. I have sifted and resifted my memories in search of a man named Black. I have looked long and hard for someone who felt sufficiently indebted to me to give me a house.

Doris shook her head. "I don't know a thing about him, Mr. Dunn. Nothing. A&I managed the property. When they went out of business, Martha Murrey seems to have taken it over. I asked Jake about her after you left, and he said she used to work for A&I and took everything it had left when Mr. Isaacs retired."

"What was his first name?"

"Mr. Isaacs? I have no idea."

"Mr. Black."

"Oh, him. You have the deed, don't you? It should be on there."

"It isn't. The previous owner was a corporation, GEAS Inc. Since everybody talks about Mr. Black, I assume that he owned the company or controlled it."

Doris looked thoughtful. "You know I believe Jake mentioned Mr. Black's first name, and it was something perfectly horrible." Her fingers tapped the table. "Not Zeke. Zeke's funny, and this was just dreadful. I'll ask Jake when I get back to the office. You haven't seen him?"

"Seen Jake? I suppose I did when I went to your office, but I don't know which one he was."

"Seen Mr. Black. You could introduce yourself. You know, 'Hi there! I'm Baxter Dunn.' Then he couldn't very well say 'I'm Mr. Black.' He'd have to give his first name, wouldn't he?"

I said, "Don't you think he'd mumble? He's dead, after all."

That brought the sly smile again. "Some people say he's still in there, living in your house."

(Winkle is peeking at me through the window, George, which means she is still outside. I shall tell you about Winkle in a moment.)

Doris clearly retained a schoolgirl's delight in gruesome urban legends; I had to smile. "Perhaps he'll help with the dishes."

"You don't scare easily, do you?"

"On the contrary. I'm a rather timid man, and I know it, Mrs. Griffin. Much too careful, if anything."

She surprised me, reaching across the table to touch my hand. "You're wearing Ted's ring, Mr. Dunn. It doesn't seem right that we're still Mr. Dunn and Mrs. Griffin. I'd like you to call me Doris. Will you do that?"

I said, "Certainly, if you wish it, Doris. It will be a privilege."

"And I'll call you . . . Do you know, I think I've lost your first name?"

"It's Baxter, but nobody says that. Please call me Bax."

Our lunches arrived—the Lakeshore Hat Trick for me and coconut shrimp for Doris. Hunger is the best sauce, or so they say, and I had a large bottle of it. Doubtless anything would have tasted wonderful; but with that said, I really think my lunch was far above average.

Doris laid aside a shrimp tail. "It's good, isn't it, Bax? I didn't steer you wrong?"

"It's superb. I've been eating like a starved dog, I know. But this is even better than the fish I cooked at home last night, and I was very hungry."

She smiled. (I was always looking for that smile, George, always eager to earn it.) "You know there's nothing about you to remind me of Ted. He was taller and quite a bit heavier. Your hair's sort of yellow-brown, and his was almost black. Your faces are different, and so are your voices. But you do remind me of him. Why is that?"

"His ring, of course." I displayed it.

"No, that's yours, not Ted's. Besides, I wouldn't have given it to you if you hadn't reminded me of him already. There's a warmth, and— and I get the feeling there's courage to back it up."

Here I laughed aloud, George, although I had to cover my mouth. "I've been accused of a great many things, but never of being brave."

"You've been living in the Black House."

"Quite uneventfully. Peacefully, in fact."

"Have you explored the basement? Or the attic?"

That took me by surprise. "Do you know, I haven't. I never even thought of doing it. I've been thinking about the garage. It's locked—a large padlock that looks like trouble. I don't have a key, and I've been wondering how I can get inside. I never even thought about the cellar or the attic."

"Will you go in them now?"

"Yes, certainly." As soon as she had mentioned them, it had occurred to me that there might be old furniture stored in them. In the attic, particularly.

"At midnight?"

I shook my head. "Why wait? I'll look as soon as I get home."

Doris sighed. "I wish I could join you, but I'll have to go back to the office."

She would, I believe, have joined me had I given her the least encouragement. Not wishing her to see how I live here, I did not.

I had a stroke of luck on the way home. Only two houses from my own (granted, the houses are widely spaced here) a neighbor had set out a perfectly good recliner for the garbage collection. It was almost too heavy to lift, but I recalled that the old lady who had let me borrow her lawn mower had a wheelbarrow. I asked to borrow it.

"I really don't think I own such a thing. Do I? You may certainly borrow it if I have one."

The wheelbarrow was in her garage, where I had seen it when I returned her mower. I loaded my new recliner onto it, brought it home, and am sitting on it this minute while I write on a book in my lap. It has clearly seen some use, but it is by no means worn out.

Furthermore, I found fifty-five cents in the crack between the seat and the back. You will laugh, George, but fifty-five cents is a significant sum to me just now.

Well, my check should arrive in three days.

You will be eager to hear about the attic—or perhaps only eager to burn my letter. To be honest, I would like to know much more about it myself. There are a great many things up there, and after my first discovery I undertook no further exploration.

Before I get to that, I ought to explain that I had a great deal of trouble finding my way into it. There are six rooms upstairs, I believe, although the correct number might be seven. There is a short hall, and another hall beyond it, reached (I would judge) by the stairs from the side door I nailed shut. Some rooms open onto both halls, others onto one or the other—but not both. Another (or perhaps two) can be reached only from other rooms. Allow me to change hands.

.　.　.　.　.

The entrance to the attic was in a closet. Perhaps I ought to have written that the only entrance I have found thus far was. The ceiling of this closet is a trapdoor. I used the pole on which clothing once hung to push it up. Rungs in the form of oak rods had been mounted on the wall of the closet.

That said, I must add, George, that I feel certain there must be another entrance. There are chests and massive articles of furniture up there. They can hardly have been brought up through the trapdoor I found.

I have never been athletic, as you know, but I mounted the oak rungs without great difficulty and managed (rather less easily) to clamber into the attic itself. At once I heard scrabbling and scratching sounds that made me think that squirrels had nested there.

Conceive of my astonishment when I discovered their source. There was a cage of steel wire, not large, on the floor not far from the trapdoor. In it was a large fox. There was no food in the cage and no water. (Nor is its bottom soiled, something I observed only a moment ago.)

As you will easily understand, I could not and cannot imagine how it got there. Someone must have entered the house while I was having lunch with Doris and carried the cage and its occupant into my attic. But why in the world would anyone do such a thing?

Certainly Winkle cannot have been there long or she would have starved or died of thirst. (Do you recall Mother's pretty white cat, George? The one whose kittens you killed? Never having been an original thinker, I have borrowed her name.)

My first thought was to open the cage at once, but the fox (or vixen, which I believe is the technical term) might have hidden in a thousand places in that attic. I could not descend the ladder while holding the cage, which would have required both my hands. My solution—for I did solve it—I think rather clever. I removed my belt and put it around a bar at an upper corner, lay on my belly, lowered the cage as far as my arm and my belt would reach, and dropped it.

I would have fed the poor creature if I had any food, but I have none; after thinking things over, I found that my only recourse was to free her outside. There she could certainly drink from the river and feed herself, catching field mice, rabbits, and so forth. After climbing down, I carried her into the wood between my house and the river and opened the cage.

Winkle remained inside, huddled opposite the door—I suppose because she was afraid of me. I walked some distance away and waited; when I returned, the cage was empty. Why did I bring it back into the house? I confess I have no immediate use for it; but when one is desperately poor, one conserves everything.

Since then, I have seen her half a dozen times at the windows. Most of them are closed or boarded up, but I have opened a few for ventilation. They are screened, and the screens keep her out. She must believe that there is food inside, poor creature. I only wish she were correct.

You dislike me, George, I know; and I cannot blame you for it. You are in the majority, after all. I know, too, that you believe all my misfortunes to be my own doing. In that you are at least partially correct— nor shall I argue about the rest.

Honesty compels me to say that I am not fond of you, either. Perhaps I have less reason. *I am your brother even so.* The face you see in the mirror is mine. Have you thought of that? I have never sought to do you harm, and have done my best to keep my misfortunes from reflecting upon you. I would help you, if I could, any time that you needed help.

Can you say the same?

Yours sincerely,
Bax

Hey, Prof!

Got this paper from the chaplain. You know, I never thought I would be writing anybody from here except my old lady. Feels funny. But good. I liked getting your letters.

I got another hearing coming up in Sept. If God's on my side I might get to this haunted house you got before Halloween.

It is not that I hate being in here a whole lot. I know it bothered you a lot more than it ever bothered me. It is that it is not what I want. I want to be able to do whatever I want to do, and what I want to do is get away someplace where there is no sidewalks or streets or phone wires or any of that crap. A place where you listen and what you hear is the wind and birds singing.

When I was a kid I got sent to this summer camp one year. I do not know how long I stayed, but it seemed like a long time back then. We played ball and went canoeing, and it was all right, especially the baseball which I was pretty good at.

But the best part was getting lost when we went on hikes. I would drop back and drop back until I could hardly hear them, then go off to one side and hide because I knew they were going to send a couple of guys back for me. I would watch them going down the trail. Then I would watch them coming back. After that I was free. I would be back in time for supper most times, but one time I spent the night in the woods. That was the greatest night of my life. You are the only one I would tell this to, Bax. With the other guys I say it was the night I screwed some bitch, and sometimes it is a bitch I really screwed and sometimes just one I wanted to. But I have told you the truth.

Please keep this. Or else burn it.

———————————

Sheldon Hawes

Dear George:

Why does Bax torment me with his letters? I can hear it even as I write. You know the answer, and know equally that I might ask questions of my own.

Last night I had the strangest dream of my life. Tell poor Millie, please. I feel quite certain that you have no interest in dreams; but Millie may, and if she does she deserves to hear about this one.

Before I begin, I ought to say something about Winkle. (I intend my Winkle, not Mother's.) Yesterday I implied—or think I did—that Winkle was not truly a fox, although that was what I had first thought her. My implication was based upon glimpses I had gotten of her as she tried to enter the house by various windows. At the time I hoped she would tire and go to another house, where she might find food. I knew, however, that she would find her way inside eventually if she persisted. The house is large and old. There are many windows, odd corners, and nooks, and Winkle is an expert climber.

Now that I know her better, I think her midway between a fox and a monkey. She is red, with glossy black markings and a white tip to her tail. Her green eyes seem to me rather feline; but there are fingers behind her tiny claws, and her delicate paws are more monkeylike than doglike. She has long canines, but both foxes and monkeys have those, I believe. She seems to me, in short, a rare animal of some kind, most probably from Africa or Asia.

In my dream I lay asleep until Winkle came and woke me, wanting me to look out the window. I rose readily enough, followed her to a window, and looked out. The lawn behind the house was bathed in moonlight, and the oddest possible figures were dancing in a ring there. Some were grotesque, some quite attractive.

Most impressive was a tall, broad-shouldered man with a full beard. He was crowned like a king, and his crown gleamed in the moonlight. He danced stiffly, but with great dignity, keeping time (as I saw) to music I could not hear. Beside him danced a Junoesque woman nearly as tall as he. She wore a long gown and many jewels, and there was something beautiful and mysterious in her dance; I longed to see her more closely, and to follow the intricacies of it. With them danced a lean, capering fellow who seemed all arms and legs, a dwarf with the face of an ape, a half-naked girl with flying hair, and others I find I cannot recall distinctly.

I do remember this, however. The nearly naked girl seemed to be aware that I was watching them. She met my eyes once, and danced so wildly afterward that it seemed she might lose the animal skin that served her for a dress.

Having no food, I had no breakfast to bother about. I drank water from the tap in the bathroom, washed, and shaved. Returning to the living room to dress, I found three dead birds on the hearth—birds I know were not there when I woke. Two were pigeons, and the third a quail. I hurried out to collect wood and discovered that a ring of mushrooms had sprouted on my lawn.

And that is really all I have to say, George. I cleaned and gutted the birds as well as I could, removed some skin, and stewed them with dandelion greens in an old pot I discovered in one of the kitchen cabinets.

Winkle appeared when my stew was nearly ready. She was clearly apprehensive at first, but I spoke gently to her and offered her a bone with a good deal of meat on it. Soon she was sitting beside me, eager for her share of the stew.

Now she watches as I write, fascinated it seems by the movements of my pen. I am glad that you are not here to despise her.

But what am I to make of her?

. . . . .

Rereading this letter, I see there was one point about my dream that I neglected to mention. I sleep in my living room, as you may have gathered. Nights can be cool here at this season, and the living room has a fireplace. I cook over the fire there and sleep in front of it, waking when I am cold to put more wood on.

The window to which Winkle led me in my dream was in the living room; but when I looked through it, I was seeing the lawn behind the house. None of the living-room windows offers a view of the backyard.

Possibly I should say they do not normally show it.

There is something about the windows in this house that perturbs me, George. When I am intent upon something else and see a window from the corner of my eye, it seems to me—sometimes—that what I see through it is quite different. Once I saw a pale face; but when I looked directly at it, it was the moon. Perhaps I am too much alone.

I went out this morning after breakfast. Before I left, I asked Winkle, "Will you protect the place in my absence?"

It seemed to me that she shook her head, so I said, "In that case, will you hide from intruders?" I looked away for a moment; when I looked back, she was gone. I have not seen her since.

. . . . .

If I had closed my letter above, it would have been better, perhaps. But what would I do now? My eye is swollen . . . almost shut, but I am in too much pain to sleep. I shall tell you about it. It is best, I am sure, if I have some occupation.

It would be better still if I had food.

Well, then. About midmorning I hiked into town. It is only too likely that my allowance, when it comes, will come to the post-office box I rented when I realized that Mutazz had tried to forge my signature to my allowance check. I have written to Mother's attorneys and provided them with the address of this house, but letters can be slow and attorneys even slower. It is too soon, but it seems it must come too soon or I shall starve. Which would not trouble you.

A man in the post office stopped me and asked to see my ring. I did not recognize him at first, and said simply that both the rings I wore were mine.

"Oh, I know that! Are there two? The gold ring with the large stone."

"And why do you want to see it?"

He smiled. "You don't remember me, do you? You brought in a ring—costume jewelry—for me to look at yesterday. I'd like to see the one you're wearing now."

I remembered him then and held up my left hand.

He bent over it. "I won't ask you to take it off."

"I wouldn't," I said.

"That's a fire opal, I believe, the best I've ever seen. What did you pay for it?"

"I'm sorry, but I don't have time for this." I went to my box. No check. I had not really expected one, but not getting one did nothing to improve my mood. When I turned around, the jeweler was still there. I went past him without a word.

The truth, George, is that I was terribly tempted to sell him Doris's husband's wedding ring. It is plain gold, but wide, and large enough to be a little loose on my finger. I would think that even the pawn shop would give me a hundred dollars for it.

I am very glad now that I did not. Both sides of my face are swollen, and the pain on the left side is really quite bad; but I think that if I had sold or pawned that ring I might very well be dead.

What I did instead was return here and go back up into the attic in the hope of finding something I might use or pawn.

There is a good deal of old, heavy, black furniture up there, filthy with dust. Much of it I could have used, and still more of it might have fetched a decent price from an antique dealer.

Which did me no good whatsoever, since I could not possibly have gotten any of those old beds, dressers, and chairs down the trapdoor. There must surely be another entrance, but I searched for it in vain.

As daylight faded in the dormer windows, it occurred to me that though the house is large, the attic seemed larger still; I went to one of those dormer windows and peered out, more than half expecting to see something very strange indeed.

In a way I did, George. I saw treetops. Only the leafy green tops of trees in every direction.

My first thought, naturally, was that I was at the back of the house and looking down upon the wood in which I had freed Winkle. And yet, that could not be.

I see I got blood on the paper. Sorry! I have bathed the place—what a blessing it is to have running water! I have torn up an old shirt—all my shirts are old. Your old shirts would fit me and would be treasured; I hope you will consider sending a few.

·　·　·　·

The bleeding seems to have stopped.

·　·　·　·

He roused me by slamming the closet door. I jerked awake and sat up, disoriented and badly frightened. After that, I heard the crash of breaking glass. Is there a more frightening sound in all the world?

I jumped up and saw that he had broken one of the windows I had repaired. Rage displaced my fear, and I rushed at him. What I intended to do, I have no idea.

Whatever it was, I had no chance to do it. He was only a boy, a head shorter than I; but he was strong and fought like a wild animal. I hit him more than once, and he pounded and kicked me.

Then I was down and he kicking me again and again. I tried to protect my head with my arms, tried to roll away. I remember his shoes, low black shoes with gold buckles and thick soles. Isn't that odd? Please excuse the blood.

.   .   .   .   .

That will do it, I think.

A big man appeared—out of nowhere, it seemed. For a moment or two he stood between the boy and me, and the boy fled. I sat up and the man was gone. You will believe none of this; but it is true, every word of it. I have the bruises and the bleeding nose to prove it.

To say nothing of the broken window.

The big man must certainly have been the boy's father. At the time, because of his ring, I thought him something else; but now that I have had a chance to consider, I feel quite sure that I understand everything that happened.

The boy returned looking for the bronze apparatus I have described. He expected to find it in the coat closet, though I cannot say why. Perhaps he assumed that I would keep it near me, and not finding it in plain view in a room almost entirely empty, he thought it must be in the closet. He looked inside, but it lay flat on the shelf intended for hats, and it was pushed back a trifle. Since the shelf is higher than his head, he failed to find it. Enraged, he broke the window as I have described.

His father had followed him, feeling no doubt that his son was up to mischief. He got into my house as his son had, through an entrance I must find and secure. Hearing the breaking of my window, he would have run toward us; and finding his son in the act of kicking me, he forced him to desist. I must have lost consciousness at that point; and he (intent upon punishing his son and perhaps fearing that I might sue) left with the boy.

I hope you and Millie are well, and faring better than your poor brother.

Yours sincerely,
Bax

Dear George:

Doubtless you will resent this second letter, coming as soon as it does. But then you resent everything, or nearly everything. I have all sorts of news! Why should my letters be exempt?

When I studied my face in the mirror this morning, I decided I really ought to seek treatment. I have no money for a doctor, as you know; but I recalled that under the law anyone who goes to the emergency ward of a hospital must receive treatment. I would walk to a drugstore I had noticed on earlier walks and inquire about the nearest.

I had traversed no more than a block or two, when a car screeched to a stop beside me. "What happened to *you*?" It was Martha Murrey.

Smiling bravely, I declared that it was nothing.

"You get in here this minute. I'm going to take you home and put ice on that."

Of course I obeyed.

"Did you win?"

I shook my head.

"You see, that's what happens when a man goes to bars. My postman used to do it, too, that biker bar in Port—I won't tell you where it is."

I explained that I had fought an intruder.

"Did you say he was a boy?"

"Half grown." I shrugged. "He seemed strong for his age. At any rate, he proved more than a match for me."

"Most men would have told me there were two of them."

"As would I," I said, "if there had been. As it was, I was saved from a worse beating by his father."

"You should have called the police."

"I don't have a telephone."

"Still? I'll call them. Get a cell phone."

I nodded and said I suppose I would have to.

"There's this wonderful place that will give you one. Did you know about them?"

I certainly had not known, and said so.

"If you'll sign up for their service, you get a free cell phone. It's bottom of the line, of course."

She waited for my reaction, and I said, "Good."

"If you don't want to take pictures with it, or watch sports or any of that . . ."

"I simply want to call the police," I said. Honesty forced me to add, "And my friends."

The truth, George, was that I was thinking it might be possible for me to obtain assistance from Doris and Martha now and then if I had a telephone.

Nor was that all. During the time I was living at the Riverman, I pretty well gave up my job search; months have elapsed since I stopped looking, and it seems possible that something has opened up. Doris or

Martha may know of employment opportunities I would never have discovered for myself, for that matter.

"And your family, of course. You must have a family."

"Hardly any save my brother," I explained. "He's very busy and sometimes becomes angry when I call him." (As you see, I accorded *you* every consideration. Far be it from me to defame a family member, even when strict truth would require it.)

"That's a shame."

I agreed, and mentioned that I would soon be seeking employment.

"Not until your face heals, Mr. Dunn. Nobody will hire somebody who looks like he's been fighting."

I had not thought of that, but she is indubitably correct.

The upshot of all this, George, was that my cuts and bruises were bandaged and salved—"I always wanted to be a nurse"—and that I was Martha's guest at lunch. She spoke at some length about the advantages of selling my house and moving to an urban area in which I might more readily find employment, but I will not give that here.

What surprised me was her evident pleasure when I explained that I would greatly prefer to stay where I was for the time being. "Since you're staying, I hope to see you from time to time, Mr. Dunn. When you have your cell phone—did I give you the address?"

I shook my head, and she wrote it out for me.

"Give me a call when you have it, will you? Before I give it to anyone else, I want to make sure they treat their customers right."

Of course I promised I would.

As matters evolved, I did not actually require the address she had provided. She drove me there, waited while I signed the agreement and received my telephone, and drove me home. "Call me anytime," she said in parting. "I live alone, you know. I'm always glad of company."

Need I say that I returned home in high spirits?

At once I began a search for the means by which the boy had entered my house. I found it (or at least found one way, which may well be the correct one) immediately. Earlier, you see, George, I had searched the house from within; it was by that means that I discovered the broken side door.

Wiser now, I chose to search outside. There are at least eight rooms on the ground floor, and I may well have missed one or even two. Five of these are corner rooms.

I had no sooner reached the back of the house, than my eye fell upon an old-fashioned cellar door greatly in need of paint, the kind that the boys of long ago slid down. There is a hasp on it, but no lock.

My first thought was to nail it shut, as I had the side door. In the end I refrained for three reasons, all of which seem good to me. The first, of course, was that if I were to nail it shut I could not use it myself. In the case of the side door, that hardly matters; the front and rear doors remain at my disposal. There is presumably some means of accessing the cellar from within the house, but I have yet to discover it. Until I do, I would be locking myself out of my own cellar.

Second, I rather hoped the boy would return. I boxed and fenced at the university, as you may recall. I will not say I was expert at either; those who were regarded me with contempt. Yet I did those things. Last night I suffered defeat at the hands of a mere boy, and I find that I regard myself with greater contempt because of it.

Besides, I have his apparatus—his, assuming he did not steal it. If it is his, he should be able to tell me what it is and how it is used; and if it is his, I am honor bound to return it.

Third, my small supply of nails (I found them in the old lady's tool shed) is nearly exhausted.

Once I had rejected the notion of nailing my cellar door, it occurred to me that padlocks are not particularly costly and that I might purchase one when I receive my allowance.

After that, that the doors of the garage are already padlocked. I had given the garage little attention. Indeed, I had given it so little that I imagined it had been built to house a single automobile.

That was an error. It is a three-car garage. There are two small (and very dirty) windows, but no entrance other than the three large doors intended to admit three automobiles. I tried to peer through the windows, but the interior was so dark that I could see nothing.

No doubt it is empty—or full of rubbish. Still, one of those padlocks would be very useful once I have settled matters with the boy.

Here, George, I had planned to give you the best of my news. I find, however, that my conscience will not permit it. Earlier I concealed something from you, knowing that you would not credit it.

I told you about Winkle, the small creature—I cannot call her an animal—I discovered in a cage in the attic. I told you that indeed, but concealed the fact that she can speak.

You have wadded this letter into a tight little ball and thrown it into your wastebasket. I know it. I can only hope that you will repent, smooth it out, and read the rest. In an hour, perhaps, or in a day or two.

First, let me say that I am not mad, no matter what you may think. She speaks, and I hear her.

Second, she is no chatterer. Her words are small and generally few.

Third, I am not about to attempt to profit by her. I feel quite sure she would be like my ring. In the presence of others she would become (I believe) an ordinary fox, red with black markings. You need believe nothing of this, of course.

Nor will you. If I had not known I would not be believed, I doubt that I would have told you.

My great news is that she has shown herself again. I asked where she had been, and she said she had not left at all, only hidden. It seemed clear that she did not wish to reveal her hiding place, so I did not inquire.

"It's wonderful to have you back again, Winkle. I've missed you."

She climbed me, very quickly and easily, and laid her cheek against mine.

"Are you hungry?"

She shook her little head.

"That's good because I have nothing to give you. We might fish in the river, though. Would you like that?"

She nodded, and I carried her out the back door and put her down on the lawn. "Here's the circle where the dancers you showed me were. See the mushrooms?"

"I thee . . ." Her voice is small and soft, but I thought she sounded thoughtful.

"I've been running down to the river, then back to the house."

55

She said nothing, so I added, "Three times. If I'm going to fight the boy again—"

"One tho bad."

"I know, and if I'm going to fight him again I need to be in condition, which is why I've been doing push-ups and running down to the water and back. I was resting when you came."

She nodded, I suppose to show she understood.

"What I wanted to say was that I was careful each time to jump the mushrooms. I don't know why, but I was."

"Riverman?"

"Did I see him, you mean? No. It's just a legend, I'm sure."

Winkle looked dubious, but said no more. We were in the house collecting what I may humorously call my fishing gear when I heard footsteps from the floor above.

My first thought was that it was absurdly unfair. I had only just begun my training program. I was tired and more than a little winded. And here he was again.

My second was that I might kill him. The stick I had cut for a fishing pole is about five feet long and, though crooked, quite strong. (Before adopting it for angling, I had attempted to break it over my knee.) I grasped it then and hurried upstairs even while I knit a plan to dispose of the body.

Seeing him, I did not pause to demand his surrender, but assaulted him straight out, swinging my stick for all I was worth. My third blow knocked him to the floor, and he screamed.

It stopped me cold, George. I cannot explain why. Or rather, I *can*, but there were so many reasons I despair of explaining them all. Perhaps the primary reason was that I realized, when I heard his scream, that I was victorious. It is only rarely that I have I been victorious in life's battles, George, as you know.

"Give up?" I was so winded that it was all I could do to get the words out.

"Yes!"

"Very well." I stepped back, gasping for breath.

He sat up. "Who are you?"

"It seems to me," I said, "that it's I who should be asking you. Answer, and provide some identification, or you will regret it."

"I'm Emlyn." He was rubbing his bruises.

"That can't be all."

"The Good."

"All right, Emlyn Theegood, prove it." Even as I said that, it occurred to me that he was too young to have a driver's license. Was there some sort of identification that might be expected of a boy?

"How can I prove it?" There was despair in his eyes, George. I have seen it too often in my own to mistake it in another's.

"Is there someone who'll vouch for you?"

He shook his head.

"What about your father?"

"If we can find him."

"I suppose he's at work. What about your mother?"

His eyes filled with tears, and I did a very foolish thing, George. You need not trouble to tell me you would not have done it. I know it.

I went to him and laid my hand upon his shoulder.

Like lightning, he snatched my stick and punched me in the stomach. I bent double, and took three hard blows from my own stick upon my head and shoulders.

I fell, and he stood over me with my stick raised. "Now you know how it feels."

Rubbing my head, I sat up. "It wasn't as bad as your kicks last night."

His eyes grew very wide when I said that, but I ignored it.

"You've won," I told him. "Doubtless you would like the apparatus you dropped returned to you. You may have it, and need not believe me when I say I would cheerfully have returned it without a fight."

"The triannulus? Yes, I want it back. My longlight, too."

Would you have looked wise at that, George? I confess I did not; I felt a fool, and no doubt looked like one. "Is *triannulus* what you call that apparatus? What in the world is a longlight?"

"I had one when you surprised me. You must have seen it. I—I dropped it and ran. I thought you were Ieuan, and you'd have a sword or a knife."

"Ieuan?"

Emlyn nodded. "He's my brother."

You may imagine, George, how I felt when I heard that. I coughed and stammered a bit. At last I said, "Is your face bruised?"

"I don't think so. It doesn't hurt."

"Would you, as a favor to me—I realize that I am in no position to give you orders—stand nearer the window?"

He nodded slowly and did as I asked.

"I am a twin," I told him. "My brother's name is George. You need not ask his appearance, because you're seeing me."

Emlyn laughed. "I saw you took a thumping. That was Ieuan?"

"I believe so. He beat me, as you see, but I did not go down without a fight. I hit him hard, more than once. He would show signs of it, I'm sure."

"You're telling the truth," Emlyn informed me.

"Thank you. I'm glad you realize it."

"I'm good at that, and I might as well tell you. Do you like your brother? The truth now."

"No. You want the truth and you shall have it. I love my brother. We shared our mother's womb. . . ."

"But you don't like him."

"May I explain? He's terribly afraid people will think him weak. Why, I don't know—I only know he is. He's bad mannered, because he thinks good manners are a sign of weakness. I . . ."

"Yes?" Emlyn struck the floor with the butt of my stick. "Now tell the truth!"

"I won't say I have good manners. That's for others to judge. But I try to be well mannered, and I'm quite certain George thinks I'm weak. Not just because of that, or even largely because of that. There are other reasons."

"Does he hurt people?"

"Yes, but so do I, only too often."

"And animals?"

I shrugged. "I eat their flesh."

"So do I." He hesitated; and I tried, unsuccessfully, to guess what he was thinking. At length he said, "I gave you my name and my brother's. What's yours?"

"Bax." I held out my hand "I don't suppose you want to risk shaking hands with me, but I'm entirely willing to shake yours if you are. There will be no treachery."

He smiled and we clasped hands; then he said, "Want your stick back?"

"It doesn't matter now, does it?"

He shook his head and handed it to me. "You said you'd give me the triannulus back."

"Is it yours?"

"It's Father's. I borrowed it, and I have to return it."

I said, "Then I'll certainly give it back to you."

"The longlight's mine. I made it. I'd like that back, too."

"Are you sure I have it? I don't know what it is."

"When you first saw me, when I dropped the triannulus, I was carrying a light. Did you get it?"

"Your candle? Yes, I did." I tried to recall what I had done with it. "Is that the longlight?"

He nodded. "This is somewhat technical I'm afraid. Have you used the triannulus?"

"I wouldn't know how."

"Give it back to me and I'll show you."

I asked a few questions about his father after that. Emlyn described him and explained that he had tired of his sons squabbling and gone away, leaving them to settle their differences.

"I take it you haven't."

He sighed and shrugged. "He's my brother. I hope someday he'll understand that I'm his."

We went downstairs together, and I got the apparatus down from the closet. "Your brother looked in there for it," I told Emlyn, "but he missed it. He was so angry he broke my window. That woke me up, and we fought."

"He broke your window?"

I showed it to him.

"He isn't like that." Emlyn sounded thoughtful.

"Not like what?"

Emlyn sighed. "There's hot anger and cold anger. Hot anger is when you yell and stamp and break things. That's the way I am when I'm angry."

I said, "I understand."

"Cold anger is when you smile and wait. An hour later, or a week, you do something horrible. That's the way Ieuan is. Do you understand that, too?"

I said I thought so. "That's why you gave me back my stick, isn't it?"

"You're right. Lies almost always sound false to me. So I didn't think you were lying, but I wanted to be sure. Why did Ieuan break your window?"

The question surprised me, I admit. I said that I had thought he broke it because he was angry; and if it was not that, then I had no idea.

"It wasn't, and it would be good for us—for me, anyway—to know why he did. Breaking it made you so angry you attacked him? Didn't you say that?"

"Yes. Hot anger."

Emlyn nodded absently. "Is there someone you can get to repair it?"

I knew there was some putty left and tried to recall how much glass I had. "I'd rather make the repair myself. I repaired it a few days ago."

Emlyn jumped as if struck. "*You* repaired it?"

"Yes, I did. I'm not a skillful worker, but—"

"I understand. This could be important. I hope so. The window possesses some property that Ieuan doesn't want you to control. That has to be it. Think very carefully now. Did you repair it before—or was it after—you got my longlight?"

"Before."

Emlyn smiled. "Let's hope that's right. You're quite sure?"

"Certain." I pointed to the apparatus. "I got your longlight when I got this. I had neither when I repaired the window."

"Good. You'll understand why I say that when you understand the triannulus. Where's my longlight?"

My eyes fell on the lamp. "I was sitting in here reading. . . ."

"Yes?"

I snapped my fingers. "A neighbor came and gave me that. It's an oil lamp."

Emlyn waited.

"We lit it and he blew out the candle. Blew out your longlight."

"You hadn't—never mind. Go on."

"He gave me a spare can of oil for it, too. I was afraid of what might happen if the oil got too close to the fire, so I put it in the kitchen after he left. Put the oil and the long light in there together, side by side."

I felt quite proud of myself for remembering that, George; but when we went to get it, it was gone. I looked and Emlyn, and he at me.

"This is where I put it," I said. "Right here next to the oil, on this shelf in this cabinet."

I had never heard the sharp bark of a fox before, but I heard it then and spun around.

The fox was Winkle, of course. She was standing in the kitchen doorway with the longlight in front of her; her expression was more mischievous than ever.

I said, "Well! I wondered what had happened to you," and went to get it.

At which, George, she picked it up and ran.

Emlyn yelled, "The facefox!" and sprinted after her.

We chased her, I believe, through most of the rooms on the lower floor, and there are a good many of them. Emlyn, who can run far faster than I, was always in hot pursuit. I tried to get ahead of her and block her exit.

Neither of us succeeded, and at last we gave up and sat down on the floor, panting.

At which Winkle sat, too, carefully set the longlight down in front of her, and grinned at us.

"Please, Winkle." I gasped for breath. "Let us have it. It belongs to Emlyn here."

Emlyn said, "I've been trying to find you because I learned that Ieuan had caged you. I was going to set you free. Doesn't that prove I'm a friend?"

"Ahhh! Tho?"

"If you'll give it back to me now—it's mine, it really is—I'll always be your friend. I'll never try to force you like Ieuan did." Emlyn raised his hand. "That I swear by wind and tree, by grass, river, and hill."

Winkle nodded and looked at me. "Ahhh, tho?"

"You don't need a friend as poor as I am, Winkle. I know that. I was the one who needed a friend, and you were that friend for a day or two. I—I'd like for us to be friends again. Won't you be my pet? You'll always be free to come and go, and if there's any way I can help you, I'll do it. Any way at all."

At that, Winkle picked up the longlight, trotted over to me, and set it down in front of me.

I must end my letter here, George. This is my last sheet, and my eyes ache after so much writing by lamplight. I shall recount to you the rest when I have obtained more paper.

Please remember that I long to hear from you, whether you will assist me or not. How are you? How is Millie?

Yours sincerely,
Bax

Number 9

SORCERY

Dear George:

This paper itself is interesting. You may recall that the first boy (Emlyn) promised to show me how his father's triannulus operates. Once we had reclaimed his longlight from Winkle, he did so.

"Each ring is a want list," he explained. "The inside ring has the shortest list, because it has the least room to put things in."

I nodded.

"The middle ring has everything that's on the inside ring and some more things of its own. Look here. See this symbol?"

I did. It was an oval surrounding something that might have been a flame.

"It's not on the inner ring, but it is on middle ring. See?"

I remarked that it was on the outer ring as well and asked what it meant.

Emlyn looked up at me. "I don't know. Do you?"

Lacking your imagination, George, I could only confess that I had no idea.

"See if you can find this snake on the outer ring."

I did, without much difficulty.

"Right. Everything that's on the middle ring is on the outer ring, and a few more."

(Winkle was between us, and bent over the triannulus with as much interest as I.)

"Tell me something you want," Emlyn instructed me, "and we'll use this to try to find it."

"Stationery," I said.

He looked up. "What's that?"

"Writing paper and envelopes. I've been writing my brother from time to time, and I've only a little left."

"That's terribly trivial, and I'm certain it's not on the inner ring. What we want now is something that's on all three."

"What about money? I need money badly."

Emlyn nodded. "That's on all three, I believe. Yes, here. It's on the inner, so it must be on all three. We'll line them up."

At this point, George, I recalled my fish; but I said nothing about them then. Each of the glyphs he aligned showed three small circles of varying size. I suppose they represent coins.

"Now move the pointer so it points to them. You're the one who wants money, so it will be better if you do it."

I did. "Does this mean I'll get it?"

"Not yet. You have to light the longlight."

I had obtained several folders of matches at the Lakeshore Inn. Producing one, I struck the match.

Winkle sniffed and backed away.

"That's a good trick." Emlyn's voice was icily calm. "A good trick but a bad spirit. Snuff the flame."

I blew it out.

"There's still a coal or four in there." He pointed toward my fireplace. "Puff them, and light the longlight from one."

I did.

"Good. Now listen carefully. The longlight must burn until you get what you want. If it goes out before then, you will acquire numen. Do you want it?"

I said, "I don't even know what you mean by it."

"That trick with the little stick made me think you might want it."

"Numen? Is that what you said?"

He nodded. "I've got it already because of you, and I think you've got it, too. We're both dangerous—dangerous to ourselves and to each other. Sorcery is the power wielded by a sorcerer, someone like Father. Do you know what a sorcerer is?"

"Yes, I think so."

"Good. For an object like this to work, it must have numen. The making of it endows it with numen. If it fails to, the object is useless. When it's used, its numen creates sorcery and directs it. Directs it mechanically, I ought to have said. Not intelligently, unless the device possesses intelligence. Intelligence is very rare."

I nodded. "I know."

"When the object is a triannulus, lighting a longlight begins the process and snuffing out the longlight ends it. I assume you know about swords? Lighting the longlight is like drawing a sword and snuffing out the longlight is like sheathing that sword."

I was not sure I followed that, and I said so.

"You mustn't draw a sword too soon, and sheathing it too soon is even worse. That's all I meant. Suppose—"

"Wait!" I can be forceful when I want to be, George, and I was forceful then. "There are fish on there. Fish on all three rings. Suppose I lined up the fish, and moved the pointer, and lit the longlight to read by."

"That would be very foolish."

"But say that I did it. Then, before I'd gotten any fish, a neighbor came to the door and gave me an oil lamp, then blew out the longlight. What would happen then?"

"Is that what happened?"

I nodded.

"I want to blame you," Emlyn sighed. "I want it so much I'm going to do it. You should never, ever, have toyed—which is what you did—with sorcerous things you don't understand. It's all your fault! Everything's your fault and you deserve everything that happens to you."

Winkle barked and snarled at him.

"Yes, he does! By marsh and mere, he's got it coming to him." Emlyn stamped. "He's a dirty donkey, and you know it."

Winkle shook her head.

Emlyn turned back to me. "My own disaster is your fault, too, Bax. You got into my father's house and came upstairs with your blinding torch and made me drop the longlight. It went out, and that's how I acquired numen I'm too ignorant to wield."

"I deeply and humbly apologize." I know I must have sounded contrite, George, because I felt contrite. "If there's some way I can make it up to you, I'll certainly do it. On one point I must correct you, however. This isn't your father's house. It's mine."

Winkle ran to the window, jumped up onto the sill, and barked.

"I think someone's coming." Emlyn went to the window and looked out.

I followed him. "That was the postman, I believe. The flag's down."

He looked at me quizzically.

"The flag on my mailbox," I explained. "Last night I wrote a letter to my dear brother George. He never writes to me, but I hope to soften his stance eventually."

Emlyn nodded. "Do you have a courier or a page to run with your letters?"

"The postman takes them. That's what I'm trying to make clear. When I'd finished my letter and stamped it, I put it in my box and raised the flag. The flag tells the postman to stop even if he hasn't any mail for me. When he's picked up my letter—or she has, postmen are often women—he puts the flag down."

"I don't see the flag. Can you show it to me? I think I've finished reviling you, for the present at least."

We went out to the box, and I showed him the little metal flag, raising and lowering it. Several cars passed, and I have wondered since what they thought of the three of us gathered around my rusty mailbox in the bright summer sunshine—of Emlyn in his knee breeches and wide-sleeved shirt, and Winkle, an animal of flame, ice, and night.

There was mail, including—oh, wonder of wonders—my allowance. I opened it when we had returned to the house, and explained what a check was to Emlyn.

"There! It's money, you say?"

"It certainly is, and very welcome money, too."

"Then we must snuff the longlight." He held it up. "Moisten your fingers and pinch the wick. That's the best way."

I did.

"Now the operation is over." Emlyn smiled. "If you had put out the flame too soon, the numen would have been directionless and unfulfilled. That's what happened to me when I dropped the longlight and the flame went out, and it's what happened to you when you let someone put the flame out before you got your fish. I ought to warn you that fish may keep coming until you get three of them. That could easily happen."

Here, I felt, was confusion that should be dealt with. "I got three that night," I explained. "The neighbor who gave me fish actually gave me three of them."

"Is that so?"

"Yes, three fish. I recall that distinctly. Each was about so big." I indicated their length with my hands.

"Did they differ in some other way? In any way at all? That may be important."

"They were of three different kinds, I believe. One was a catfish. I believe both the others were bass, but—but . . ."

"Yes?"

"Different kinds of bass, perhaps. I don't know much about bass, but they didn't look quite the same."

"This could be bad." Sighing, Emlyn resumed his seat on the floor.

"Do you mean that the numen might continue to get fish for me?"

"Exactly. It may get you three fish three times, for example. What's the matter, Bax?"

"I think perhaps it already has. I lunched on fish chowder. First, I mean. Before the entrée I had a cup of fish chowder. They might easily have chopped up three fish to make a big kettle of fish chowder. Wouldn't you think so?"

Emlyn nodded.

"Then for my lunch, I had three sorts of fish. There was blackfish, which I'd never eaten before. It was quite good. The others were . . ." I stopped to think.

"Were they two different kinds?"

"Yes, I'm certain they were. One was pike, I'm sure. The other was quite dry and served with black butter."

"That may have done it. Three wheels, you see. Three pictures of fish. So three fish for the three pictures, and three occasions for the three wheels. If that's it—I'm not saying it is—you may be free of the entanglement. We can hope you are, at least."

"But what about you?"

Emlyn nodded. "I was about to get to that. Do you remember what I told you about my twin? About Ieuan?"

"Cold anger? I recall that."

"I said he would wait for an hour or longer, then do something quite horrible. Well, he has." For a moment, Emlyn smiled at Winkle. "Your friend here is a facefox, so I assume you know about them. One—"

"I don't know what they are!"

"Really?"

"Yes, really. I know what a fox is, of course."

"Do you know what a werewolf is?"

I was about to say I did, George, but that I didn't believe in them, when I realized that I do. Too many strange things have been happening to me. My old disbeliefs have been crumbling.

"If you do, it's quite simple. Make it a fox instead of a wolf and do it backwards."

Winkle smiled at my confusion and put her paw in my lap. "Tho thimple . . ."

"It may be so simple," I said, "but it confuses me just the same."

"It really is simple," Emlyn told me. "A werewolf is a man or a woman who puts on a wolf's skin. A facefox is a fox who puts on a human face."

I stroked Winkle's head. "Is this true?"

She nodded.

"A werewolf may look like a wolf," Emlyn told me, "but it's really a man. Or a woman. When I was small I thought it would be fun, but there's nothing fun about it. They want human flesh, as much as they can get. They'll do just about anything to get it. Brave any danger."

"If you're saying Winkle's like that, I don't believe it."

"Oh, she isn't. Facefoxes are foxes who become human. As foxes they may kill poultry and so forth—do the things foxes do. But when they become human, they act like other women." Emlyn rose. "They're nearly all women, and there may not be any men. I've never heard of one, though there might be some." He picked up the triannulus.

"Where are you going?"

"Up to the attic. It's where I was going when you hit me with your stick. Ieuan caught a facefox, you see, and caged it. I think it may be in the attic."

"It's not. That's where I found Winkle."

"Really?"

"Yes," I said. I got the cage and showed it to him.

"I wish Father were here."

"So he could discipline your brother?"

"So he could explain things to me." Emlyn sighed. "To tell you the truth, Bax, Father's not much of a one for explaining. Or for disciplining, either. But if he were here, I'd know that someone understood. Just knowing that might make me feel better."

"If you were to explain it to Winkle and me, you might understand it better yourself."

"I suppose. What I did, you see, was to set up the triannulus to find a facefox. I'd never tried it before. Never tried anything like that before, really. Only I know it can be done. Father could have done it in a wink."

He got the triannulus to show me. "Here in the outer ring is a fox. See?"

It was certainly a rough picture of a four-legged animal with a tail.

"And here in the second ring is a face. I lined that up with the fox. Then the first ring has an arrow. See? I put that in line with the other two. Find the facefox. Then I moved the pointer to them and lit my longlight."

I cleared my throat. As you know, George, I have been a substitute teacher in the public schools when there were no alternatives on the horizon; and at that moment I felt that I was once more in a classroom. "I feel compelled to point out," I said, "that your longlight was extinguished before you found Winkle."

"Exactly." To judge by Emlyn's looks, he certainly had the wind up. "I have found a facefox now. Or perhaps the facefox found me. She stole my longlight just to get me to chase her."

"Us to chase her. I remember."

"Girls enjoy being pursued, and so do foxes. It may be that was the end of it. I hope so. But I ought to go up to the attic just the same. I may find another facefox there. There could even be more than one. In entanglements, you never know."

"You won't object if Winkle and I come with you?"

"I was hoping you would mend the window Ieuan broke while I was gone."

I shook my head. "I can't keep replacing the glass over and over. I'm not going to do it again until I get some sort of commitment from him."

All of which was true enough, George; but my chief reason was that I hoped Emlyn would show me an easier route to the attic.

As he did. At the back of the butler's pantry was a door to which I had never given the least attention. Emlyn opened it to reveal a helical staircase I had not known existed. He and Winkle went up the steep steps much faster than I—which gave me an opportunity to open a door on the second floor.

The room beyond was large and dirty. A four-poster stood somewhere near the middle; it was surrounded by other furniture, which appeared to be paying homage at a polite distance: chairs too many to count, small tables, chests, and wardrobes. A dead animal on the floor appeared to be a rabbit; another, sprawled over a chest, was clearly a large fox.

"That's Ieuan's bedroom," the boy called. "I wouldn't go in there."

I rejoined him in the attic, where he had stopped to wait for me.

"Ieuan doesn't leave that door unlocked often. When it is, it's usually because he's hoping to catch something. You, for example."

"I'll remember that."

"You'd better. You're an intruder in my father's house, after all. If Ieuan were to slash your throat, nobody could breathe a word against him."

(You always ridicule me for failing to get to the point, George, and I am about to hand you a capital opportunity; but I feel that this should be said, and I have no better place to say it. Ieuan—it is pronounced "*yai*-yan"—never seemed to me a particularly euphonious name; but it sounded positively sinister in that attic.)

I said I hoped he would not and asked what had become of Winkle.

"Oh, he went off that way." The boy waved vaguely. "He'll yell if he finds something, I'm sure."

"We had better go after him," I said.

"Good idea. Lead the way."

"I should introduce myself." I offered my hand. "I'm George Dunn."

(You will pardon the liberty, George, I feel certain. You will doubtless recall that we often did the same thing in school.)

"My name's Emlyn."

"It's a pleasure to meet you, Emlyn." I raised my voice. "Winkle! Come here, Winkle!"

The boy stepped back and put his fingers in his ears. "Must you? You'll deafen me."

"Hurry!"

The boy turned and bolted down the stairs with Winkle in hot pursuit. I believe she sank her teeth into his calf once at least.

"What's all this?" It was Emlyn.

"Your brother was waiting for me at the top of the steps," I explained. "He pretended to be you, though I fear he has no future as a thespian."

"Really?"

I nodded. "Yes, really."

Winkle favored me with a smile more attractive than I would have supposed any fox could manage. "Tho withe!"

"No, not really. Emlyn has the triannulus. Ieuan did not. He could have put it down somewhere, of course, but that started me wondering, and there were other things."

"What were they?" Emlyn asked.

"He gave his name an ugly sort of emphasis I've never heard you use, for one thing. It sounded like a curse."

Slowly, Emlyn nodded. "I don't imagine Ieuan likes himself much."

"His shirt was a bit soiled, too. Yours looks as if you put it on fresh this morning. His looked as though he had worn it yesterday. I decided to test him, and said my name was George Dunn."

"Your brother's name?"

"Correct. He accepted that without a qualm, although you knew my name and had used it. At that point, I felt quite sure. I called for Winkle, fearing that he had done something to her."

"He must have slipped in behind us on the stairs. You didn't hear him?"

I shook my head. "I neglected to say that his face showed fading bruises. They were hard to see in this light, but they were there. Also, he assumed that Winkle was male, calling her 'he.' I noticed that, too. Why did he run when she appeared? Do you know?"

"He knew she was female," Emlyn said. "He just didn't want you to know it. He ran because she'd have denounced him, of course."

"I wouldn't have fought him, only asked why he broke my window."

Emlyn sighed. "You don't understand him. He tried to deceive you and failed almost from the start. He's deeply humiliated, and if he had stayed, it would have been worse—or that's what he thinks."

"I believe I understand."

"He'll hate you now, because you saw through him. He may hate you worse because you saw him run away."

"If he hates as easily as that, he must hate a great many people," I said.

"He hates everyone, himself included."

. . . . .

(I abandoned this letter for something or other, George, and have only now come back to it.)

After the conversation related above, we searched the attic for more foxes. Or at least, Emlyn and Winkle searched it for that purpose. I am afraid I only feigned to be looking for foxes, George, when in fact I was simply looking for anything that might be of use or interest to me.

The first thing I found was a massive old four-poster heaped with dusty blankets and sheets. Winkle at once set her teeth in the mattress and gave it several good yanks. Releasing it, she told me solemnly, "For theep."

"You're right," I said. "We'll see about that."

The next thing was a dormer window, a very small and rather dirty window made to open with a crank. Peering out, I could see nothing but miles of trees. And then, far off, a hilltop crowned with a single pointed tower, as if a needle had been thrust into the very summit of the hill. I called Emlyn over then, and asked what the tower was.

"That's Goldwurm's Spire," Emlyn told me.

I asked him to explain.

"He's a warlock, that's all. He killed his master and took his home— and other things, too. Everything that his old master had, though I've heard that he could never find his master's weapon of sorcery and is still looking for it."

"I've never heard of a weapon of sorcery. What is it?"

Emlyn shrugged. "It's complicated, and I certainly don't know everything there is to know about them. A sorcerer can take a part of his power and put it into an external object for safekeeping."

"Like putting money in the bank?"

For a moment Emlyn looked blank. "Maybe it is. Like putting gold in a chest instead of holding it in your hand. It makes it harder for anybody to attack the sorcerer, because they can't touch that power unless they know what the object is and where it is."

"Like opening an account under another name."

"I suppose. Anyway, the early ones were just about all weapons. Swords, mostly. That's why they're called weapons of sorcery. A lot are staffs and wands these days. I've heard of cups, too. I imagine Goldwurm thought he'd find his master's without much trouble, so he didn't keep him around to question. Just strangled him and threw him in the river. It was before my time, but I've heard that the old sorcerer's name was Ambrosius."

"I doubt that it matters now," I said.

Emlyn shrugged.

"I suppose this Goldwurm was acquitted."

Before Emlyn could reply, my cell phone chimed. I pushed a button that I hoped (not exactly fervently) was the correct one, and said hello.

"Bax? This is Martha Murrey. How's your phone? Are you satisfied with it?"

I said that I was very satisfied, although the truth was that I had never so much as attempted to use it.

"Wonderful! I don't suppose you're free for dinner tonight?"

Recalling my allowance check, I said that I was. I would have to walk to the bank before it closed and deposit it in my checking account—an account that eight pathetic little dollars are holding open at present; but once I had, I would be able to write a check for our dinner. Any area restaurant, I felt reasonably certain, would accept a local check for dinner.

"I'm not inconveniencing you?"

"No, not at all. There are several questions I want to ask you. About the house, you know."

"Wonderful! Pick you up at six?"

When we had said good-bye I asked Emlyn whether he would help me drag the mattress down to my fire.

"You say you're not a sorcerer, Bax?"

"No, indeed."

"But you can talk on that thing?"

"Sometimes. Whenever someone calls me, or I call someone." It occurred to me that I might give him the number of the Riverman; Mutazz would answer, and their conversation might be amusing. "If you'd care to try it . . . ?"

"No, no!" He backed away.

I returned the cell phone to my pocket, and we had gone off to find the bed when something caught my eye. "Look at this."

He nodded. "I've seen it. Do you know what it is?"

"Certainly. It's an escritoire, a writing table. Quite a nice antique, too." On impulse, I pulled out the uppermost drawer, and to my delight found a small stack of stationery and a dozen or so envelopes.

"Didn't you say you needed those?"

"Yes. We didn't set your father's triannulus to find them for me, but here they are anyway. If this is what numen does for one, I'm heartily in favor of it." Well before I completed that sentence I had taken this paper, thinking to roll it up and put it in a pocket. Beneath it lay three gold coins.

Although I heard Emlyn's sharply indrawn breath, I paid that little heed, picking up the coins instead and examining them with interest. Winkle leaped onto the escritoire so that she might look, too.

"This is Greek." I displayed the coin so Emlyn could see it. "I believe the city must be Corinth, but I've no idea whose head that is."

"It's gold." Emlyn sounded as though he were choking. "Don't you understand what this means?"

"Yes, I understand. But you can't possibly understand how much this gold means to me."

Winkle echoed my sentiments, barking joyfully. "Tho thcrumptiouth! Thuperb thilkth! Oh, tho thuper!"

"It means that something's gone terribly wrong," Emlyn declared. "We asked for money, you got it, and you put out the longlight. It should have stopped there."

"Are you sure?"

"Absolutely! You think this is good news. It could hardly be worse."

I feared then that I understood what he was getting at, and I dropped the coins into my pocket and declared that I intended to keep them.

"You may have them," Emlyn declared. Then, like his brother, he turned and fled.

Later, as you may imagine, I searched the telephone book in the drugstore for a coin dealer. I found an ad for one, and was overjoyed to find it—then plunged into the depths of despair when I perused the address. The dealer was in Port Saint Jude, some distance away.

Leaving the drugstore, I called him, described the smallest of the three coins, and asked what it might be worth.

"You want to sell it to me?"

I said, "Yes, I might."

"And I might buy it, but I'd have to see it."

"I understand. What if I didn't want to sell it?"

"Then I'd charge you fifty dollars for an appraisal. You'd get that in writing, and notarized."

"But you'd have to see it."

"Correct. You say you found it in your house?"

"Yes, I did."

"I see. I'll have to check it against the reports of stolen coins. If it matches, I'll have to call the police. Do you still want to show it to me?"

"Certainly. Very much."

"Fine. I close at five and open at nine."

You can easily guess what I did next, George. I went to the office in which Doris worked, hoping that I could persuade her to drive me to the dealer's. She was showing houses, however, and was not expected to return until morning.

At the pawnshop, the pawnbroker told me quite frankly that he could advance me no more than the value of the gold if I left it with him. I did, and received a pawn ticket. That was perhaps three hours ago.

Here I shall explain my reasoning, George, though I doubt that you require it. With the money I received from the pawnbroker, I will be able to pay for dinner and have a bit left to tide me over until my check clears. Tomorrow, surely, I will be able to contrive some means of reaching the dealer. Doris will drive me, or Martha will. If worse comes to worst, I will hitchhike; although I do not enjoy that, I have done it before and emerged unscathed. Possibly there is someplace in town where I might rent a bicycle; I'm told the distance is only about fifteen miles.

Once there, I will sell one of the larger coins. It should bring a considerable sum, and with that I can redeem the smallest.

And that is where I am now, George. Assisted only by Winkle, I was—barely—able to drag the mattress down the spiral stair I have described and into this room. I am seated on it now, and sit proudly. Bottom-of-the-line or not, my new cellular telephone has a time feature, I find. It is a pleasant surprise indeed. The time is five forty-two, and I eagerly await the sound of Martha's horn. I have promised to bring something back for Winkle. As I shall, if it is humanly possible.

Wish me luck?

Yours sincerely,
Bax

PS: How do you like this paper? I believe it must be hand-laid.

Number 10

TOUGH QUESTION

Dear Shell:

It was great to hear from you! When I wrote you I wondered whether you would ever answer. I misjudged you, and I apologize. This is one time when I find it a real pleasure to be wrong. Remember how we used to sit and talk and play checkers until Lights Out? Half the time we'd get so busy talking we would lose track of whose turn it was to move. When I read your letter, I felt like I was back there with you, talking about how we might get a better cell and what our lives had been like when we were kids.

Or marriage. You would tell me never to do it, and I would point out that your wife stuck by you all through the trial and was still writing you every week. And you would explain that was the best reason there was not to do it.

I can hear you now: "Come clean, Bax!"

No, I am not about to ask somebody to marry me; but I have met a couple of nice-looking women. More about this when I know more.

Meanwhile, I have a tough problem and will welcome any help you can give. I have found three gold coins. Yes, I found them; I did not steal them. I am pretty sure they would bring a couple of thousand and perhaps more. The problem is that if I try to sell them I may find myself in trouble with the law again.

I telephoned a rare-coin dealer and described one of them. He said he could not make an offer without seeing the coin, and he warned me that when he had he would check it against reports of stolen coins. If it matches, he will call the police.

As I said, Shell, I did not steal them. I found them in the drawer of an old table in the attic. I do not know who put them there or whether they are hot. Sooner or later I am going to try to sell them—to him or to someone else; I need money too much not to try it. If I do and they are hot, I may find myself on trial again.

And again dependent on a pro-bono lawyer appointed by the court. I have done that, and you know how it turned out. Is there anybody you know in this part of the state who might help me? Please let me know.

———————————

Yours sincerely,
Bax

Dear George:

A great deal has happened since I last wrote, and I confess I am at a loss as to what may be important. I must issue a warning, however. You may not wish Millie to read this. Women—some women at least—are so easily offended by anything of an Anacreontic nature.

Get to the point, you will say. Since when have *you* had truck with women?

Patience, George. Patience. It is a great and a most noble virtue.

Martha, it transpired, had not intended that we should dine in a restaurant at all. She had prepared a dinner for us at her house, and though it was plain American cooking, I found it exceeded my expectations: a lamb roast with mint jelly, glazed carrots, and a fine salad.

Our cheesecake (which she confessed to buying) was a bit heavy, I thought, but by no means contemptible. I will not describe our small talk during dinner; it would only bore you.

Now that the time had come, I found myself embarrassed by the need to describe my destitution. Not for my own sake, George, but for yours. I knew that should I describe it, I should soon find myself launched into a description of your affluence. Martha would urge me to seek your assistance, and I would be forced to lie. *Oh, George would help me in a moment, if I were to apply to him,* and all the rest of that sorry charade. I have very little pride left, George, but the dregs remain. I could not do it.

Instead I was reduced to asking Martha quite casually whether she often had occasion to visit Port Saint Jude.

"Oh, that awful place! No, I go there only when I must, Bax. Have you seen it?"

"No, I've never been there. But I collect coins, and I'm told there's a dealer there. I thought I might see what he has to offer."

"How fascinating! I'd love to see your collection."

I laughed. "You'd be disappointed, believe me. If—"

At that moment there was an odd sort of noise outside, half moan and half whimper. I asked whether she owned a dog.

"Not anymore." She sighed. "You have one, you grow attached to it, and then . . . Well, we are all mortal, but it breaks my heart each time. I don't want to go through that again."

I stood up. "I'm going to look out. I'd swear I heard an animal out there."

Outside, I saw nothing and heard nothing; but there was an odor—a faint, musty stench.

You will wonder why I mention this at all, but I have a reason.

Martha had left the table when I did, and when I returned she suggested coffee in the living room. Of course I acquiesced.

"You said on the phone that you had questions about the house, Bax."

"Yes, I did. Do you know how I might get into the cellar without leaving the house? There is an outside door, I realize, but that's bound to be inconvenient in winter."

Martha shook her head, slowly at first, then more positively. "I've only been in the house once—no, twice, I think. I wasn't showing it you understand, just holding it for you. And then when the maintenance money ran out . . . Well, you can understand. What was the use of my knowing that something needed to be fixed when I had no money to fix it with?"

"I do understand. But you were in the house twice. Do you have floor plans?"

"No. I had a survey, showing the property lines. I gave that to you with the deed. Nothing else."

"Did you go into the cellar?"

"I don't believe I did."

"What about the attic?"

"I—this is embarrassing, Mr. Dunn. I meant to. I intended to and I tried to. But I couldn't find a way to get up there. I—I wanted to see if the roof was leaking. There had been some wind damage, shingles blown off, you know. Eventually I had the roof repaired without ever going up there. The roofers didn't need to get inside. They hardly ever do."

"I've found two ways," I told her. "One is a stair off the butler's pantry. It's—"

"Is there a butler's pantry?" Martha looked a trifle shocked.

"That's what I call it. Quite possibly you would call it something else. It's a smallish room between the dining room and the kitchen."

It was about then, George, that we heard the first siren. There was a screech of brakes, and the spinning red light of a police car filled Martha's picture window with a fitful glare. Another siren wailed in the distance.

Martha hurried outside, doubtless fearing that one of the neighboring houses was on fire. After putting several small pieces of meat into my pockets and sternly ordering myself to fall flat in the event of shooting, I followed her.

For my peace of mind, it proved a grave error; I saw the victim, and wish I had not. That she was dead was beyond question: a leg had been torn away, and there was a great deal of blood. I shall leave it at that.

Martha became hysterical. I omit those details also; no doubt you have had some experience of hysteria. In the end, she was undressed by a female officer who put her to bed after administering a sedative she found in Martha's medicine cabinet.

After quizzing me about my bruises, she said, "Do you have a car, sir?"

I explained that Martha had picked me up at my home.

"Is it far?"

"Not really. Four or five miles, I suppose. Thirteen hundred Riverpath Road?"

"That's more like seven. Want a ride home?"

"Yes, indeed. It's very kind of you."

In her squad car, I inquired about the dead woman, saying that she must surely have been a friend of Martha's.

"A neighbor, but they may have been friends, too. You new in town, sir?"

"I came in January, so I'm still quite new. I—well, I've spent most of my life in cities, I'm afraid. After a while, one becomes dreadfully tired of cities."

"I wouldn't know. What do you do, sir?"

"Right now? Look for a job." I outlined my degrees. "There is never much demand for scholars, I'm afraid."

"Ever tried acting?"

I could only stare.

"I'm not joking. You'd be good at it. You'll be nice looking when your face heals, and you said thirteen hundred Riverpath like I'd say eight eleven Walnut Street. That's the Black House, and you must know it."

"I did. Martha told me, but I thought you might never have heard of it."

"All us cops know about the Black House."

"I see . . ."

"It used to be for rent, years and years ago. This is what I've heard. I wasn't a cop then."

"Obviously not."

"Thanks. People would rent it and find bodies. Ever found one?"

I shook my head.

"They'd call the cops, but when we got there the body'd be gone. No body anywhere, and no blood. They'd been hung, mostly. Some had been stabbed, but mostly it was hanging."

"Neater, I suppose."

"Right. Then the same renters would find another one, and when it disappeared, too, they'd move out."

"One can hardly blame them."

"I wouldn't." She smiled at me, suddenly pert and pretty. "You're renting it from Mrs. Murrey?"

"No, I own it."

"Wow."

She was quiet after that until we reached the house. Then she said, "You left some lights on."

"The electric company must have restored power to the house," I said. "It was still off when I left."

"Good news then." She offered her hand. "I'm Kate Finn."

I was greatly tempted to say, "Of eight eleven Walnut Street," but naturally I introduced myself instead, though I had given her my name and telephone number earlier.

As soon as she pulled away, the lights in my house went out. All of them. I have rarely been tempted to curse, but at that moment it would have been an enormous relief.

· · · · ·

Should I tell you this? I will be handing you a weapon, but then you have a great many already. Will I ever feel the sting of this one? I doubt it. If I were wise—but we both know that I am not. To this point I have told you everything of moment, and I hate to spoil my record.

Very well.

George, I stumbled over a human leg in the dark. It was on my porch, two steps in front of the door.

At first I did not know what it was. I tried to kick it away, and found it softer than I had expected and heavy. Stepping over it, I went inside and got my flashlight. The leg was a woman's, or so I would judge. All clothing was gone and there was a spattering of blood, but it appeared hairless.

Here, I admit, I acted exactly as you would have in my place. I (or so I would have predicted) would have called the police—who would have found me penniless, living in a house without furniture. Who would soon have discovered that I had pawned an antique gold coin that very day, even if I had hidden the other two. Who would have known as a matter of course that I had been very near the scene of the woman's death.

For those reasons and more, I carried that leg down to the river, threw it into the water, and returned to the house, terrified. I had expected to be apprehensive, but I had certainly not expected what I experienced; my walk through the little wood separating my lawn from the river was one I shall never forget. There were things in that wood, things I heard whisper and move.

Do you believe me? If you do not—if you believe I am spinning fancies for my own entertainment—so much the better. You did not see their eyes or hear their voices, George. I did.

I bathed by the light of the oil lamp my neighbor had kindly loaned me, and tried to think only about washing clothes. With the money I had gotten in the pawnshop I would be able to wash and dry everything at the Laundromat (this I told myself over and over). On the way home, I would deposit my allowance check—something I ought to have done already.

I had been sleeping on a pad of old newspapers, as you may remember. The mattress that had cost me so much labor was somewhat lumpy and far from new, but how I luxuriated upon it! Had it been dark, I believe I might have been terrified; it was not—one of the advantages of sleeping before a fire.

There can be few things more surprising than waking to find that there is another person in your bed. It had never befallen me before, but it did that night, when I was roused quite pleasantly by the caresses of a small hand.

You are a man of wide experience, George, or at least you say you are. You would only be irritated by a recital of my clumsy fumblings. Suffice it to say that I quickly learned that my partner was small but by no means a child, slender but pleasantly curved. Other than that, her nails were long, as was her hair. It was all I knew, and it was more than enough for me.

Much later, when we had both slept for some hours and the morning sun had come to supplant my dying fire, I was able to admire her delicate oval face and long black hair. My admiration held more than a little curiosity, as you may imagine. Who was she? Where had she come from? How had she gotten into the house?

How, for that matter, did Emlyn and his brother do it?

Why had she chosen to give herself to me?

It was not until I saw my own clothing, folded and stacked beside my shoes, that I thought to wonder about hers. A few glances showed clearly enough that it was nowhere in the room.

She woke, opening her eyes and smiling; her smile (how well I recall it!) was gentle, sly, and utterly enchanting. Elfin, George. You do not know what that word means, but I do now.

"So nice . . ." It was a whisper, and her whisper is enchanting, too.

"So beautiful," I said. "You're lovely. Yes, truly lovely, and I knew you would be."

She giggled, and her little hand stroked me beneath the blanket; I tried to explain that I could not cooperate, although I hoped to later.

"It was nice . . ."

"Thank you. For me it was quite wonderful."

"So nice we tore the mattress. Did you see?"

"Did we? I don't care."

"The stuffing leaked."

"Did it? I hadn't noticed. It's an old mattress, however. It must have been in the attic for a very long time, and I'm afraid that some structural weaknesses are to be expected."

"This leaked out. See?" She held up a handful of currency.

I accepted it from her, and when I had counted it, she gave me another. "Are you going to wash?"

"Not now," I told her. "In a moment."

"Then your little pet's going to wash first." She rose, managing to drape herself in the blanket as she stood, and fled giggling into the master bedroom.

That was the last time I saw her, George. Eventually I went into the master bedroom myself. The bathroom door stood wide. The blanket she had taken lay on the floor, and the window had been opened.

She was gone.

What am I to do? Place an ad?

> Lost, a young woman. Long black hair, oval face, dark brown eyes, tiny nose, delightful little mouth, perfect complexion. Long nails painted black. Accent. Wearing nothing when last seen. Reward.

Of course I have done all the obvious things. I have looked around outside for footprints or something of the sort, and found nothing. I have tried to look into every room on both floors, and though I cannot be sure I visited them all—there must be at least forty—I did the best I could. I have scoured the neighborhood twice.

These things have kept me on my feet all morning, and now I sit, writing you about them. I can only hope she will return.

Yours sincerely,
Bax

Number 12

A Big Deal in Prospect

Dear George:

Another letter so soon? Well, yes. It's evening now—no, night. Full dark.

And she has not returned. Winkle did, and gratefully received the scraps of meat I had brought her from Martha's table. I had never expected to have a tame fox. Indeed, I have never heard of anyone who did, although there must be others.

You will laugh, but I told her about the girl who had visited me, how lovely she was and what she had meant to me while we were together. Winkle looked as sympathetic as it is possible for a fox to look, laid one neat black paw in my lap, and whispered. "She cometh. She cometh. She cometh thoon."

I telephoned Martha. "This is Bax. I wanted to make sure you're all right."

"Oh, yes. Thank you, you're very thoughtful. You kissed my hand." She sighed. "Did you really, Bax? Or did I dream it?"

"Yes, I did, but you were asleep by then."

"I knew it. I felt your kiss. I'm fine now. Not quite my old self, but recovering rapidly. How are you?"

"Oh, I'm perfectly fine. Rearing to go, isn't that what they say? This morning I want to phone the electric company—though I suppose it must be nearly noon. This afternoon, then."

"Have you found a way into the cellar?"

It was a question I had not anticipated. "No. Or at least no way other than the door in back I told you about—the outside door. I haven't even looked for one today."

"This morning it occurred to me that the best way to find one would be for you to go into the cellar through the outside door and look from the bottom up. There will be steps. There'll have to be. Go up them, and see where you are."

"You're right. I should have thought of that. There was something else I wanted ask. Do you have keys to the garage?"

"Garage?"

"Yes, there's a big garage with three doors. They're all padlocked."

"I don't have the keys. The only key I've ever had was the one to the front door, and I gave it to you." She hesitated. "Couldn't you call a locksmith?"

"Yes. I'll do that."

After that our talk wandered off into generalities.

When I hung up, I smiled to think that it was the truth. I *could* call a locksmith now. I will not tell you, George, how much money that beautiful girl and I took from the mattress. She brought out two handfuls. I believe I said that. I brought out more shortly before I began this. When I counted all I had, the sum was so great that I grew frightened. I put most of it back into the mattress, got out my little sewing kit, and sewed the mattress back up. My stitches were not as sturdy as the factory's; nor were those of the person, Mr. Black, or whoever he may have been, who had ripped out the factory stitches and inserted the money. It was why they had burst while the girl and I enjoyed each other's company.

But I have kept out enough to make me feel very rich indeed, a man who can summon a locksmith without a second thought.

As I have. He will come tomorrow.

· · · · ·

Up there I was interrupted by a call from a young lady. "Mr. Dunn? Is this Mr. Baxter Dunn?"

"Speaking," I said.

"My name's Cathy Ruth, Mr. Dunn, and I write for the *Sentinel*. May I ask you a few questions?"

"You may, Miss Ruth, if you'll answer mine. How did you get my number?"

"Mrs. Murrey gave it to me, Mr. Dunn. She felt sure you'd be delighted to talk to me."

"I see. I was just speaking with her. I'm surprised she didn't mention it." I was striving to recall to whom I had given my number.

"She probably forgot about it. Are you living in the old Black House, Mr. Dunn?"

"Yes, I am. I own it."

"I know! She told me. And you were present when Star Paxton died?"

"Star Paxton was the poor woman last night?"

"That's right. Mrs. Wesley Paxton. You were there?"

"As I understand it, she was killed on the front lawn of her house. I was next door, at Mrs. Murrey's, talking with Mrs. Murrey."

"This is great! You ran outside when you heard the screaming?"

"Mrs. Murrey did. I followed her."

"What did you see?"

"Mrs. Paxton's body, and a great deal of blood. Also Mrs. Murrey looking down at it and screaming."

"You didn't know Mrs. Paxton?"

"No. To the best of my knowledge, that was the first time I'd ever seen her. Now I'd like you to answer another question for me, Miss Ruth. What—"

"Call me Cathy, please."

"What do the police say killed Mrs. Paxton, Cathy?"

"There's been no official statement, Mr. Dunn. That will come from the coroner's office."

"I understand, but you have sources of information on the police force—one at least whom I could name. What does she say, Cathy?"

"Has anyone ever told you you're scary, Mr. Dunn?"

"Never. In my entire life no one has ever called me frightening, Cathy. It's a word that people reserve for my brother George. What does your contact say?"

"You're not supposed to know about her."

The pronoun made my conclusion certain. I said, "If you don't tell me, Cathy, I'll tell Officer Finn that you revealed her identity without being asked."

"Mr. Dunn . . ."

"You may well decide to risk it. I'm a poor liar, and I'm inclined to think Officer Finn will soon realize that I am lying. Why don't you chance it?"

"Suppose I tell you now? Exactly what she said?"

"Then I will keep your secret, upon my honor."

"All right. She said everybody thought it was a big dog. Nothing else. Just a big dog."

"I see. Did she agree?"

"No, she didn't, and now you're going to want to know what she thought it was. And I can't tell you because she doesn't know. But one of Star's legs was torn off. Did you know that?"

"Go on."

"She said she grew up with Saint Bernards. Those are big dogs."

"I know."

"Her father bred them. She said the big males are as strong as any dog on earth, and they couldn't have done it. They could have grabbed a leg and dragged the body for miles, but they couldn't have torn a leg off like that."

"I'd say she has a point. Shall I wait for you to ask whether I own a big dog?"

"Do you?"

"I do not."

"Any kind of a dog? A little one?"

"I have nothing against dogs. I rather like them, in fact. But I have never owned one."

"You saw Star's body, Mr. Dunn. I didn't. What was your first thought? What did you think had happened to her?"

"I shouldn't answer that." I paused, hoping Miss Ruth would speak again. "I will, but only because I'm a trifle ashamed of having bullied you. I thought that she had been attacked by a bear."

"Why did you think so?"

"I can't tell you. It just popped into my mind."

"Do you still think that? What do you think now?"

"At present, I don't know what to think. If you'll excuse me, I have to—"

"Please! Just a couple more questions."

"All right, two. No more than that."

"What is the connection between Star's death and the Black House?"

"There is none that I know of." (I was lying, to be sure; but I was not under oath.)

"Have you seen a ghost? In the house, I mean, since you've been there?"

"I'm not certain," I said, and hung up.

I dialed Directory Assistance immediately and was soon connected to the power company. I provided my name and address, explained that I had been occupying the house for several days, and suggested politely that the house could now be reconnected to their grid.

"Let me check this, sir. It will just take a minute."

I waited.

"You've asked to be reconnected before, haven't you, sir?"

"I have not, but I've been told that the real-estate agent made the request on my behalf."

"I see. What this shows, sir, is that you've already been reconnected. It was done yesterday. You don't have power?"

"Correct."

"You checked today?"

"Yes. This morning."

"Could you try again now?"

I could and did, flipping switches in the living room, the dining room (two switches), the butler's pantry, and the kitchen without result. "No power," I told the woman who had answered my call.

"We'll send a man over as soon as we can, sir."

I thanked her, and turned off my cellular telephone.

Now, George, you are bound to be curious regarding my final sally to Miss Cathy Ruth. I confess that I spoke as I did to discomfort her; but upon reflection, I fear there was more substance to it than I intended. I shall not enlarge upon that until I learn more. And perhaps not then.

·　·　·　·　·

I have bought her a gift, George. You will say that does not sound like me, but I have.

I walked downtown, you see, after writing to you. You might suppose I would be too tired to do anything of that kind after combing the neighborhood for her, and searching (however inadequately) this house as well. You would be quite correct, too; I was tired, but hunger is a great spur. It was nearly noon, I had money in my wallet, and I had not eaten since dinner last night at Martha's.

So I found a little place with a salad bar and enjoyed a bountiful lunch. After that, I went to the pawnshop, reclaimed my coin, and would have reclaimed my laptop if I could. The time had run out, however, and it had been sold. I will buy a proper computer soon, never fear. Then you can send e-mails berating me once more.

Nor was that all. I found a Laundromat and bought a laundry bag, and tomorrow I intend to carry all my dirty clothing there and wash it.

After that, it occurred to me that I ought to have invited Doris Griffin to lunch—that I owed her a meal. I telephoned her and suggested dinner, promising to pay for our dinners if she would provide our transportation. Very much to my surprise, she asked me to come to the office in which she is employed, saying that someone there needed to speak with me.

I was footsore, I admit, and the distance was at least six blocks; I asked her to pick me up early. We will go to her office and have dinner afterward.

Should I then have bought a gift for another woman? You will say no. Millie—a better judge, I think—might well say yes. I felt that if I was going to buy Doris's dinner, I ought to do that much and more for the young lady who had spent the night with me.

As I have. My original notion was simply to give her a robe to replace the blanket she had borrowed for her dash to the bathroom. When I described her to the saleswoman, however, she insisted that I ought to buy her a silk one of the type she showed me, an Oriental robe with wide sleeves. She had several of these sized for small women. I sat in near-royal majesty (you will not believe this, George, but it's true) while another clerk of the correct size modeled each. In the end I chose the simplest, though it was also the most costly. It is white, and prettily embroidered with a nature scene: a golden pheasant on the limb of a pine watching a fox in pursuit of a rabbit. The sash is crimson. This is something less than modest, I suppose, but I honestly think she will like it. If she does not, I can return it; I have the receipt.

·   ·   ·   ·   ·

Well, George, I had a most interesting time last night with Doris. She arrived earlier than I had expected, but I laid aside my pen and trotted out to meet her.

"I hope you don't mind," she said.

Of course I assured her that I did not.

"We can have an early dinner. The restaurant won't be crowded, and we can enjoy each other's company."

"Believe me, I'm looking forward to enjoying yours. You are a most charming woman, and I can't be the first to tell you that."

She smiled. "Afterward, we might go to my apartment for a drink and a little more talk. Will you be free?"

It took me by surprise, but I managed it well enough, I think. At least I acquiesced without stammering.

"But first Mr. Hardaway wants to talk to you." She backed out of my driveway and pulled onto the road. "We had a staff meeting this morning."

"Yes?"

"Your name came up." Here I received a delightful smile. "Would you do me a great, great favor, Bax? It will be a very small thing to you, but a very big one to me. And I'll be ever so grateful."

Of course I said I would do whatever I could if it would be of the least assistance to her.

"You're still wearing Ted's ring. I noticed that, and it makes it very hard for me to ask you for anything else, because that was a maxi-favor, too. Hard, but I'm asking just the same."

"You will get whatever you ask for," I assured her.

"Mr. Hardaway's my boss, Bax. Do you remember how we discussed all those real-estate matters over lunch? Well anyway, you must remember that I was going to say we did on my expense account."

"Certainly."

"I'd like you to make it clear to Mr. Hardaway that I'm your agent—that I take care of real-estate matters for you."

I assumed, as I believe anyone would, that Doris had been put on the carpet concerning her expense account, and I swore that I would back her to the hilt.

Although she was driving, we shook hands on it. "You see, Mr. Hardaway happened to mention a tract between here and Port Saint Jude, and—what's the matter?"

"Nothing. Nothing at all. Go on, please."

"Anyway he mentioned a missing owner, and that was when I said, 'Would you repeat that name, sir?' And he said, 'The name is Dunn, Mrs. Griffin. Baxter Dunn.'"

"Well, well."

"Yes, indeed. So I said, 'Why I had lunch with Baxter Dunn just the other day, sir,' and everybody froze. They've been looking for you for three years."

I smiled, trying to make it charming. (*You* look like a shark when you smile, George.) "Not in the right places, apparently."

"Obviously not. There's an attorney named Trelawny involved. Do you know him? Urban Trelawny?"

I shook my head.

"And a man named Skotos. Alexander Skotos. What about him?"

I said, "It sounds familiar, but I can't place him." I said that, George, because I judged it contrary to my best interests to commit myself one way or the other so early. How was I to know whether I had, at some time in what I know you will concede has been a checkered career, come across an Alexander Skotos? Perhaps I had. Or more likely, Alexander Skotos was a name assumed by someone I had known under another appellation. I knew a man called Sandy Scott at Churchill Downs, for example.

"Ahhh," said Doris. She was clearly impressed.

"Will he be there?" I asked. "At your office?"

"No. Definitely not. Have you a place in mind, or do I get to choose the restaurant?"

"You get to choose, of course."

"Fine. We'll want a quiet spot with slow service."

"And good food."

"Absolutely. Mr. Hardaway didn't exactly open up with me."

"I quite understand."

"But Olga told me afterward that they've been looking for you for three years. For a Baxter Dunn, anyway. And there's this big tract of un-developed land." Doris took a deep breath. "What we're talking about here is a big, big commission, Bax. You've probably guessed that."

"From what you said, it seemed likely."

"Right. Nobody's said that. Nobody's mentioned any figures at all, but it was in the air. I could smell it. Have you ever been poor?"

"No," I said, "but I've been broke. It's not exactly the same thing."

"You're right, it isn't. And now that I think about it—" She stopped at a traffic light and turned to give me another most fetching smile. "I believe I was broke, too. I still am, or almost. Ted made good money, but he didn't have much life insurance."

"What a pity!"

"Yes, isn't it? It took a lot of what we had just to bury him, and there were medical bills. There *are*, I ought to say. I haven't paid them all yet."

"I know the feeling. Did we just pass your office?"

"Yes, I'm looking for a parking place. They're not easy to find at this hour."

We pulled into one, and she turned off the engine. "I was going to say I was glad I put gas in this last night, because I was thinking of a place way out of town, but . . ."

"Yes?" I asked.

"But that's really wrong. It would be foolish, in fact. What I want—what I need, Bax—is a place where people from my office will see us eating together. The place I've got in mind is fairly expensive. It's not terrible, but it is a little pricey. Would that be all right? I promise to order something cheap."

I said it would be fine, and that she could order anything she wanted.

"It's the main dining room at the Hilton. They have a great chef."

"In that case, let's go there."

"Our people take clients there when there's a big deal in prospect. I'll make a reservation."

Which she did when we reached her office, telephoning from her desk. After that, we spoke with Mr. Hardaway; but this letter has grown too long already.

Yours sincerely,
Bax

Number 13
MOUTHPIECE

Okay, Prof, you asked about a lawyer that might bail you out even if you were broke. I did not know of anybody in that jerkwater town, but I asked around.

Remember Rick? Tall guy, boosts cars, bad complexion. He said his cousin had this guy and he had talked to him. He is good, Rick said, and he might do it. He likes to see his name in the paper, you know what I mean? The name is Ben Ramsey. Rick said you might want to try him.

You seem to be messing around with women. You will not listen and I do not blame you, but there are only two kinds. There are women who make trouble for you and women you make trouble for. Just those two. You will find out, so let me know what you do.

Sheldon Hawes

Dear George:

My dinner with Doris—I'll tell you about it in a moment—made me realize that my wardrobe needed more than a few improvements. My clothing is of good quality for the most part, but quite thoroughly worn. I have three suits on order now, and I've bought a sports coat, three pairs of shoes, underwear, some shirts, and four pairs of slacks.

Emlyn has not returned, though I would be glad to see him, and Winkle has vanished once more; but there have been other developments. I shall attempt to describe them in order.

Did I mentioned Nicholas the Butler? While Doris was making our reservation, an older woman asked me about the Black House and whether I had seen him. Her manner implied that this butler was a boogeyman of some sort; so I said, "No," which was all I had time for.

Mr. Hardaway is a large, tweedy man, quite bald; he smokes cigars, although a pipe would fit him better. He welcomed us, shook my hand heartily, and invited me to take a chair.

Doris said, "May I sit in, sir? I feel I should."

"That's up to Mr. Dunn." Mr. Hardaway gave me a quick professional smile. "Will you feel outnumbered, Mr. Dunn? You can believe me absolutely when I say that Mrs. Griffin and I have your best interests at heart."

I said that if what we were going to discuss concerned real estate, I would certainly want Mrs. Griffin present.

"It does. You knew the late Mr. Skotos?"

"I prefer to reserve that, Mr. Hardaway."

He frowned. "We're not likely to get very far if you mean that."

"As you wish. I came here at your request. If you've nothing to say to me, I'll be happy to leave."

"You are Mr. Dunn?"

I nodded.

"Mr. Baxter Dunn?"

"Correct. I can show you a driver's license. Would you like to see it? The picture is less than flattering, but it is a picture."

"Could you, if asked, produce a birth certificate?"

"No, sir."

Mr. Hardaway raised his eyebrows. "You couldn't?"

"No. My brother and I were adopted. Presumably there are birth certificates somewhere, but the names they carry will not be George and Baxter Dunn."

"You have a brother?"

I nodded.

"He would be able to vouch for your identity?"

"Certainly. And there will be school records and so on. I have two Ph.D.'s, and various other degrees. There should be no difficulty."

"I see. Would you care for a cigar, Mr. Dunn?"

"No, thank you. But I have no objection to your smoking."

He laughed. "Mrs. Griffin would object, I'm sure. She wouldn't say it, but all the same . . . I'll wait."

Doris said, "Thank you, sir."

"Is there anyone else who could vouch for your identity, Mr. Dunn?"

"My sister-in-law would be an obvious reference, I'd think. Millie's known me for years. My parents are dead, but I have several cousins. Other than that, there's Mrs. Murrey. Mrs. Murrey gave me the deed to thirteen hundred Riverpath Road. Murrey and Associates? You must know of her."

He nodded. "She was satisfied that you're Baxter Dunn?"

"Yes. Obviously."

Doris coughed apologetically. "So am I, Mr. Hardaway. When I met Mr. Dunn he knew nothing about this."

"He knows almost nothing now," I added. "Would you mind telling me what we're talking about?"

Mr. Hardaway cleared his throat. "We're talking about the Skotos Strip, Mr. Dunn. It's a tract of land on the other side of the river. A tract roughly three miles long and half a mile wide."

I sensed, rather than saw, Doris's reaction.

"Let me tell you the whole thing from my point of view. Fifteen years ago I was just Jim Hardaway, another real-estate salesman. Do you shoot, Mr. Dunn?"

"Birds, you mean?" I shook my head.

"Handguns. It's my hobby. I collect old pistols and revolvers. There's a range outside of town, and I shoot a bit. At the range, I became friendly with Alex Skotos."

"Yes?"

"He was a shooter and a collector, too. We had a lot in common, and we did some trading. Say that I had an old dueling pistol. I might trade it to him for a Peacemaker. Sometimes we just got together to talk."

"I understand."

"When we'd known each other for a year or so, he asked me about investments. He was thinking, he said, of putting some money into real estate. Short term?, I said, or long? He said long, so I told him what I always tell everybody. The best long-term investment a man can make is undeveloped land fronting on water. He asked me to look around."

Doris said, "I know it must be a good property, sir. You would never advise a client to buy one that wasn't."

"I didn't find the Skotos Strip all at once," Hardaway told her. "I did find him a good-sized tract that became the nucleus of it. After that, I handled the negotiations for him. He wanted the property on either side, and it took four or five years to get it." Mr. Hardaway paused, clearly wishing he could light a cigar.

"Alex passed away, and I was surprised to find out he'd made me his executor. Thunderstruck, in fact. But when I thought the matter over, it made a great deal of sense. He'd had no wife and no kids. No other relatives, so far as I could discover. His gun collection was nice, but not terribly valuable. You could duplicate it today for about thirty thousand, in my judgment. Other than that and his furniture, his estate consisted of a sizable bank account and the Skotos Strip. That's what we've been calling it here at the agency."

Doris asked, "Didn't he own a home, sir?"

"No. He leased an apartment. His will was a simple one, but it hasn't been simple to carry out. He directed that his furniture should be auctioned. The same thing for his collection, except for one nice set of cased dueling pistols. He was particularly fond of them and wanted them to go to his heir."

"And Mr. Dunn is the heir?"

"I think so." Hardaway turned to me. "There's better than a hundred thousand in the account. A hundred and five thousand and change. Are you impressed?"

"Tolerably."

He laughed. "I agree. There's also the Skotos Strip of one and a half square miles. One square mile is six hundred and forty acres, so nine hundred and sixty in the Strip. Allow a hundred and sixty for streets. That's four hundred two-acre building lots. Two acres is a large lot."

I said I knew that.

"For two-acre lots in that location you could, in my judgement, average about ten thousand dollars today if the operation were handled right. So, four million. There'd be commissions to pay and other expenses." He smiled. "You'd be looking at well over three million even so."

"If I sell now," I said.

"Exactly. Are you going to?"

"I don't know. To begin with, Mr. Hardaway, I don't require the money. My needs are modest, and I have more than a sufficiency. The best investment a man can make, or so I've heard, is unimproved land fronting water. It might be wise for me to hold the land for a few more years before I cash in."

"You're right. I was about to advise you, in fact I do advise you, to sell those lots off slowly. If we do that—pardon me, I misspoke. As executor, I could not be a party to the transaction."

I objected. "But Mrs. Griffin is my agent."

She took my hand.

"Okay, but she's an associate here at the agency. She doesn't represent me as a person, in other words. You can, if you want to, and I hope you will, engage the Country Hill Agency to act in your behalf. Naturally the agency can and will have Mrs. Griffin take personal charge of your account."

Doris said, "When will Bax get the property?"

But I have gone on too long about this, George. I shall summarize. I told Mr. Hardaway that I would make no decision regarding the Skotos Strip until I was thoroughly familiar with it. Doris and I will look at it in a day or two. (The locksmith is coming today, and I want to buy hiking boots and so on.) Mr. Hardaway will contact the lawyer and ask him to schedule a reading of the will as soon as possible.

No doubt you are happy for me, George. How fervently I hope so!

On to other matters. Doris and I dined at the Hilton as planned. We discussed the Strip until one of her coworkers stopped at our table. "Have you two heard about the Hound of Horror? That's what they're calling it."

We asked for details.

"It's killed another woman, a nurse who was half an hour late getting off shift. The story was on the five o'clock news. Got her in the hospital parking lot. They've found part of her body."

"Only part?" Doris asked.

"Right. The report I saw didn't say which part, just that part of her had been found next to her car. I didn't mean to scare you, but both the victims have been women and both were caught outside alone not long after sundown. You be careful, Doris." He left before she could reply.

She looked at me. "Well, I *am* scared."

"I don't blame you. So am I. I saw the first body."

"Did you really?"

I nodded and explained.

"Let me get this straight. You inherited the Black House from Mr. Black?"

"No, not exactly. He put it in my name and told the agency Martha worked for at the time that I would be along to claim it. When the agency dissolved, Martha took it over."

"Alexander Skotos did the same thing, or almost."

"I suppose you could say that, although Mr. Black simply gave me his house."

"His haunted house."

I shrugged. "Did you hear that woman ask whether I'd seen the butler?"

"Alice? Yes, I did. She was just being friendly. She's a nice person."

"I'm sure she is, but I haven't seen him. Is he a ghost?"

"I suppose. There was a story in the paper last Halloween. That's all I know about it, and I imagine all that Alice knows, too."

"Tell me, please."

"I'll try. Supposedly Mr. Black had this horrible butler, who went out at night and stole clotheslines."

"What?"

"Stole clotheslines. That's what the piece in the paper said. If you didn't take the clothes in before dark, this butler—I forget his name— would come around and steal the line with the clothes still on it. Then when Mr. Black died or moved away or whatever he did, the butler stayed behind. People would see him once or twice a year."

I swallowed a bite of steak. "Isn't this rather tame for Halloween? I was expecting something, well, stronger."

"I'm getting to that. One day a bunch of kids decided they'd spend the night in the Black House. I don't know how . . . They were going to climb in through a window. That was it. They went to the window, and inside they saw the butler with a human head on a tray."

"Ah hah!"

"They ran away, and in their panic they got lost. The article was written by the daughter of one of the girls. I remember that now. They wandered around until they saw an old man sitting on the ground under a tree. He called them over and asked what they were doing, and they told him the whole story. He nodded and laughed and said he could explain everything. The butler had worked for King Herod in biblical times, and he was the one who had carried in the head of John the Baptist. God punished him by making him stay down here, always as a butler, until he found somebody who would eat the head. Is this bothering you, Bax?"

"It certainly is," I told her. "I wanted to laugh, but I was afraid I'd choke."

"Then the old man invited them to come into his house. He said he'd get them something to eat and drive them home. They went inside and ate, and one of them asked his name, and he said, 'I am Mr. Black.' "

"At which point," I said, "they realized that they had been eating the head of John the Baptist."

Doris giggled. "I'll bet you're right. You got me talking about this to get my mind off the Hound, didn't you?"

I disclaimed any such intention.

"I know you did, and I've got a question for you. If I have a whiskey sour, will you be afraid to ride with me?"

"Absolutely not."

"Want one?"

I explained that my past experiences with alcohol had been less than fortunate.

"But it won't bother you if I do?"

"Not at all."

She had three before we left, and thinking it prudent, I drove. I was badly out of practice, but I managed well enough. Doris gave me directions and showed me where to park, and we were very good friends indeed by the time we went up to her digs.

For Millie's sake, I will spare you the interesting details; but I slept soundly last night, and this morning Doris (only a trifle hungover) kindly returned me to this house before going to work.

. . . . .

I was about to give you four or five pages of incisive reflections upon my recent adventures, George. And now I am badly tempted to write them anyway. You will admit they have been extraordinary? I have much of substance to say about them, but you are spared.

The locksmith arrived while I was meditating. His name is Les Nilsen, and he's a big blond fellow who seems quite competent. I took him to the garage. He glanced at the locks and asked whether I wanted to save them. I said that I saw no point in it, after which he took an acetylene torch from his truck and burned through all three shackles.

After that, he helped me open the doors, which are heavy and were in every case stuck tight with paint. The first bay contained gardening tools, neatly arranged and all quite old. There was a reel mower, a scythe, a sickle, a collection of spades, and so on. The second—we could see into it from the first—contained old furniture and pictures, very much like the attic.

The third surprised us both. Amazed would not be too strong a word. In it was an automobile, and I believe it must be the largest I have ever seen. It is covered with dust and cobwebs, but seems to be in fine condition. The headlights are huge; beyond that, George, it truly beggars my poor powers of description. There are three seats. The first, with room for the driver and a single passenger, has a leather top which can (could?) be folded back. There are three axles, one front and two rear. There are six doors, and the trunk is an actual trunk, a huge piece of luggage that could not possibly be carried by fewer than four men.

"This," Les whispered, "is worth a ton of money."

I was still taking it in and said nothing.

He tried to open the driver's door, but it was locked. After that, he tried all the rest in turn. "All locked," he reported. "Could be they're just corroded shut, but I don't think so. She's in too good a shape for that. I'm going to pick it."

Which he did in short order.

"I could make you a key, maybe. My guess is the same one would work for all six. Probably the ignition, too."

I encouraged him to do so.

"It'll cost. I might's well tell you. I'll take the lock out now and take it back to the shop. No extra charge for that, but making a key's goin' to run you forty dollars per each hour. Could be as much as eighty or a hundred."

I gave him my number and told him to call me if it appeared that his charges were liable to exceed one hundred dollars.

Now a confession. I became curious about the contents of the trunk, but became curious too late. The trunk was locked; I had paid Les and he had gone. So I will have to wait. It is probably empty anyway.

As am I, George. I had a very sketchy breakfast with Doris and have not eaten since. A large lunch figures in my immediate plans. After that, I will deposit my check (which I still have not done), put some of the money from the mattress in the bank, and endeavor to purchase hiking boots, a pair of stout jeans, mosquito repellent, and so forth—all that I will require to explore the Skotos Strip with Doris. A hunting knife should not be terribly costly, and will look virile.

It would be well, perhaps, to send flowers to Doris. Why not? And perhaps I could get something else for the girl who joined me on my mattress. I have the robe, and it is by no means a trifling gift. But still—

Perfume? Chocolates? I'll think things over during lunch. Meanwhile, love to you and your dear and beautiful Millie. I hope you are both well.

Yours sincerely,
Bax

Number 15

WOMEN

Dear Shell:

Thank you for the tip. I will keep it in mind, even though my financial situation is much better these days.

Let me tell you, that is a great relief. During the time I was inside I had forgotten just how important money is out here; my first few months out were a sharp refresher course.

Have I said I am trying to keep my nose clean? I am. I have even phoned my parole officer about my change of address. Now I have to remember to see him next week. I still haven't gotten a job, but I am starting to see some possibilities. Not office work, but something that might keep him off my back.

As to women, I have become intimately acquainted with two

recently. (That is not the way you would phrase it, Shell, but it is the way I am going to phrase it. I think you know what I mean.)

One is a small oriental, very pretty and very, very far from frigid. I am quite sure that I am not the first man in her life and almost certainly I will not be the last. I feel tenderness toward her just the same. Love, and I know she loves me. Beyond that, I know nothing at all about her, not even her name.

The other is a widow. Doris has chestnut hair and hazel eyes, and although she is not slender she is not at all bad looking. I know her name and where she lives—I slept there the other night—but every so often something surprises me. She has tattoos in unexpected places, for example. She likes money, but I cannot hold that against her. So do I.

No, I do not pay her. I did not mean that. She is not particularly intelligent, but quite shrewd. I am more intelligent but less shrewd, and if I am really as smart as I like to think I am, I can learn something of shrewdness from her.

As for technique, I have learned quite a lot from both of them.

Thank you again, Shell. Do not forget to write. Tell me about your new cellmate. All those things. You are a part of my life I do not want to lose.

Yours sincerely,
Bax

Dear Bax,

George has shown me some of your letters. I find them very interesting and really creative, but you must know the effect they have had on George.

He is furious. Yesterday he said that he would see you back in the penitentiary if it was the last thing he did, and today he said that he was going to fly out there and force you to see a psychiatrist. He is trying to find out what city has the nearest airport, and arranging for a two-days' leave from work. It will have to be a Thursday and Friday or else Monday and Tuesday so that he will have four days. Or else Friday and Monday, but not Monday and then Friday. You know what I mean, I feel sure.

Also is there a good golf course?

I wanted to go with him but he said NO.

So I talked all this over with Madame Orizia. She is my psychic adviser. I said, "Do you think George will hurt his poor brother?" She tried the cards and looked terribly frightened. After that, the little crystal. That is the real one, as she told me two years ago. There is a big one, too. It is plastic but it looks like crystal and it tells everybody what they want to hear. She uses that one all the time.

But the little one is real. She said she saw great danger for George and his brother (you), too. BE CAREFUL. She said for me to keep George at home if I could, and I will try. He will be safe here and sometimes I wish that something bad would happen to him. I lie awake wishing that sometimes, but you cannot pray for bad things so I pray for JUSTICE.

Most of your letters I have gotten out of the garbage are interesting, too, even though I have had to piece them back together with tape and sometimes the grease makes that hard. I do not think I like Doris. If I were you, I would say Mrs. Murrey. But you have seen them both, which I have not. Seeing a person changes everything, and perhaps I would feel different if I were to have Doris to lunch at the Tapestry Tea Room. Only I do not think so.

Besides, Doris is a trashy name.

I am very glad you found all that money. Life is such a chore without it is what my father used to say.

Your letters tell me all over again that I married the wrong brother, but I have known that ever since George said so many bad things about my family!

Fondly,

Millicent Kay Dunn

PS: If I can find George's plane tickets I am going to tear them all up and flush them in my bathroom. He will not know. If I cannot find them something else. If you were to write to me George would not see it. The mail is at three and he does not get home until six. Or later. I would hide your letters, so please write.

———

Kisses,
Millie

Dear Millie:

It was marvelous to hear from you. What a treat! My brother has never understood what a wonderful, wonderful woman he married—I know that. I have told him more than once, but he just sneers. You know that expression, I feel sure.

Let him come, please. If I thought he were really in any danger, I would not say that; but he will be as safe here with me as he could ever be at home, and it has been years since I last saw him. He will have a chip on his shoulder, I know; but I will be prepared for it and will do everything in my power to make peace. Has he gotten fat?

Not a lot has happened since my last letter to George, which I assume you have read. Les the Locksmith made keys that fit the doors and the ignition of my car, which I think very clever of him. He also recommended a friend ("Joe") who restores old cars. Joe will come to-morrow to look at mine. Les says—correctly, I feel certain—that it will fetch a much higher price in working condition; an antique car in working condition can be taken to car shows more easily, driven in parades, and so on.

Here is a sad piece of news, I fear. I believe I have mentioned in some letters that tramps appear to have camped in my house from time to time. I find empty cans, soiled rags, and so forth. There is a bedroom on the second floor that has a fireplace, and it seems to be a favorite spot of theirs.

Today I went up there wishing to see Emlyn's brother's room again, and perhaps have it out with him. He was gone, as were the dead ani-mals. You may be shocked to learn that I was tempted to pry; some of his possessions looked quite interesting. I resisted and left, pursued by curses from a dwarf whom the brother (his name is Ieuan) has chained to a staple in the door frame.

Need I say, Millie, that I would have freed the dwarf had he not at-tempted to attack me as I went out the door? He was not expecting a stranger to come out of the room—that much was quite clear—and though he snatched at my belt I got away.

In another room I discovered an ugly old tramp playing with his dog, a mongrel resembling a small terrier. The old man begged piteously, but I insisted he must go, and at last threatened to call the police. (I do not believe I would have had the fortitude to carry out that threat, but I said it.) He agreed, gathered his meager possessions, and hobbled away, leaning on a crutch. I saw him and his dog down the front stairs and out the door.

To confess the truth, I was tempted to give him a few dollars, al-though I knew that he would certainly return if I did. I felt horribly guilty about turning him out, as I still do; but I simply could not see let-ting a tramp share my home. The old man (Nick is the name he gave) will have to find shelter elsewhere.

Shortly after that, my gloom turned to sunshine. The mail carrier came; I went out to my box expecting nothing, and discovered your letter. Have you any notion what it means to a friendless man to learn that he has one friend after all?

Only one friend, but what a friend! Thank you! I will never be able to repay you. If only George knew what a treasure he has!

With sympathy and admiration,
Bax

Number 18
LUPINE

Dear Millie:

George has disbelieved out of hand many things I have confided in my earlier letters. I know that. This letter I would surely disbelieve myself, if I could. By the will of the gods, I cannot. I was there.

Yesterday I chased a poor old tramp out of my house. Today he hobbled into my living room bearing a rusty tin tray covered with a shining silver bell. When I looked up in astonishment, he made me a small, stiff bow. "I bear ill news, I fear, sir."

I rose and got my stick. "Indeed you do. I ordered you out and told you what would happen if you disobeyed. You have disobeyed, and can only blame yourself for your bruises." I can be stern, Millie, when I must; and I was stern then.

"I returned, sir, out of concern for your welfare. If you choose to beat the harmless old servant who strives to do you a good turn, I cannot prevent you. Yet the nobility of your countenance, sir, and the forthright gaze of those blue eyes, say plainly that there is no touch of the brute or bully in your character. There is a mechanic, sir, an electrician, working at the rear of our house. Were you aware of his presence?"

"No. I was not."

"From the painted side of his truck, sir, I conclude that he was dispatched by the Conjoined Edison Corporation. Upon his arrival, he went to the connection box. There is a lever on the connection box which, when pulled, deprives the house of its electrical energy, sir. Doubtless you are aware of it."

I shook my head.

"He went there, sir, as I said." The old man's manner was as grave as a bishop's. "I, for your sake and at great personal risk, arrived before him. What I took from that locality, sir, I bear upon this tray. Allow me to display it to you. After I have done so, you may thrash me if you wish."

He bowed again, handed me his tray, and removed the silver cover. Beneath it lay the severed head of a woman. I have seen a great deal in the course of a misspent life, Millie, but I had never seen the expression of mingled fear and horror I beheld then.

"You would not wish the electrician to trip upon this, sir. So it appeared to me."

I conceded that I would not.

"Which might have occurred, sir, had I not forestalled it." He replaced the cover. "You will not wish to look at this much longer, sir, and I hear boots upon our porch."

As he spoke, chimes sounded in the hallway. I put down the tray and would have started toward the door, but the old man said, "Permit me, sir. It is my office."

He soon returned, followed by a middle-aged technician in coveralls. I said, "Please excuse our appearance. Our furniture hasn't arrived, and my man and I have been trying to clean the old place."

"Sure. Must have been hard with no juice."

I nodded. "It is."

"I come here a couple days ago and switched it on for you. Only somebody turned it back off. Did you do that?"

"Certainly not." I paused to reflect. "I'd been at Mrs. Murrey's, and had caught a ride back here. When I got here, there were lights on all over the house. Before I reached the front door, they were extinguished, leaving the house dark again. At the time, I thought your company had done it."

"No, sir. I'd have known, 'cause there'd have been a order on my computer. There's a master switch that can be locked either way. Up and you're on." He illustrated by a gesture. "Down and you're off."

"I see."

"When I was here before, I unlocked it and pushed it up. Then I locked it again like that. You're not supposed to touch it. It belongs to the company."

"I haven't touched it," I said.

The old man added, "Nor have I, sir."

"Well, somebody did. Somebody busted our lock and shut you down."

"Why would anyone do that?"

He shrugged. "Just mischief, most likely. Now I need you to try the lights and sign for me. I couldn't get you to sign the first time 'cause you wasn't here."

I had been forcing myself to keep my eyes away from the tray, but as soon as he had left I told the old man, "We ought to dispose of that."

"My own thought precisely, sir. I might bury it in the wood behind the house. Have we a spade?" The contrast between the old man's exceedingly correct manner and his torn and soiled clothing could not have been greater.

"We do. But that—that thing would still be here and might eventually be found. I'll throw it in the river, but I don't suppose I should do it before dark."

"I would counsel you against it, sir. A prudent act may be less prudent by day."

"Doris is coming, too. Doris Griffin. We're going to have a look at some property I seem to have inherited."

"If I may offer a suggestion, sir?"

At that very moment, Millie (I do not blame you in the slightest if you do not credit it), Doris's horn sounded in the driveway. If I left, I would be leaving a destitute old tramp alone with a mattress stuffed with money; I have never been so tempted to call the police in my life.

I got out two twenties instead and gave them to him, saying he had earned that much and more.

"Thank you, sir! You needn't keep your lady waiting. Rely upon me."

"What are you going to do?"

"You have purchased groceries, sir. I observed the plastic bags in which such commodities are packed in the kitchen."

I nodded. "What of it?"

"I shall tie that"—he glanced toward the covered tray—"in one of those bags, sir, after adding stones to weight it. When it has been thus prepared, I shall cast it in. You may rely upon me, sir."

"And you can rely on me to be properly grateful for your help," I told him.

Doris's horn winded again, and I dashed out.

She smiled at my breathless entrance and we shook hands; but I do not believe either of us spoke until we were a mile or more outside town. Then she said, "You've got boots, I see. That's probably wise."

"Blue jeans, too, and a manly shirt."

"Not to mention a hat fit for an explorer."

"Precisely. I feel sure it will be too warm, but as a fan it should serve me well."

"Aren't the sides mesh? I thought I saw that."

"Yes, but I can fill it with fallen leaves when the weather grows colder. You know where this place is?"

"Of course I do. Have you always kept your hair as short as that?"

"Not really. It's often been shorter. Since you know, how about telling me?"

"We drive down to Port Saint Jude and cross the river there. Turn left on State Thirty-seven and head back up. Mr. Hardaway briefed me on the Skotos Strip this morning, and it begins at Greenwood Road and ends at Old Willow."

"Its southern edge is the river?"

"That's right. It's one of the things that makes it so valuable."

I considered that. "I'd like to go down the river in a boat sometime."

She glanced at me, a slight smile playing around her lips. "So would I. We'll do it as soon as I can set it up."

"Good."

"I'll pack a picnic lunch. It'll be fun."

"Provided we watch out for poison ivy. You say we're going to Port Saint Jude. Could we stop at a coin shop there for a moment or two? I believe the address is one sixteen Main."

"Of course."

"It's fifteen miles to Port Saint Jude, isn't it?"

"From town? That's right. Probably eleven or twelve from here."

"So that's thirty miles of riverfront, counting both sides—thirty miles of woods and farmland. I'd like to see what makes a three-mile strip on the wrong side of the river so valuable."

"I'll be happy to show you, but I can tell you right now. First, it isn't all woods or farmland, on this side particularly. There are homes here and there. If you wanted to put in a major development, you'd have to buy them."

I nodded.

"Which is bad enough. Then you'd have to tear them down, and all the woodsheds, and barns, and detached garages, and so on. All that costs, and you'd be sure to find a few owners who wouldn't sell at any reasonable price. We cuss them in my business."

I said, "I imagine you do."

"But they've lived there for thirty or forty years. Pretty often, they grew up in that home. Would they sell if the offer was high enough? Sure they would, but you wouldn't want to buy a home for twice what it's worth."

"I understand."

"Swell. Second, a lot of it's flood plain. Land that's covered with water every time the river rises. People will build homes on flood plain, and people will buy homes there. But not pricey homes. We're talking two-bedroom starter homes, mostly."

"Yes. Go on."

"You still haven't heard the worst. A whole lot of it's swamp. There's nothing worse than swamp. If you can build on it at all, you've got to bring in tons and tons of fill, and that costs more than tearing down the old homes. If it's protected wetlands, you can't build on it at all. You can own it, sure. But you can't do anything with it that might scare the ducks."

I started to speak, but she said, "I'm not finished. The Skotos Strip's not like that. Not at all. It slopes up, away from the river. Slopes pretty steeply, but not too steeply. Because of the slope, it's never been farmed. There are big old trees that could be left when the homes are built. It's ideal, and you don't want to be on this side of the river. There's too many gas stations, garages, and groceries." Doris pointed. "Knitting supplies, honey, and live bait. Did you see that?"

"Yes, I did."

"Look at this one coming up. Saws sharpened. This's where poor people live. The north side's a lot more rural, which means less spoiled. You'll understand what I'm saying better when we take that boat trip."

I had hardly heard her second and third statements. "I find it hard to look down on those poor people," I said. "After all, I'm one of them, a poor man living in an old house on the wrong side of the river."

"A poor man who just might buy a rare coin to add to his collection."

"You have that backward, I'm afraid. I have a coin I might sell. I probably won't, but I might. I want to hear what a professional has to say about it."

"May I see it?"

Remembering the ring, I hesitated. "You're driving, Doris. I don't think you should."

"I'll pull over."

She did, and I handed her the coin.

"Wow! Is this gold? How old is it?"

"It's certainly gold—not pure gold, of course. As I understand it, pure gold is too soft. As to its age, your guess is as good as mine, so let's hear it."

"What have you got, Bax? Two Ph.D.'s? I think you said that."

I nodded.

"I was a home-economics major and never got a degree. So my guess *isn't* as good as yours. But I think this goes way back to ancient times. I don't know what the shop in Port Saint Jude will say, but my guess is that Saint Jude in person would call this a really old coin."

A gnome ran the coin shop, a stooped, bald man with glasses and enormous ears. I showed him my coin; he scrutinized it through a large magnifying glass, weighed it, and scrutinized it again through a jeweler's loupe. "You say you found this?"

"Correct. I live in an old house on this side of the river." I cleared my throat. "I own the house, so the coin is legally mine. I was looking at some furniture in the attic and found this coin in a drawer."

He said nothing.

"It looks old and I'm interested in ancient history, so I put it in my pocket. I'd be very grateful if you can tell me anything about it."

"Very little." He sighed. "Very, very little, sir, and I cannot provide the appraisal we spoke of. I've never seen one like this. I have reference books, and I will go through them tonight. If you'll leave your number with me, I'll call you. That's if I find anything."

I gave him my number.

"The helmeted woman on the obverse . . ."

"Yes?"

"Presumably, she is Athena. A woman wearing a helmet on a Greek coin is always Athena, in my experience. The other woman on the reverse—"

Doris interrupted. "Is that a woman?"

"It is, madam. You failed to observe her breasts. Breasts, plural. So would I, without a glass. But they are there." He sighed. "She engages with a spear in one hand and a sword in the other. No doubt you both saw that. Thus she is not a second depiction of Athena, who would

127

surely bear the aegis, the shield of Zeus. Nor is she an Amazon, since an Amazon would have but one breast."

Doris looked surprised, and he added. "That is what the Greek means, madam. Without a breast. One breast was burned away in infancy."

He turned back to me. "Do you wish to sell this, sir?"

"Perhaps. I don't know."

"Knowing no more than I do, I dare not offer too much. Would you consider three hundred dollars?"

I shook my head.

"Then three hundred and fifty, and that is my final offer. Until I know more, I can go no higher."

"No," I said.

"He's a poor man," Doris told the shopkeeper, "who never seems to need money."

He ignored her. "If you like, sir, I will take it on consignment, with a price of five hundred dollars. If it sells, my commission will be twenty percent. Shall I do that?"

I declined, and we drove to the Skotos Strip.

It was larger and more heavily forested than I had imagined. The slope was slight, but perceptible. We drove slowly up Route Thirty-seven until we found a good spot and pulled off the road. As she locked the car, Doris asked what I wanted to do.

"I'd like to walk south from here until we reach the river, then walk along the river a bit. After that we can turn north, find this road, and follow it to the car. It should be two miles or less, I would think. Would that be agreeable?"

It was, and we set out. The oaks—they were nearly all oaks—were large and in full leaf. They protected us from the sun so well that the time might have been an hour after sunset. I had come prepared for mosquitoes. There were none, and a large flashlight would have been a more useful provision. I said as much, and added that I was afraid of stepping in a hole.

"Are you as lost as I am?"

"Not at all, I'm following the slope down. If we do that, we're certain to reach the river."

As I spoke, a hand slipped into mine.

It was pleasant, of course; but a few minutes later when Doris said, "I think I'll turn around and go back," it seemed that she was some distance behind me.

"I'll meet you at the car, in that case," I told her. The hand in mine squeezed it, which I took to mean that she would not actually leave.

Almost at once, a big, heavyset man stood frowning in front of us. I should scarcely have been able to see him, yet I saw him quite distinctly—his white shirt and dark patterned tie, as well as his fleshy, not-unhandsome face.

My companion muttered something, and he vanished as abruptly as he had appeared.

I said, "Did you see that?"

"We are not far from the water."

I looked, but could see only the trees and a little underbrush; listened, but could hear no sound that might have been flowing water.

"A man was standing right in front of us."

She said nothing.

By then I had recovered sufficiently to be frightened. "Tassels on his loafers, dark slacks, and a white shirt." I was babbling.

A fox barked, and my hand no longer held a woman's. Something raced away, too big and too dark, too near the ground. It vanished in an instant.

I pressed on, thinking in a dazed fashion that Doris had to be somewhere ahead. For an interval that felt like hours, nothing more happened. I walked on, always down the slope, sometimes feeling my way with my hands, periodically cursing my stupidity for not bringing my flashlight, and reminding myself over and over that the distance should be no more than half a mile. I felt that I had walked five miles at least, and if you had said eight or ten I might have believed you.

The undergrowth grew thicker; I pushed through it and saw sunshine glaring from water.

Then a young woman, reclining on a fallen log. For one insane instant I thought her back was covered with hair. A moment later I realized it was only that her hair was long, dark, and tangled, seeming never to have known a comb; and that she wore the shaggy pelt of some animal.

Without looking at me, she said, "Sit down. You need a rest."

I thanked her and sat down on the log near her naked feet, panting. The water appeared far clearer than it was when it flowed past my house; if there were houses, garages, or barns on the opposite bank, I could not see them.

"I like you."

"And I'll like you, I'm sure, when we've come to know one another better." It was all I could think of.

"I will do you no hurt."

I said, "That's good. You are quite safe with me, believe me. I've never forced a woman."

"Do you think I fear you?" Her snicker was almost a snarl.

"I hope you don't," I told her, "since you've no reason to."

"Your kind always think themselves dangerous. What have you done with my head?"

I understood then—as I should have the moment I saw her—that she was psychotic. Now I feel sure that she is a psychopath. I sincerely hope you have never had to deal with such people, Millie. I have, unfortunately, and more than once.

"Have you no answer?"

"I haven't touched your head. As I said—"

She sprang up and faced me, all high cheekbones and blazing eyes. "Your servant carried it in to you. What have you done with it?"

"Oh, that head. I didn't know it was yours. Didn't it belong to some unfortunate nurse?"

"It's mine!"

"I understand. Old Nick—I suppose that's who you mean by 'your servant'—had it when I left the house. I'll get it back for you if I can. Would you like me to keep it for you? I would turn it over with pleasure and alacrity anytime you asked."

"Throw it in the river. It will come to me."

"I . . . see."

"You don't believe me." She laughed, and there was everything a laugh can have in hers except humor—beauty and ugliness, mockery, cruelty, and madness. "Listen now. Hear me."

I listened, and heard precisely nothing. A minute dragged past.

Something was struggling up out of the river; it was mostly white, touched here and there with carmine. Not until I caught sight of the foot did I realize that it was a human leg. As it struggled onto the mud bordering the water, its stench came with it.

"This was to be a gift for the boy who calls to me. Sometimes gifts go astray." She had risen and turned to face me. "It found its way to the water instead. To the water and to me. What is your name, man?"

"Bax."

"I am Lupine." She did not offer to shake hands, at which I felt a surge of joy. "The boy lives in your house. Tell him I hunt for his sake. I will kill again soon."

"Not me, I hope."

"Not you. I will have you for a friend." She smiled; her smile was terrifying. "Whether you will or no."

I said, "I'd like it very much if we were friends." It seemed safe.

"Then do not disturb my gifts. Let him find them." A fox barked some distance away; she looked angry but made no motion.

"Believe me, I shall. May I tell him they're there?"

"That will help." She smiled again.

I rose, backing away. "I think I'll go back to the car I came in. If you don't mind."

"Wait." She pointed to the leg. "Would you like that?"

"No, I—no."

"I don't relish carrion myself. Will you need these?"

They were keys, half a dozen a least, on a key ring from which a pink plastic rabbit dangled; after a moment, I recognized them. "Please let me have them," I said. "I'm sure Doris will want them back."

It evoked the terrifying smile.

"Where did you get them?"

She laughed and tossed them at my feet. When I stood up she had gone, leaving the leg rotting in the mud.

·　·　·　·　·

Millie, I nearly abandoned this letter at this point. What I have written already is enough to make you think I have gone mad, I know. I know, too, that George thinks so already. In a way, I am glad he does. I have not seen him in ages, and from what you say he is coming here because he believes I have taken leave of my senses.

But you—I have not the smallest wish to deceive you, but you must surely think me as mad as a hatter. What I am going to write next will put the seal on it.

·　·　·　·　·

Joe came for the car. I know I wrote to George about that. It interrupted me, and to tell the truth I was glad of it.

I have told you about the barefoot girl on the log who had Doris's keys. Did I say that she had gone when I straightened up?

Yes. Here it is.

When I saw she had vanished, I cut a staff for myself. The camp knife I had thought little more than an ornament proved sharp and capable. When I had hacked down a sapling and trimmed it, I walked back the way I had come, going up the slope a good deal more slowly than I had gone down it, and feeling my way through the darkest stretches with my staff. It must have taken me an hour or more to cover that half mile, if half mile it was.

At last I struck the road. I had no idea in which direction Doris's car was but turned right at a venture, which proved correct.

My passenger came up just as I was unlocking the door. At once I offered to return her keys. She said, "You will have to drive, Bax."

"Then I will. You must be terribly tired."

She said nothing.

"We should never have separated."

"We are together once more."

I slowed, and turned to look at her; she would not meet my eyes, staring straight ahead.

"Why don't we stop and get something to eat?"

"No."

"My treat, of course."

She did not reply.

I had started to say that I would take her back to her apartment, where she could have a nice bath, when I caught sight of a woman standing by the road and waving.

My passenger saw her too, and laughed.

After that, one glance was enough; and when I stopped for Doris, the seat was empty.

"Thank God, Bax! I'm so tired I could cry." Doris got in. "What have you been carrying in here?"

I said, "It will be hard to explain."

"Don't you smell it? You must."

I sniffed. If I had used my nose earlier, I would not have been deceived.

"Did I leave my keys in the car?"

I shook my head.

"I didn't think so. I took them out of the ignition and locked the car. I know I did. How did you get them?"

"A girl I met down at the river's edge gave them to me."

"Really?"

I nodded. "You probably won't believe me, but that's the truth. This is, too. She brought the smell that you complained about."

"She was in here with you."

"Yes. She was." I stopped and turned to face Doris. "You teased me to tell you about a ghost. There are worse things than ghosts, and I've been talking with one of them today."

"You're serious."

"Serious, tired, and hungry. Will the Lakeshore Inn take us, dirty, and dressed the way we are?"

"I doubt it."

"In that case, we're going to your apartment. You can clean up there and so can I. Do you have pictures of Ted? You must."

Have you read this far, Millie? You are an angel! I must say this before I close: those parts of my letter which you must think most fantastic, I have actually toned down. What I suffered was far more fantastic than I have told you.

Wilder, and much less credible.

One thing more, and I shall close. Doris showed me pictures of Ted. Several of them. He was unquestionably the man I glimpsed for a moment in the woods, the man who vanished when Lupine spoke to him.

He is, I would say, also the man I took to be Ieuan's parent.

I have told myself over and over that I must get out of this house, that I have stumbled upon a place where dreams walk by daylight and that those dreams may destroy me. But there's the money, and I have been so poor for so long.

There is a terrible fascination, too. I am a scholar or I am nothing, Millie. I knew an elderly Jewish scholar at the University of Chicago, a Dr. Kopecky. He was robbed on the street, and surrendered his wallet and his watch without a struggle; but when the gang of juveniles who had surrounded him tried to take his bag, containing one old book and his notes, he fought them all.

Perhaps you understand.

I hope you are well and feel certain you must be more beautiful than ever. For me you are an anchor of sanity in a world gone mad. Please, please write again.

Forever your friend,
Bax

Mr. Dunn:

My name you will have gotten from my stationery, and the skills I proffer as well. Your sister-in-law is my client. She has described your difficulties in detail, and I have warned her—as I warn you—that you stand in grave danger. Mrs. Dunn suggested I contact you psychically. I mean to act upon her suggestion, but it seems best to write you first in order that you may prepare.

From what Mrs. Dunn says, your home is a node. It may well be possessed. I am an experienced exorcist, certified by the International Occult Council, A.S.P. My fees are reasonable, and refundable in the unlikely event of client dissatisfaction. I cannot specify an exact amount without first inspecting your premises, but my fees typically run between $500 and $5,000. Because your home is more than 100 miles distant, you would also be required to compensate me for travel expenses. (Non-refundable.)

Should you wish to engage me, you may write me or reach me at the number above.

But you need not. Rest assured, you and I shall soon be in psychic contact.

————————————

Yours truly,
Mrs. O. Pogach
"Madame Orizia"

Number 20
A Very Strange House

Dear George:

Your gracious wife dropped me a note the other day saying you planned to come here. That is why I have not written you sooner. You have not; thus I feel I should write you now to say that I understand entirely. Your career must keep you exceedingly busy. Nose to the grindstone and all that.

It has been a terrible disappointment just the same. How I would love to see you! I would employ my newfound wealth to pay you a visit if I thought you would receive me. You called the police last time, remember? It was profoundly embarrassing, and they held me for most of the day. I only hope that time has relaxed your edgy reflexes.

Interesting events have taken place here. Have I told you about old

Nick? I feel certain that I told you (was it in my last?) that I intended to inspect the Skotos property with Doris. We did, had a good dinner afterward, and spent a pleasant evening.

When I returned home this morning, I discovered that old Nick had been busy in my absence. An Oriental rug now covers most of my living-room floor. There is a table in the dining room, and the escritoire in which I found my coins and this paper lords over an adjacent room.

"I trust you approve, sir?" he said. "I hoped you might find this more comfortable."

I said that I certainly did, and asked as casually as I could what he had done with the mattress.

"Returned it to a bed, sir. The one we installed in the master bedroom. I—um . . ."

I felt sure that he had found the money. "Yes?"

"We have no sheets as yet, sir. Nor blankets of the correct size. I have, um, selected a few of each from our attic, sheets as well as blankets which I hope will suit, sir. They are dusty, however. I have washed a few, sir, and dried a blanket." He coughed. "Only the one blanket thus far."

"I understand. Might I have a look at the master bedroom?"

"Certainly, sir. But you must make allowances. As I hope you will, sir. I have scarcely begun."

"Let me see it," I said, "and I'll tell you." Do I have to explain that I was worried about that mattress, George? I was. Worried sick.

He led the way, his crutch thumping the floor at every stride. A door in the little hall between the dining room and the kitchen admitted us to a longer hall, and that to the master bedroom. It is capacious and at present more than a little bare; but the high, black four-poster from which I had taken the mattress stands at its center. I walked around it, pretending to examine the bed while I actually looked at the mattress. It seemed intact; as I scrutinized it, it occurred to me that the old man would certainly have decamped if he had found the money.

"A formidable piece of furniture." I smiled.

"Indeed, sir."

"I've gone through here to shave and bathe, but I've never paid much attention to the room. It's rather nice."

"May you spend many a restful night here, sir."

"The house is unheated, I believe."

"Not wholly, sir. There is a furnace, sir, though its, ah, salubrious breath does not attain to every room."

"In the basement, I suppose."

"Indeed, sir."

"Is there gas for it? Has the company restored our service?"

"Not to my knowledge, sir. It is a coal furnace in any event."

"I see. Have we coal?"

He shook his head. "No, sir."

"Then perhaps we should return this mattress to the living room. The nights are still quite chilly."

"That will scarcely be necessary, sir. There are fireplaces in this bedroom, sir. I doubt that you will require both, though of course you may have both if you choose."

I looked around without seeing either.

"Behind this, sir." With obvious pride, the old man rolled aside an antique washstand on casters, revealing a small fireplace in which a fire had already been laid. "Ieuan assisted me, sir, helping carry your furniture and your carpets. He also supplied this wood. A most obliging young man, sir."

"Ieuan?"

"Yes, sir. Young Ieuan Black. He lives nearby, I believe."

"So do I. Do you happen to know his brother Emlyn?"

"Ah." The old man sighed. "He's a bad one, sir. By repute at least. I—um—have not had the pleasure, sir. And don't want it."

"I see. I have so many questions to ask you that I don't know where to begin."

"Perhaps I may assist you, sir. The, ah, object we discussed prior to your departure yesterday has been cast upon the flood, sir, in the manner proposed."

"No doubt that's for the best. You say you've washed sheets? Several sheets?"

He nodded. "Six, sir."

"And at least one blanket."

"Quite correct, sir, though there are others awaiting my attention. Three more, sir, and a quilt."

"You cannot have washed any by hand, I think. That would've left you no time to fetch them, and to fetch down all this furniture. Did you take them to the Laundromat?"

"No, sir. I, ah . . ."

"Yes?"

"I, um, pledged your credit, sir. No interest, sir, and the first payment will not be due until July, sir. We have a washer and a dryer, sir. Now."

"I understand. No doubt they are in the basement?"

"Quite correct, sir. In the laundry room. Both are electrically powered."

"You intend to use them to wash your own clothing as well, I hope."

"Indeed, sir. Quite correct. My first wish, however, was to render you more comfortable, sir. I had hoped to have your bed in order before you returned."

"Surely you expected me last night."

"Not, um, really, sir." He colored. "The lady was young and attractive. I glimpsed her through our window, sir. You are, if I may say it, sir, a young man of—"

"Let's leave it at that. You said there were two fireplaces. Where is the other?"

"Across the room, sir. In the corner behind that screen."

It is of painted silk, George, and might well be in a museum. When the old man had folded back its mist-wrapped mountains and sinuous dragon, a second fireplace was indeed revealed—as well as a hearth on which two animals sat as primly as porcelain figurines upon a mantelpiece: one was Winkle, the other the small dog with which the old man had been playing when I first saw him.

I glanced at him to see whether he had been expecting them, but he appeared at least as surprised as I felt. I said, "That is your pet, I believe?"

"It—ah—he is, sir. My, um, little Toby."

"He is housebroken, I hope."

"Yes, sir. You do not object to him, sir?"

"I'll answer that in a moment," I said. "I have a question of my own first. Clearly you saw the fox."

(Winkle rose to rub herself against my leg.)

"Oh, I did, sir. I do indeed."

"Here is my question. Do you object to her?"

"From her behavior, and yours, sir, I take it that she is yours? If that is so, it is scarcely my place to make objection, sir. Rather, I shall care for her as though she were my own."

I was too occupied with my thoughts to speak.

"Better, sir, I hope. My, um, straitened means have compelled me to neglect poor Toby more than I should wish to confess."

"Then I will say this. I do not object to Toby at present."

The old man smiled, revealing teeth I feel quite sure are false. "Thank you, sir. Thank you very much!"

"If you—and Toby—want to continue living in this house, it cannot be as a guest. Do you seek employment with me?"

"Precisely so, sir. I have endeavored to prove my worth. As your servant, I shall redouble my efforts."

"Commendable. What terms of employment will you accept?"

It cannot be easy for someone who needs a crutch to bow, but the old man managed it. "First, sir, that Toby and I be permitted to continue here. We have no other home, sir."

"Certainly," I said.

"Other than that, our food, sir. We must eat or starve."

"Will you undertake to prepare mine?"

"Gladly, sir, though I am no chef. Simple food will present no difficulties, however. Welsh rabbit, omelets, *hamam bil zaytun*, and the like are within my range, sir, though it does not extend far beyond them."

"Can you make coffee?"

"Indeed, sir. Would you care for some?"

"Good coffee?"

"Yes, sir. I can, sir. But excellent coffee . . ." He sighed. "I cannot, sir. Not with the materials at hand."

"I understand. Please make me some good coffee, and we will continue our discussion."

He left, with Toby at his heels. Too late I added, "Close the door, please."

Winkle giggled as I shut it myself.

I said, "You can talk, Winkle. I know it and you know I know it."

"Yeth."

"Dogs and foxes are mortal enemies—or so I've been given to understand. When the old man moved that screen, you and Toby were certainly not at each others throats."

"He ith a familiar."

"The old man's familiar? Are you saying he's a witch? Or a sorcerer?"

"I am yourth."

"My familiar?"

Winkle giggled again. "I go outthide?"

"You need to go out?"

She nodded vigorously. "Pleath open the window, Bakth."

I did, and she bounded through it.

As you may imagine, I was very busy indeed with a painstaking examination of the mattress until the old man returned. It was just as I had left it. I seated myself upon it when his soft knock told he had returned, and he hobbled in, pushing a small serving cart.

"Coffee, sir. Cream, sir. Sugar, sir. Since you purchased the latter commodities, I assume that you will employ both."

I nodded, and he filled my cup from a silver pot. The coffee smelled wonderful, and tasted even better.

"It is nothing out of the ordinary, sir. Clean equipment and good water. I was forced to employ a percolator, sir. It is all we have at present."

I said, "As long as your coffee remains as good as this, I will not complain of it. What salary will you accept?"

"If you will supply my small needs as they arise, sir, that will be entirely sufficient."

"I would greatly prefer to pay you a weekly stipend," I told him. "Please propose a figure."

I was prepared to bargain, but the compensation he asked was so modest that I agreed at once. After that I told him that I intended to take a nap, adding that I had gotten little sleep the previous night.

"I quite understand, sir. I am too old for such things now, but in my younger days . . ."

"Of course. Could you fetch my luggage? My pajamas will be in my bag."

"I have attended to that already, sir." He opened the door of what proved to be a very large closet. My bag and my clothing were in there, as was the oil lamp I had almost forgotten.

There were bolts on both doors. I shot them as soon as he had left; then, with trembling heart, ripped out the stitches I had sewn earlier in the mattress.

The money was still there, and for the first time I counted the entire sum. I will not give you the total, George, but it was quite large.

Reassured, I sewed the mattress up again, put on my pajamas, and lay down. Doris had exhausted me, but the coffee I had drunk kept me awake for a few minutes at least. I recall thinking about buying her something, and about getting the old man a new crutch. (The one he has is little more than a forked stick, with rags knotted around the fork to pad it.)

I woke after an hour or so, and found I had company. The almond-eyed young woman for whom I had bought the robe had rejoined me, lying quite naked beside me. Still half asleep, I mumbled, "What are you doing here?"

"Cuddling."

"As I see." I sat up. "It's good of you. I find that I'm quite chilled."

"No fur." As she spoke, she spread her hair with both hands. It is jet black and very long indeed; I imagine she could sit on it.

"No fur to speak of, but I have a flannel shirt in here." I got it out of the closet. "And something for you. I hope you'll like it."

I gave her the silk robe. She opened the box as eagerly as any child, slipped into the robe very quickly indeed, and dashed around the room with wide-spread arms to show off the wide sleeves, an exercise she completed with a dozen kisses.

"I'm very glad you like it," I told her. "I wanted to get you something more, but I didn't know what you might like. Shoes seemed the obvious choice, but I didn't know your size." Her feet are tiny.

"Not really needed."

"We'll make a tracing of your foot. I can take that to the store." I opened my bag and got out my stationery and this pen; but when I turned around, she was gone.

I went to the window and looked out. That window, I know, had shown nothing more surprising than a stretch of lawn, a wilderness of weeds and brush, my neighbor's neatly clipped hedge, another expanse of lawn, and his house. It opened upon a forest now.

A real forest of immense and ancient trees, shadowy, silent, and brooding.

The young woman to whom I had given a silk gown was gone, and the gown as well. I wanted to call out to her, but I did not know her name. It occurred to me that she might be in the bathroom; its door stood open, and there was no one inside.

The house felt so silent that I felt certain that the old man and his dog had gone.

You know me, George; you may well know me better than I know myself. Can you guess what I did next? I know that I could not, if I were in your shoes.

I resumed the clothing I had worn from Doris's, found the staff I had cut in a corner of the closet, and climbed out that window.

Try as I will, I cannot explain it. No, not even to myself. There is a streak in my makeup that seems to have no connection with my conscious mind. You will regard what I did as no more than one more instance of self-destructive behavior, I know. I only wish I knew how to regard it.

Before I had taken a hundred steps, I realized that there would be every chance of my becoming lost if I went far. The course of wisdom seemed to be to return to the house; when I had found it again, I might circle it, locate the front and rear doors and so on, and so gain some idea of the position of the forest.

I turned around, retracing my path to the best of my ability. After a hundred steps (yes, George, one hundred; I counted them), the house was nowhere in sight. A hundred more, counted as carefully as the first . . .

Nothing. Only trees, huge and silent, sleeping giants robed in moss. And then—

"Mr. Dunn! Where are you? Mr. Dunn!"

Someone was calling me. I could hardly believe it. "Here!" I shouted. "Over here."

I saw her before she saw me, a stout, middle-aged woman in a long, loose dress. There was a shawl around her shoulders. I called and waved, but it soon became apparent that though she could hear me, she could not see me. She was groping; I decided that she must be blind, or nearly so.

When I was quite near her, she said, "You're here. I know you're here. I sense it."

"Right here," I said, and took her arm.

She blinked, and focused on my face. "I see you! I see you, Mr. Dunn. But you're Millicent's husband. Where is your brother?"

"I'm Baxter Dunn. George and I are identical twins. Didn't she tell you?"

The woman shook her head.

"Well, we are. May I ask what you're doing in this forest?"

"You dream, Mr. Dunn. This is your dream, and I have entered it in search of you. I myself am in a trance—"

My cell phone chimed. I pushed the button and said hello.

"Mr. Dunn? This is Jim Hardaway. I hope you remember me?"

"Yes, of course."

"Could you speak up? You're very faint."

I raised my voice. "Is this better?"

"A little bit. You must be quite a ways from the tower."

Looking around at the forest, I agreed.

"Can you meet with the lawyer tonight? About the will, you know. He's busy, but he's going to keep his office open for us. His name's Trelawny."

"It is in the laps of the gods, but I'll try."

Mr. Hardaway laughed. "God willin' and the creek don't rise."

"Precisely."

"It's two seventy-one Wilson, third floor. You won't have any trouble. That's very near the corner of Wilson Street and Railway Road. Six o'clock sharp."

Recalling a radio station I had heard far more than I ever wanted to, I said, "Be there or be square."

"Oh, I will, Mr. Dunn. I'll see you at six tonight."

He hung up and I turned back to the woman. "You are in a trance, you say?"

"Even so. My corporeal body is in my own parlor. The thing that you see, the thing you grasped, is my spiritual body."

I ventured that it had felt quite solid. She was, to be offensively frank, of substantial girth; I doubted that I could have lifted her, unaware that I would soon have to try.

"We are spirits, you and I. Do you recall my letter? I am in a trance, as I said. You sleep."

It was rather annoying, since I knew that I did not. "I'm in a forest," I told her, "and it seems to me a most sinister place. But I'm not asleep. I've wandered into this forest—which was foolhardy of me—and I'm trying to get back to my house, quite a large house."

She said nothing.

"It's painted white but in need of fresh paint. Have you seen it?"

"I have come to see it. I am Madame Orizia."

About then I heard a fox bark. I looked around for Winkle and saw the girl who had joined me in bed. I saw her, George, but what a transformation! She wore the silk gown I had given her; but her glossy black hair, which had been loose, was elaborately coiffured and held by two long, ivory-colored needles. Her face had been powdered, and liberally; it was far whiter than my house. She smiled and advanced trippingly, on high platform shoes. "I'm back, Bax. All dressed. Do you like me?"

I embraced her. "I will always like you, dressed or undressed, with makeup or without."

"I love you!"

"I love you, too. And you're Japanese!" One more hug. "I think I must have known, deep down."

"Oh, yes!"

Madame Orizia said, "Won't you introduce me to your pet? I love animals."

I had begun to say something about having heard Winkle nearby when the girl I had been hugging bowed. "This lowly person is called Winker Inari."

"I am Madame." Madame Orizia offered her hand; the girl who called herself Winker Inari sniffed it, smiled, and backed away.

"She is shy," Madame Orizia explained. "That is only to be expected in a wild pet, and is no bad thing in any pet. I would have to prove my peaceful intentions, which I should be glad to do if only I had the time. It might take weeks, however, while I will scarcely have an hour."

I protested. "You're talking as though she were an animal."

"She is a fox, Mr. Dunn."

"I know the expression, but still—"

Madame Orizia raised a hand. "You are about to say she is a person. Of course she is. Many animals are."

Winker kissed my cheek. When I turned to look at her, she smiled. Then she barked. "I'm sorry, Bax. Oh! Very sorry! I love you."

"I love you, too." It was the second time I had said it. I touched her hair, and we kissed. I have never been kissed, George, as I was there in that brooding forest. I never expect to be kissed so again.

Here I wish I could recount our search. I will not, because I have neither paper enough nor time. Strolling for miles through a noble forest spread across whispering hills, we discovered hidden springs and beautiful glades, arching ferns higher than many a noble tree, and caverns we dared not enter. We saw white deer (and once a bear with a leering human face) as well as many other creatures that I will not describe because you would not believe me.

At last, guided by Winker's nose, we found the house and the very window through which I had come. I offered to help her in, but she dived through with one amazing bound.

Madame Orizia was another matter.

I heaved, my shoulder against her hips; she clawed at the window frame, and Winker lent her small strength from within the room. It was comic, I suppose, though not for us.

And in the end—no pun intended—we failed. I told Winker to remain where she was, and said that we would walk around the house until we found a door.

"It is a terribly strange house," I explained as we walked. "For one thing, it seems to grow bigger all the time."

Madame Orizia nodded. "Strange, but not unique, Mr. Dunn."

"Also, the rooms seem to move around. Or perhaps it is only that—"

I had heard a mechanical noise I did not at first identify as an automobile horn. "What's that?"

"A Klaxon, I believe. Should I take it that the fox is your chief difficulty, Mr. Dunn?"

"Winkle? No, not at all. Winkle's no problem. I'm not quite sure I have a difficulty, but if I do it's a girl called Lupine. Lupine frightens me, I confess."

Madame Orizia pointed, and I saw that the old man was tapping on a window we were approaching. We stopped before it, and he raised the sash. "Mr., ah, Joseph is here, sir. He has returned our automobile."

"I see. We're trying to get into the house, but we haven't found a door."

"The window, sir?"

I shook my head. "I could climb through, but Madame Orizia could not. We tried."

"I see." The old man was silent for a moment. "Mr. Joseph desires his, ah, quittance, sir. His remuneration."

"Yes, I understand."

"May I propose a solution, sir?"

I said, "I wish someone would."

"Permit me to climb out this window, sir. You might then enter the house by it and attend to Mr. Joseph. I shall guide the lady to a more commodious entrance."

"If you can."

"It is false confidence, perhaps, sir. Yet I am confident."

Madame Orizia said, "I must remain with you, Mr. Dunn."

"You will soon be with me again," I told her, "if you make haste to follow my man."

He was already coming through the window, and doing it remarkably well for a man of his age. A moment later, he knelt and offered me his knee as a step. I declined, jumped and pulled myself through with my phone ringing all the while.

As soon as I had gotten out of bed I answered it, more than a little out of breath. "Yes?"

"This is Doris, Bax darling. You'll be at the reading of the will tonight? Mr. Hardaway just told me about it."

"Yes," I repeated. "Excuse me. I've been exerting myself."

The Klaxon sounded somewhere outside, and I made my way through the kitchen to the back door.

"What was that?"

"A horn. Ask not for whom the horn blows, Doris. It blows for me."

"Another woman's picking you up."

"Hardly."

"A temptress. A seductress. Alice Vrba." Doris giggled.

"No, but I like her name." I opened the door, knowing that it was quite unlikely that I would see the old man and Madame Orizia. Instead, as I expected, I got a fine view of my own sunlit backyard; the wood beyond it prevented me from seeing the river.

"Alice or Vrba?"

"Both." I set out for the garage.

"Can I pick you up for an early dinner? My treat."

I said, "I owe you."

"You *don't*. You paid last time, when we got back from the Strip. Besides, I'll put it on the expense account."

"What about a late dinner, after the will?"

Joe was seated behind the wheel of the huge car Les and I had found. He got out as he saw me approaching.

"I was hoping you'd say that, Bax. Meet you at Trelawny's office?"

"Yes, but wait. I want you to talk to Joe. Joe, please tell Doris that you are neither a temptress nor a seductress." I handed him my telephone.

"This is AAAA Autos of the World, ma'am. You got a foreign car?"

. . .

"Sure. Like you've got a Porsche. There's no dealer here. Or a Fiat, maybe. Same thing."

. . .

"Well, you ought to get one. Or you want an antique car restored, like Mr. Dunn here. We do that, too." He covered the tiny transmitter with his thumb. "She wants to know if you'll drive your car to the lawyer's office so she can see it."

"Can I?"

"Sure." Joe returned to Doris. "He says sure, if you want him to. He says anything for you, babe." He winked at me.

. . .

"You bet. I'll lay it on thick." He returned my phone. "I didn't hang up. You better do it."

Hearing only a dial tone, I did.

"She gives you all her love. Kissy, kissy. She says dress nice this time, not like yesterday, and she'll take you to a real uptown spot. That probably means the North Portico. She said to say she'd pay, but I bet she sticks you with the check."

"She wants me to drive this?"

"Yep. You know how to drive a stick shift?"

I shook my head.

"Okay, we'll talk about that, but let's get the old stuff out of the way first. This baby's in great shape. I cleaned it up, checked all the rubber, and put you in a new battery. See that leather top?"

"Yes, of course."

"It was gettin' ready to crack, so I oiled it up good for you. Neatsfoot oil. Feels like a good fielder's mitt now. I lubed all the struts, folded it back, and put it back up again. No problems. You want to try it?"

I nodded. "I see the seats are leather, too."

"Right. They were in better shape than the top was, so I just sprayed 'em with Mink Oil. That soaks right in and dries fast. If the lady's got on a white dress, she might get a oil stain on her butt, but probably not. Anything else, forget it. You get in there, loosen the clamps, and push it straight back."

I did, and the leather top folded with remarkable ease.

"You want to leave it back? Going to be a nice night."

"Yes." I was looking at the dashboard; I had expected it to be simpler than that of a modern car, but it was more complex.

"Swell. There's a strap here with a buckle. See it? You buckle that around it so the roof won't come forward if you have to make a quick stop."

I did.

"Want to look at the inside? It's not as roomy as it looks, but it's still pretty big. Lots of legroom."

Joe hopped down from the steel step. I left the front seat with more decorum.

Joe threw open a door. "The boss and his lady rode right here, see? His chauffeur drove for him. The jump seats were for servants. Or kids, maybe. See that? For a picnic hamper, and there's another one here. You got a special compartment for golf clubs, too."

"What about the trunk?" I asked. "Did you open it?"

He shook his head. "I didn't have a key. I'd have had to bust it open, which I would never do. I took it down there, though, and put it back up. Clem and me did." Joe fell silent.

"Yes?" I said.

"There might be something in there, but it can't be much. It rattled a little."

"I see."

"Les could pick it for you. A trunk lock? Candy for him."

"No doubt." I paused, thinking. "You drove it over, didn't you, Joe? I don't see another car."

"Sure. I was hopin' you'd drive me back."

"Wouldn't we get a ticket? The license plates will surely have expired."

His teeth flashed beneath his mustache. "No way. Brand new. Let's go around back and look."

We did. The plate was new and shiny: AQ1313.

"See the letters? It means antique. Gets a special low rate from the state, only twenty bucks." He coughed apologetically. "It's on my bill."

It was I, I felt, who owed the apology. "I must tell you something, although I would rather not. I can drive, but I don't have a valid license. Mine has expired."

"No big deal, probably they'd just give you a warning the first time. Tomorrow, maybe, you could take the test. Only don't drive this. Borrow your buddy's."

"Yours?"

Joe looked thoughtful. "One of my loaners. Only I'd have to charge you. You goin' to sell this?"

"Eventually, I suppose."

"Okay, you listen here." Joe had come to a decision. "You had me to work on it, and I did it right. Pulled the head and all that. Lubed the transmission, put in radiator fluid. You name it, I did it. You pay my bill now, no bellyaching or bullshitting. And you let me put my sticker on it, 'Maintenance by AAAA Autos of the World.' You do that, and I'll teach you to drive the stick and let you have a loaner to take the test in. It's a real good deal, and I wouldn't do it if I didn't like your car so much."

I can drive that car now, George. Its floor-mounted shift lever (with a knob I take to be genuine ivory) is no mystery to me. We drove about ten miles altogether, and received at least fifty admiring stares. Are you proud of me? I confess that I am proud of myself.

Yours sincerely,

Bax

PS: The old man returned as I was about to seal this envelope. He states that Madame Orizia vanished only a moment or two after I left. He was walking ahead of her, and when he looked behind him she was no longer there. Winker seems to have vanished as well, although her gown and shoes are in the bedroom closet. I will recount the reading of the will tomorrow, if I find time.

Dear Shell:

My life is becoming very interesting indeed, and that from every angle: money, sex, and whatever else might be specified. For one thing, I have never been present before while someone held a gun on someone else. That happened last night, and the someone else was my brother George. It could not happen to a nicer guy—I feel certain you know what I mean.

First I ought to say that I have seen my parole officer. He is overloaded, as I have been told they all are, and bought into everything I told him. I wore a get-the-money suit (dove gray with a navy blue pinstripe) and showed him a paycheck, gave him my address for the second time, and the number of my new cell telephone. The entire interview was over in five minutes.

I have founded my own little firm, you see. I call it A Plus Tutors. Our president is Henry Parkhill. (I know you would like him, Shell. You might recognize him as well.) Baxter Dunn is an employee, and good old Hank signs the checks. There is a FICA deduction and withholding for the IRS—the whole nine yards, as Lou would say.

Now the big news, and this is all straight. A kindly old gentleman called Alexander Skotos has left me a nice piece of real estate. Does that name ring bells with you? Skotos is Greek, so he would be Greek or at least look Greek enough to pass. I have been rummaging through every last memory I can turn up, and I have not found a Skotos or anyone who owed me and might use that name. Ask around, please. I could handle everything here much better if only I knew who Skotos really was.

You have been waiting for the sex, if I know you. The problem is telling you so that you will believe it. As I told you in my last, I have a Japanese girlfriend and an American girlfriend now. The Japanese girl is kitten-cute; I could tuck her under my arm and carry her around all day. Slender, sweet, submissive—and under all of that, very, very smart.

The American is, at a guess, somewhere between thirty and thirty-five, a hundred and fifty pounds, and about five foot nine. Roundhouse curves in all the right places. She is a widow and has been around. (At first I thought she might be sleeping with her boss.) Good face, great smile, brown hair with no dye in it. (I have poked around in her medicine cabinet and so on.) After a couple of drinks, she is as sweet and hot as a woman can be; they seem to loosen her up and make her forget her dead husband.

So which one?

Well, why not both? It has been working thus far.

There are other things I could tell you about, but you would not believe a word of it. It seems to me that I had better stand mute, as the lawyers say. If ever I see your smiling face around here—and I would very much like to, Shell—I may be able to show you things that will open your eyes.

What I just wrote assumes that I will still be alive.

Remember, please, that the big question is "Alexander Skotos." Who was he? Any information at all.

Have you ever heard of a Mary King? There is probably no connection, but she and Alexander Skotos lived here in Medicine Man or close to it, and both are dead. Please let me know, Shell. Pass along anything you pick up, no matter how nebulous.

———————————

Yours sincerely,
Bax

Dear Millie:

George is here and jailed. You will probably receive the letter I wrote to him yesterday before you see this one. I advise you to open and read it. You need not show it to him when he gets home—the decision is yours.

At any rate, I am going to assume that you have read it, and say little or nothing about the events I described in great detail there. You will be eager to hear about my poor brother and his legal difficulties.

Very well. You will recall that I was to meet Doris at the lawyer's. Emlyn returned while I was dressing. "I found a human head, Bax. A dead man's head." He gulped audibly. "It's been torn from its body. I thought I ought to warn you. Something or someone killed that man, and we may all be in danger."

I agreed and told him that he should tell his father.

"Oh, I will! As soon as I can find him."

There are very few things that will stop me cold in the act of knotting my tie, but that one did. "You don't know where he is?"

Emlyn shook his head. "We—we don't talk about it."

I returned to my knotting. "Who is 'we'?"

"Ieuan and I. Father said not to. Goldwurm isn't as apt to stir up trouble for us if he thinks Father's still around."

"But he's not? Do you know where he is?"

Sadly, Emlyn shook his head again.

"I see. How long has he been gone?"

"Only a few days this time." He sighed. "It probably means that he'll be gone for a long, long time yet. He does that. He goes away and leaves my brother and me on our own. He says it's good for us."

I hugged him then, Millie, and you would have, too. He is about fourteen, I suppose. Possibly fifteen, and his eyes and trembling lip told me that he might start to sob at any moment.

When he had calmed down somewhat, and we had talked a bit more, I asked about his mother.

"People say our father killed her. He says he didn't, and I know he really loved her." The thought clearly made poor Emlyn miserable. "They had some big fights years and years ago, and they never made up."

"Those things happen." It seemed wise to change the subject. "We found a head here yesterday, Emlyn, but it was a woman's head. You found a man's, from what you say."

"That's right."

"Old Nick—that's my servant—disposed of the head we found in the river. He tied it in a bag weighted with stones and threw the bag in. If you haven't rid yourself of yours yet . . . ?"

"You're right. I'll have to do something with it, and maybe I'll do that." Emlyn was blotting his eyes with a clean handkerchief. "Can I tell you what I think, Bax? Promise you won't laugh?"

I raised my right hand. "I promise. You have my word."

"I think it's a werewolf. Facefoxes are vixens who can turn into women. Remember me telling you about that?"

"Yes," I told him. "I had almost forgotten, but I recall it now. I didn't believe you, and anything one disbelieves is forgotten very readily."

"I was telling you the truth."

"I'm certain you were. Winkle is a facefox."

"Your pet? I know."

"She makes a most charming Japanese girl. Pretty, and quite vivacious."

"You agree then? About the werewolf? I've got to convince you, because I want you to help me find him."

"Do you know it's a man?"

He shrugged. "No, but they usually are."

"Never a young woman?"

"Yes, there are women. They're most often men, but—"

"In that case, I can name the werewolf. She is a woman. A girl in the broad sense."

He stared.

"That was a pun, wasn't it? I didn't mean it that way."

"I didn't catch the pun. I—I'm not good at jokes. But you remind me of Father. Are you him? Are you really my father, Bax? Tell me! Tell me, please!"

"No. I'd tell you if I were, Emlyn. I'm not. Can he disguise himself that well?"

"Yes!" Emlyn sounded as though he might start sobbing again.

" 'It's a wise child who knows his own father,' " I mused. "I didn't understand that as a boy, and because I don't know my own, it haunted me. I think I understand, now. What's your father's name?"

"Zwart." Emlyn paused. "We don't have two names like you do."

"Really? It's Zwart?"

"Yes, that's his name. What's wrong?"

"It means black. Were you aware of that?"

Emlyn shook his head.

"Your brother Ieuan helped my man the other day. He collected wood for the fires and so on. My man called him Ieuan Black."

"He will have told him that. Like I said, we don't really have any last name, but sometimes we need one and when we do we say Black."

"As instructed by your father?"

"Yes." Emlyn nodded.

"There seems to be a man named Skotos involved in all this, too. Do you know the meaning of that name?"

Emlyn shook his head. "What is it?"

"I'll reserve that. The werewolf likes you and hopes to please you. It's why she gave you the head you found."

Emlyn looked frightened. "Is this some sort of joke?"

"Perhaps it is, I don't know. But it certainly isn't my joke. She's quite attractive in human form, by the way. A piquant face and so on. Are you going to thank her for the head?"

"No!"

"You may want to reconsider. I feel foolish speaking as the representative of this town. I haven't lived here long at all, and I certainly haven't been elected to any office. But foolish or not, I hope you can persuade your new friend to leave us alone. She's killed two people here whom I know of, and suspect that the head she gave you is from one of us, too. If so, it would make three. Please ask her to go somewhere else."

"I'm sure I have no influence with her at all," Emlyn told me stiffly.

"We used your triannulus to ask for money for me," I reminded him. "Your triannulus and your longlight. You must remember that."

"Of course I do. You got some money, too, and I think you ought to be grateful."

"I am very grateful, and I'll be still more grateful if you can get Lupine to leave our area."

"Is that her name? Lupine?"

I shrugged. "She said it was."

"When you asked her to go away?"

"I didn't actually. I should have, but I did not. She would only have laughed at me, I'm sure."

"You'd rather have someone else die than be laughed at."

"No doubt I deserved that." It had hurt more than I liked to confess. "Just the same, calling me names is not going to save a single life."

He shrugged. "Getting her to change her hunting grounds isn't going to save any, either. People somewhere else will die. It won't be anyone you know, but that's the only difference."

"You're right, of course. Do you think you could get her to kill only bad people?"

"Bad people like Ieuan?" It was a challenge.

"I hadn't thought of that. He is your brother, after all."

"He is." Emlyn sighed. "Someday Ieuan may kill me. I've been afraid of that for years. But if I were to kill him, or if I were to get him killed, I'd be as bad as he is. No, I'd be worse."

"You're right. You would."

"Besides, I don't think you can get werewolves to do anything like that. It would be like training a real wolf to kill only the black sheep. Generally you've got to kill werewolves. Father told me that once, and he knows about these things."

"In that case, you're going to have to kill this one," I told him.

"Me alone? I'm not a man yet, Bax."

"Yet you brought her, and I still think that you ought to have some influence with her."

"No, I did *not* bring her!"

"I think you did. You lined up those three rings, the arrow, the face, and the animal. You wanted that alignment to mean 'find the facefox.'"

He nodded. "Go on."

"Suppose that animal on the ring wasn't a fox at all. Suppose that it was a wolf. Wouldn't that mean 'find the werewolf'?"

At that, his jaw dropped. I have not seen jaws drop often, Millie, but his did then.

"Thus I think you should have some influence with her. I used the triannulus for money, and spent it as I pleased when I got it. Earlier I asked for fish, and I ate them."

"All right, I'll try. I'll try if I can find her." Emlyn backed away.

"Don't forget to thank her for her gift!" I called as he turned and fled.

You will wonder whether I really drove that enormous antique to the lawyer's office, Millie. I did, and it was the first time I had ever driven it by myself. Believe me, I was very careful indeed and chugged along at a most moderate speed, although I nearly panicked when I could not find either Wilson Street or Railway Road. I very politely asked a policeman instead, and he was so taken with my car that he got in and directed me. It was only three blocks away, and he never asked to see my license.

I was the last to arrive. Urban Trelawny is a bony man of fifty and more, with side whiskers. His eyes say quite plainly that he once trusted someone, that he has been repenting it for longer than you or I have been alive, and that he will never take the chance again.

"Sit down, sir," he said as his secretary left us. "The chair between Mr. Hardaway's and Mrs. Griffin's will do. You present yourself as the heir?"

I sat. "Yes, I suppose I do."

"You cannot prove it?"

I shook my head. "I can prove that I'm Baxter Dunn. I can't prove I'm Alexander Skotos's heir."

"We had hoped that the late Mr. Skotos had written you, expressing his intention to leave you his property."

I shook my head again.

"Also, that you would present Mr. Skotos's letter for Mr. Hardaway's examination as well as my own."

I said that I was sorry to disappoint them.

"I urged that course upon him." Trelawny sighed. "He told me he did not have your address. It may possibly have been true, although he was not, generally speaking, what is called a truthful man."

Doris murmured, "I'm sorry to hear that, sir."

"Nor was he a man, generally speaking, who complied with his attorney's advice." Trelawny paused to wipe his nose. "That is of no consequence to us tonight. I asked how his heir might be positively identified. He described the man, but in terms so vague that I positively refused to incorporate them in his will. I insisted that he—"

Doris interrupted. "He described his heir to you, sir? Don't you think we ought to hear his description?"

She was seconded at once by Mr. Hardaway.

"You are here by sufferance, my dear young lady. You are *not* so entitled."

At this point, Millie, I found myself wondering how I might bring Trelawny to Lupine's attention. I rose. It would be pleasant for me to write at this point that Doris and Mr. Hardaway fell silent at a mere gesture and a stern glance from me, but it would not be truthful. Doris was shrill and Mr. Hardaway furious; I outshouted them.

"As the heir to the estate, I believe that I am fully justified in having an adviser present. Mrs. Griffin and I will engage another adviser, an attorney. He or she will contact you in due course. In the meantime, I intend to file a complaint with the American Bar Association. The late Alexander Skotos described me to you, but you will not permit us to hear his description? That's outrageous!"

Trelawny shaped a steeple of bony fingers. "The description will only delay us, Mr. Dunn. But if you insist."

"Whether Mr. Dunn insists or not, I do!" Mr. Hardaway had risen, too. He pounded Trelawny's desk as he spoke.

Trelawny nodded. "I am outvoted. I hope that it has occurred to all of you that since Mr. Skotos's description of his heir was never committed to paper, I may now say whatever I wish. I might state that his Baxter Dunn was one-legged, one-eyed, and bald, for example. I do not, yet I might."

Mr. Hardaway said, "Pah!" and we sat down again.

"Permit me to mention as well that I will be repeating a vague description heard years ago. If my reconstruction of it is something less than exact, that will scarcely be surprising."

"Let's hear it." Mr. Hardaway was brusque.

"Lastly, I shall mention that prior to his demise the late Mr. Skotos vouchsafed other particulars concerning his heir—more precise particulars that were in fact committed to paper as parts—or a part, a section—of his last will and testament."

Trelawny waited for some objection, and hearing none vouchsafed us a frosty smile. "Baxter Dunn, the late Alexander Skotos said, was a man of moderate height and average build. He had sandy hair, blue eyes, and regular features."

Doris's ladylike fist thumped the padded arm of her chair. "I've always believed Bax was the heir, and now I'm totally positive."

Mr. Hardaway nodded vigorously. "In my judgment as executor, Urban, this matter is no longer in dispute."

Trelawny's bloodless smile was chilling. "My oral recitation of a description I heard years ago means less than nothing, Jim. The proofs demanded in the will are significant. Not sandy hair or regular features."

He turned to me. "You think ill of me, Mr. Dunn—if that is indeed your name. But consider. There are no near relatives to dispute the will. As things stand tonight, it is unlikely that the matter will ever come before a court. What we will do here, this night in this office, is liable to be decisive."

I said, "I understand."

"Decisive, and the estate is worth millions. Decisive—unless another claimant should appear subsequently."

At that point, Millie, I was conscious that someone outside the office was talking to Trelawny's secretary; I gave it slight heed, however.

"Let us proceed forthwith to the proofs that the will specifies." Trelawny wiped his nose again. "The Baxter Dunn we seek, my client Alexander Skotos has declared, is a great scholar. Have you proofs of scholarship, Mr. Dunn?"

I nodded. "As a matter of fact, I have. I brought some diplomas, thinking they would establish my identity. One's been lost, a master of fine arts from the University of Chicago. The university can furnish a duplicate copy, I feel sure, if we request it."

"May we see those that have *not* been lost?"

"Certainly. How about my Ph.D.'s? Looking at those first should save some time." I handed them to him.

He took out a pair of reading glasses, put them on, and applied a fresh Kleenex to his nose. "Humph!"

Mr. Hardaway asked, "If two Ph.D.'s don't establish a man as a great scholar, what the hell would?"

Trelawny looked at him over the tops of his glasses. "This is in Nineteenth-Century English Literature." He displayed the paper to Mr. Hardaway.

"A legitimate subject for scholarship."

"While this one is in Ancient History."

"And this," Doris declared hotly, "has become pure farce. Bax fits the description. Bax is a great scholar by any sane measure. Bax is the heir."

Trelawny's smile would have wilted a tomato vine. "An heir who will not divulge his connection to the testator. That is correct, Mr. Dunn? Still correct, I mean?"

I nodded. "I will not divulge my personal affairs, and I will most certainly not divulge your client's when he is no longer alive to defend his reputation." Strictly speaking, Millie, that was the truth. I did not want to divulge my own, and could not have divulged Mr. Skotos's if I had wanted to, since I did not know them.

"I see. There are two further proofs we have yet to touch upon."

Trelawny's secretary was arguing with someone in the outer office; he paused for a moment to listen, then said, "We proceed to the second proof. Baxter Dunn—I intend Alexander Skotos's heir—is ambidextrous. Are you, Mr. Dunn?"

I shrugged. "I can write with both hands, if that's what you mean. It was quite useful in college. When one hand tired, I wrote with the other. Shall I demonstrate?"

"Please do." He handed me this ballpoint pen and a tablet.

"I'd like another one," I told him. "Another pen, please, and another tablet. Or a book or something else that will give me a writing surface."

Doris and Mr. Hardaway watched with great interest as I positioned a tablet on each knee. Have you ever seen me write different things simultaneously, Millie? One with each hand? It is a parlor trick, I confess, but since I have very few I am absurdly proud of it.

In this instance, I composed notes of thanks to each of them, employing cursive for Doris's note and print for Mr. Hardaway's.

Trelawny wiped his nose more thoroughly than ever and leaned back in his swivel chair. "Impressive, Mr. Dunn. Most impressive, I confess."

Doris rose. "Want to hear mine? 'Doris, you are a pillar of strength, and a pillar far more lovely than any Greek caryatid.' It's signed 'Bax.'"

She laid it on the desk. "You can look at it if you want to, but you have to give it back."

"Mine thanks me for my friendship and support," Mr. Hardaway said. "It's signed 'Baxter Dunn.'" He laid his note on Trelawny's desk as well.

"Mr. Dunn." Trelawny leaned forward again, glanced at the notes, and reprised the finger-steeple. "I would like you to understand my position. Everyone present, yourself included, seems to have the notion that I seek to discredit you. It is erroneous. I personally believe that you are the Baxter Dunn to whom the will refers. I have given you credence—if we may call it that—from the moment you walked into the room. With no support from the executor, I am attempting to do my duty as attorney for the estate. I do not ask for your friendship, Mr. Dunn. Only for your understanding."

"You have it. Shouldn't we proceed to the third proof?"

"We should. The Baxter Dunn specified by the will is a twin. Although the will does not say it, Mr. Skotos once referred to him as an identical—"

His secretary was screaming. Trelawny stood up, strode to the door to the outer office, and flung it open—

—admitting George, your husband, who shoved him quite violently. "Are you the lawyer? Well, by God I've got a few things to say to you and you'd better listen."

Trelawny pushed past him and hurried through the doorway; his secretary's screams faded to loud sobs.

George fastened on me. "I don't know what you've been up to, Bax, but if you're cooking up some scheme to defraud me again, you're not going to get away with it. Now get the f–k out of here!"

I urged him to control himself. Mr. Hardaway joined me in that, and George turned on him, shouting obscenities.

"Bax! Oh, poor, poor Bax!"

It was not until she spoke that I realized that Doris was clinging to me. I made haste to assure her that George would not become violent.

"He knocked down my secretary." That was Trelawny, behind his desk once more and (it took me a long half-second to realize this, Millie) holding a gun. "I've told her to call the police." George took a step toward him, and he added, "Sit down, you! Be seated, or I'll fire!"

"With that?" George pointed. "It must be a hundred years old."

"It is far older," Trelawny told him. "It was made in England at the time of the American Revolution, but it is in perfect working order. Do you want to find out whether it is loaded? If you don't, you had better be seated this instant."

"He can have my chair, Urban." Mr. Hardaway rose. "I'll stand behind him and grab him if he tries anything."

At that point I advised George to sit down, and he did.

"Now then, sir." Trelawny was still aiming his silver-mounted flintlock pistol. "What is your name?"

"It's George J. Dunn. I'm the real George J. Dunn."

"It appears to me that you and Mr. Baxter Dunn are identical twins. Do you deny that? Either of you?"

George glared and shook his head. I said, "We are."

"That would seem to settle the matter." Trelawny looked toward Mr. Hardaway. "It certainly appears to me that the Baxter Dunn who is here in my office is the—"

Trelawny's secretary stepped in. Her makeup was in ruins and her eyes still swam in tears, but her voice no longer quavered. "I've called the police, Mr. Trelawny. They say somebody will be here right away."

He nodded curtly. "Our time is short. I shall employ your first name, as well as your brother's, to minimize any confusion. Why did you come here, George?"

"Oh, for God's sake! To protect my interests, damn it! To keep from being robbed again!"

"At some point in the past, your brother Baxter robbed you?"

George sprang to his feet. "It's all he's ever done. He's robbed me over and over again. He's been my curse! I have a brother who looks just like me, and he's a criminal and a lunatic. Why in holy hell can't people understand?"

Trelawny snapped, "Sit down, George! Sit or I shoot!"

"I won't! Shoot, damn you! Do it!"

Doris went to him, looking very starched and prim. "Are *you* saying *Bax* is insane? Is that serious?"

"He's a maniac. You ought to s-see his l-letters. He's a g-goddamn m-m-maniac and a th-th-thief." George wept.

I went to him, patted his back, and put my arm around his shoulders. "Can't we be friends? I'm not as bad as you think."

"You bastard! You utter bastard! I've worked hard, so damned hard all my life, and your butler told me where you were. *Your g-g-goddamn butler!*" He swung at me after that, Millie, something I had been half expecting. Though jarred, I deflected his follow-up punch, and Mr. Hardaway got his arms around him and forced him down into his chair.

Trelawny laid aside his pistol. "Thank you, Jim. For a moment there I was afraid I'd have to shoot."

Soon afterward there were voices from the outer office and a policeman and a policewoman came in. The woman was Officer Finn, whom I had met before. I hope, Millie, that you saw the letter in which I spoke of her.

"What's going on here?" the male officer asked. I have since learned that he is Officer Dominic Perrotta.

Trelawny pointed to George. "My secretary wishes to charge this man with simple assault."

Mr. Hardaway said, "He burst in here and became quite violent, officer. I had to subdue him just a moment ago."

"He was crying. Then he hit his brother," Doris told Officer Finn.

I intervened. "He didn't actually hit me, and I have no wish to have him charged with anything."

Officer Finn looked exasperated. "He didn't hit you, sir?"

"No, he did not." I shook my head.

"Well, somebody did two or three days ago. Wait a minute." She grasped my chin and turned my head until my left cheek was toward the light. "That's a nice red spot you've got there, sir. I'd call it a new one, and it's starting to swell."

Doris told her, "They're twins."

"Yeah, I saw. But it won't be real hard to tell one from the other for a while."

Officer Perrotta muttered, "See if the secretary will sign a complaint, Kate." Officer Finn nodded and went into the outer office.

Trelawny cleared his throat. "She will."

"You got that right. Kate's good at getting 'em to sign."

At which, I regret to say, George sprang to his feet again, jabbing a trembling finger at Trelawny and shouting, "That man pointed a gun at me!"

"Siddown!" Officer Perrotta pushed George back into his chair. "That's a damn shame, Mack. Might even be a violation of your civil rights. Lemme see now. You came busting into his office and knocked down his secretary? Is that right? So he pulled a gun on you and called the cops? Why, it's a dirty shame. Keep your ass in that chair!"

"It was this gun, officer." Trelawny displayed it. "Please be careful with it. It is quite valuable."

"Nice! Can I hold it for a minute? I always wanted to hold one of these."

"Certainly, just be very careful with it."

Mr. Hardaway joined them. "I know something about these old guns, officer, and I ought to point out that it couldn't possibly fire. There's no flint between the jaws of the cock."

"Sure. I seen that." Officer Perrotta was aiming the antique pistol at a lamppost beyond the window and squinting at the sights.

Officer Finn returned. "Got it!" She tapped George on the shoulder. "Stand up, sir, and put your hands behind you."

He struck her then, Millie. I hated to write those words more than I can say, but they are the truth. He will have telephoned you long before you receive this; no doubt you have engaged an attorney. I find the entire affair extremely distasteful and more than a little sad; I fear it is also fairly serious.

Forever your friend,
Bax

Dear George:

I have tried (injudiciously perhaps) to reach you by telephone. You may be pleased to hear that my attempts have been fruitless. I hesitate to visit you without an invitation; but should you desire to see me, please let me know. Visiting hours are three to five Saturdays and four to six Sundays. Letters, I am informed, will reach you without difficulty so long as they contain no contraband.

I had been told of an excellent attorney here; and a call to my friend Martha Murrey has yielded his telephone number, with other pertinent facts. His name is Benjamin Ramsey. You may wish to ask some of your fellow inmates about him, a resource denied me. I will undertake to engage Mr. Ramsey, or another attorney, on your behalf should you wish it.

You believe, or at least you feign to believe, that I delight in your misfortunes. If only you knew the emotions that tore my heart as I watched you beaten with that very clever telescoping truncheon Officer Perrotta took from his belt, you would understand me better. I protested, and tried to bring the violence to an immediate halt; but with so many blows raining down upon you, you can hardly have noticed.

It would seem to me that the police ought to have sent you to a hospital, and I was shocked to learn that they did not. I trust you are healing.

I plan to speak to Officer Finn on your behalf. (She and I are distantly acquainted.) Perhaps I will be able to tell you of our conversation before I close.

After you had been taken away, Trelawny asked whether he should proceed with the reading of the will. All three of us urged him to do so. It was prolix, and I could not give it all here if I wished to. The upshot was that I am to receive everything: the Skotos Strip, a sum in excess of one hundred thousand dollars, and a cased pair of antique pistols. You may recall the one with which he threatened you.

"Alex was a gun collector," Mr. Hardaway told me, "and those dueling pistols were the apple of his eye."

Trelawny wiped his nose, something he does frequently. "I hesitate to say this, Mr. Dunn. It may be a violation of professional ethics. But from what I saw of my client—no, I will not say it. I will simply caution you regarding the firearms I am about to give you. In the heat of the moment, I misrepresented them to your brother. Neither is loaded. Jim and I have examined them with care. Their barrels are not charged, there is no powder in their pans, and as Jim told that policeman there is no flint in either pistol to strike a spark. All those things are in this case, however."

He tapped it. "You'll have powder and priming powder, flints, balls, and patches. All that is needful. I advise you to dispose of the powder. Should you choose instead to load and fire these, you must be extremely careful."

I said that if the powder were as old as the pistols I doubted that it was dangerous.

"It isn't." Mr. Hardaway had gotten out a cigar and was rolling it between his hands. "Any gun shop will sell you black powder."

Doris rose. "I've been watching Bax's cheek swell. I'm going to try to find an ice pack for him."

I thanked her, and she smiled and went out.

(You were struck much more than I, George. I realize that. More often and much more severely.)

"Jim feels that Alexander Skotos, who sometimes fired the antique guns in his collection, intended to fire these upon some special occasion. Is that correct, Jim?"

Mr. Hardaway's lighter flared. "I'd say that Alex daydreamed about it. Of shooting them on his birthday, or something like that. I don't think he would ever have done it. They're too valuable." He applied the flame to the end of his cigar, and sucked smoke.

I said, "You're saying I should not do it, either. I'll heed your advice."

Trelawny wiped his nose on a tissue, and managed to look a trifle sheepish. "My own opinion is that he may have intended to fight a duel, Mr. Dunn. You will think that fantastic, I know. I know it, and I sympathize. But Alexander Skotos was at heart a scoundrel, or so he seemed to me."

Mr. Hardaway said, "A daredevil. I'd agree with that. A daredevil, but scarcely a scoundrel."

"It is a question upon which sincere men may disagree. These pistols are yours, Mr. Dunn." Trelawny paused, as if waiting for me to speak. "You may take them now, if you wish."

I did.

"Jim has the deed to Mr. Skotos's real property, I believe. Did you bring it, Jim?"

Mr. Hardaway said, "I did, and I'll sign it over to you tonight. To-morrow I'll have a cashier's check payable to you as well."

So it was, George, that I left the law office with the deed to the Skotos Strip in my pocket and a rather heavy set of cased dueling pistols tucked under my arm. Doris had not returned; Trelawny's secretary said she had left the building in search of an ice bag, and Mr. Hardaway and I met her in the foyer returning with one.

The question—at least, after Mr. Hardaway left us—was whether we ought to abandon our dinner plans. Doris feared that I was in too much pain to eat. I was hungry and eager to talk about you, George. And about myself, as well. Women always accuse us of wishing to talk only about ourselves; I do my best to avoid it, but it seemed to me that it could no longer be avoided.

She and I sat in front after concealing the leather-covered pistol case beneath the seat. I drove slowly; she held her ice bag to my cheek, as solicitous as any mother.

"We had better go somewhere close," I said. "This is not as old as the pistols, but I'm not sure how far it is to be trusted."

"We're going to the Lakeshore," Doris told me firmly. "Will you trust it that far?"

I shook my head.

"Well, I will, because that's where we've got to go. For one thing, they have a great big parking lot, and it won't be crowded this late. We can't possibly park this car of yours in a normal spot. It's the size of a mobile home."

"Not quite."

"Oh yes, it is. It's way too big, and we have to have a restaurant with no valet parking."

I agreed.

"And if you park it anyplace in town, there's a good chance it will be vandalized. Weren't you worried about it tonight?"

"You win," I told her, "and to confess the truth, I'm glad you did. I have a good deal of explaining to do, and the front seat of this car will be a better place for it than any table in any restaurant. If we break down on the way there, or on the way back, there will be still more time to talk."

"Talk about what?"

"About George and about me." I paused to think, but could think only about you. Then, shifting gears, about Emlyn and Ieuan. "I know another set of twins, Doris. Actually, I should say I know of them—I only know one of the brothers at all well. The brother I know is clearly good. His twin seems clearly bad, from what I know of him. And yet . . . Well, never mind."

"I know twin brothers, too," Doris told me. "One is polite and decent, and maybe a teeny bit too modest. Not to mention pretty good in bed. The other one—the one I met tonight—strikes me as more than a little unbalanced. Not unbalanced in a nice way, either. Can you guess which brothers I mean?"

Perhaps I nodded to that, George, although I hope that I did not. "People speak of brotherly love, Doris."

"All the time. I know."

"But in our case . . . Well, I don't really love my brother George. I don't believe I ever have. Perhaps George loved me once. I hope so."

"He probably did, Bax. You're an easy man to love."

"Thank you. As I said, I don't love him, and it makes it very difficult for me to be fair to him. I am going to try tonight." I paused. I was in third gear, but there is a fourth. I decided not to attempt it until we were well away from town.

"You think you know us both. I heard what you said when George stormed in, 'Poor Bax!' George has a temper, and too often loses control of it; but it's the only fault he has, really."

"I'll bet there are at least a couple of others," Doris said, "but that one may be more than enough."

"You think there's a good brother and bad brother, like Emlyn and Ieuan, and you're right about that. There are. There are, but you've got us reversed. George is the good brother. Believe me, it's no secret. Everyone in the family knows it."

"I'd have to hear them say it, Bax, and even if I did I wouldn't believe it."

"You will." I paused looking for a road sign, but saw none. "May I tell you how I got my Ph.D.'s?"

"You stole them?"

"More or less. George would certainly say I did. We had a wealthy aunt, our Aunt Carla Baxter. Mother's brother George had left her millions. Aunt Carla died and left my brother and me a trust fund. The terms were odd."

"Ah ha! The dotty aunt!"

"I should tell you that we were undergraduates at the time she died. Her will specified that as long as we stayed in college we would receive money for tuition and a living allowance. When we had both left college—and only when we had both left—whatever remained was to be divided equally."

Doris snuggled closer, propping up the arm that held her ice bag to my cheek. "That doesn't sound crazy to me."

"George left school as soon as he received his degree, found a good job, and got married. I went on to graduate school."

"I'm glad you didn't get married, Bax. Please don't ever get married until you run into a really nice lonely brunette."

"Do you see what that meant under Aunt Carla's will? I continued to draw tuition money and my living allowance. George got nothing, and would get nothing until I left school, too. He was furious. I believe I've already told you he has a hot temper."

"You didn't have to say it."

"He tore into me. I was a selfish clod—which is perfectly true. I was a traitor and a parasite, and so on. That was true, too; but I didn't know it at the time and became very angry. We were in my apartment, a little two-room place near the campus that I was renting while I worked on a masters in English Lit. I told George to get out. He was standing over me then and shouting down at me. He likes to do that."

"Oh, Bax! I'm so sorry!"

"I stopped answering him. I'd been telling him over and over that if he'd just sit down and be reasonable, we could work something out. He wouldn't listen, so I stopped saying it. I told him to leave, to get out of my rooms."

(You will remember all this, George, I feel sure. I shall skip a few sordid details.)

"He hit me. Ever since we were small boys, he had always been able to beat me in a fight; and that time he beat me again. He kicked me before he left. I was only half conscious, but his kick broke a couple of ribs, and I've never forgotten it. I resolved upon revenge."

"I'm glad. What did you do?"

"Isn't it obvious? I stayed in school. I had always enjoyed that life. I went from one university to the next collecting degrees. Teaching classes netted me some extra money, and . . ."

"What is it?"

"I don't recognize this road. Did I take the right road out of town?"

"I'm sure you did."

"In that case, I must have turned off somewhere. This one keeps getting narrower and narrower, and there are no road signs. We lost the white strip in the middle right back there. I think it might be wise to turn back."

"Oh, keep going. We're bound to get to someplace I recognize pretty soon. You said you stayed in school. Was that until you got both Ph.D.'s?"

"Longer than that." I had the ice bag by then, I believe. I dropped it into my lap and tried downshifting to second, managed it pretty well, and felt quite proud of myself. "I took course after course until the money ran out. I was working on a third Ph.D. when that happened. Do you think you've heard the worst?"

Doris said, "So far I haven't heard anything bad at all."

"You will. I began looking for a tenured position at a really good university, someplace prestigious with a mild climate. There was that, too."

"Did you find one?"

"No, and I ran out of money while I was looking. I took two—no, three—jobs, and found I couldn't stomach any of them. I wanted challenging work that would require scholarship. What I got . . ." I shrugged. "It wasn't that. There was a great deal of sitting at desks in crowded noisy offices and wracking my brains for something to do in order to look busy. I lasted a month at the last one. An entire month, because I was desperate by that time."

"I've had that kind of job, too. It's why I started selling homes."

"One morning I got up, and I couldn't put on my shoes. I couldn't make myself do it—put on my shoes, go out the door, and catch the bus for the office."

"You still feel bad about it."

"Of course I do. I had applied for various jobs I might have been able to stick with. That I might have been able to tolerate, because I'd be doing something that meant something: driving a truck, teaching, or building boats. Something like that. I was overqualified. I had heard that over and over. Now I was out of work again and would soon be broke."

"What did you do, Bax?"

I motioned her to silence. I had been driving slowly out of deference to the age of the car. I stopped now, peering out. "There's a horse out there in the woods. See it? A white horse."

"Yes . . ."

I put the car in neutral and pulled up the big floor-mounted brake handle.

"What are you doing?"

"I want to take a closer look, if he'll let me. He's a beautiful animal."

The white horse eyed me and backed away. I followed it, perhaps taking a hundred steps before I lost sight of it. After that I went forward for twenty more, although I could no longer see or hear it.

When I turned and looked behind me, I could see only the headlights, and they seemed terribly far away. I know—

.   .   .   .   .

Ieuan has been here, George. That was why I stopped writing. He had put on a clean shirt this time, but I knew him at once. I think it was because of the way he carried himself, cringing at times and swaggering at others. He looked like me, painfully so, and I recognized myself at once.

"Mr. Dunn? Mr. Dunn, may I speak with you? It's terribly important."

That was another. Emlyn called me Bax.

"I wanted to talk to you about the werewolf? The one who's been leaving the—well, you know."

I said, "What about her?"

"She kills people."

I nodded.

The next sentence came in a rush. "She kills them and I'm afraid I'm going to get blamed for it."

"Are you really?"

"Yes, really. Why are you smiling?"

After that I tried not to smile. "Sit down, please, and I'll tell you."

He sat on the old recliner I had carried to the house in Mrs. Naber's wheelbarrow.

"You asked why I was smiling. It was because I'm at least as liable to be blamed as you are. Perhaps more liable. She's left a leg on my porch, and a head behind my house not far from the cellar door. Doesn't it worry you in the least that I may be blamed?"

"Better you than me, Mr. Dunn, but we should make common cause. Two have four times the strength of one. That's what Zwart says. It sounds crazy, but he means at times like this. Partners?" He stood and offered his hand.

"Not yet." I had started to take it, but I put my own hand down. "I'm rather a treacherous man, you see. Ask anyone."

"I'll chance it."

"I've betrayed my brother over and over. Betrayed various friends of his, too. Swindled them. Now I find I can't take your hand when I'm in a false position, Ieuan."

He stared.

"I knew of course. Don't you remember what happened in the attic? I knew you at once, and I knew you at once today. I . . . Well, I feel sure you could deceive many people, but I'm not one of them. You should try to become accustomed to that, to internalize it."

He muttered something and spat on the carpet.

I rose. "That I will not tolerate. You beat me once. If you believe you can beat me again. I'm entirely willing to let you try."

He shook his head. "Can't you see . . ."

"Can't *you*? Open your eyes, Ieuan! If you want me for an ally, you'll have to treat me like one. There are paper towels in the kitchen. Go back there, get one, and clean this up. Then we can talk."

He rose and went out, George, and to be truthful, I thought I had seen the last of him. Much to my surprise he was back in a few minutes with a paper towel. He knelt and mopped up his saliva, doing a thorough job. "May I throw this in the fireplace?"

I nodded and thanked him for collecting firewood.

"You knew it was me? Your fool of a servant didn't."

"My fool of a servant did. He told me you had helped him. He praised you for it."

"No, he didn't!" Ieuan did not actually stamp his foot, but I could see that he wanted to.

"Have it your way; it's not worth arguing about. Why did you come here?"

"I told you!"

"The werewolf, but that was while you were playing your brother. Why did you really come?"

. . . . .

Another interruption. I am beginning to wonder whether I shall ever finish this, George. Yet I am determined. I will win through in the end.

After reading it over, I think I made a major mistake when I left my narrative to explain Ieuan's interruption. With your permission, I will change hands and retrace my steps.

When I returned to the car, Doris was speaking with a tiny old woman. "Here he is! We'll take you, Kiki. Don't worry. He's a very kind man."

"I try to be." I introduced myself.

"She's been walking a long way, Bax, and she's awfully tired. Her home is down this road, just a few miles. I said we'd give her a lift."

I nodded. "Certainly."

"Is it near the road, Kiki? Will we see it?"

"Well away. Well away." The old woman looked frightened.

"Then you'd better ride up here with Bax, so you can tell him where to stop. I'll ride in back until you get out."

The driver and his companion (should he have one) sit quite high up. There is a running board—already lofty—and an iron step above it. Essentially, Doris and I had to lift Kiki into the car.

"Rode in a cart twice," she said. "Twice in a cart's all I've ever rode. Uncanny thing, though, ain't it? Ain't it a uncanny thing?"

I agreed.

"Hope you ain't hopin' to be paid. Not hoping to be paid, are you?"

She was barefoot, and her clothes were rags; I assured her that we were not.

"You do a kindness, and your kindness pays you."

"Often," I said, "and perhaps always."

"It does that. That's what it does. This goes fast, don't it?"

"Not really."

"Don't it go fast though! Not far from my house now. Slower, 'cause the house ain't far. . . ."

I slowed, not only because she had spoken, but because there was a car with large, bleary yellow headlights at the side of the road. As we passed it, I saw Doris on the high front seat, and myself standing beside it with pistols in my belt.

"Slower . . . Now my house ain't real far."

Doris opened a hatch (or small window) behind us. "This tilts up, so the boss can talk to his driver. How are you two getting along?"

I said, "Fine. I like her."

And she: "I like him, m'lady. We gets along fine. Doin' fine, m'lady. I like him."

"You must've walked a long way."

The old woman cackled. "Way home's never long. Never a long way home. T'other one, he back there with you? You have t'other one in back there, settin' with you in the dark?"

"There are only the two of us," Doris said.

"T'other's back there, settin' in the dark, thinkin' I can't see him. I kin see him back there, dark or no." She pointed. "There 'tis! 'Tis my path right there."

I thought I could make it out in the headlights, though I may have been mistaken. I stopped.

She leaped down like a monkey, a feat that astounds me still. "Back there somewhere's t'other, m'lord." She was looking up at me; her small face, made hideous by countless years, was somehow captivating. "He's waitin'. M'lord, he's settin' in the dark. Waitin' . . . Wary. Be you wary."

Then she was gone. As Doris clambered back into the seat next to me, I said, "We ought to have asked her about the restaurant."

"I did. She'd never heard of it, but I said it was on Brompton Lake, and she said Brompton Lake was right up ahead, just follow the road. She said it was where she washes—where she washes . . ."

"Her face?" It had stuck in my mind, and certainly it had looked dirty.

A wolf howled. I had heard the sound on television and in films, George, but never in reality. It howled and it could not have been far away. I knew then an ancient fear that the first settlers knew, and wished mightily that I had brought my knife.

"Bax . . ." Doris grasped my arm.

"Yes?"

"I'm scared, Bax. She said she washed her shroud. I wish Ted were here with us."

I nodded. "We could certainly use another man."

There had been a faint knocking when I spoke. Doris asked, "What was that?"

"The engine, I suppose. I'm probably in too high a gear." I usually make a mess of downshifting, George, but that time I got it nearly right.

"I've been thinking. . . ."

I nodded. "Probably a good thing."

"Who do I know that I'd like to have here with you and me right now, because of the wolf? Ted, but he's dead."

I said, "I'd like to have him, too. Anyone else?"

"No. That's just it. I've got girlfriends and they'd be company. Good company, some of them. We'd hug each other and tell each other not to be scared, which would be great until the wolf came."

"The old woman said we had somebody else with us."

"Kiki? Yeah, she did. Somebody sitting in the dark. Tell him to stand up. We might need him."

"I'd rather not. If I—"

"What is it, Bax?"

"Water. I thought I saw the sheen of water through the trees."

"Go faster. It might be the lake."

Because of the age of the car and the roughness of the road, I did not. We descended into a tiny valley, losing all the stars; but when the road rose again, as it did, we went through a thick stand of trees and saw the lake spread before us.

"She was right," Doris said. "Kiki was. It wasn't far at all. Look over there."

I looked. There were lights, remote but real. As I watched, the headlights of a distant car came on, two more pinpoints of light. It turned its back, showing faint red taillights, then vanished as it pulled away. "It's a long way over," I said. "The other side of the lake."

"But the road goes that way."

It did, though it had become no more than rutted dirt. We bounced along it for about a mile, which took a quarter hour or so.

And we were there. The asphalt of the parking lot was under our tires, and the building no more than fifty yards away.

"It didn't look this close," Doris murmured.

I got the dueling pistols out from under the seat.

"Are you going to bring those inside?"

"Yes. I haven't had a good look at them. We can look them over while we wait for our food."

"Let's hope we don't scare people."

"I won't even take them out of the case," I promised.

Inside, a discreet sign read OPEN UNTIL MIDNIGHT. Doris glanced at her watch. "We'll have plenty of time. It's only ten."

We asked for and got a booth. There were more dirty tables than diners in the dining area.

"I want fish chowder," Doris told the waitress. "You going to have fish chowder, Bax?"

I shook my head, looking down at the case and wishing the waitress would leave so I might open it.

"Appetizer, sir?" That was she.

"Thank you, but no."

"The special tonight is Salmon Rangoon. That's grilled salmon with Rangoon sauce, garnished with crabmeat, tomatoes, diced peppers, and hard-boiled eggs."

"Nine ninety-five," I said.

"No, sir. Eleven ninety-five, only the kitchen may be out of it already. I can see."

"I'll have steak, medium-rare."

"Yes, sir. New York strip or filet mignon?"

"Filet mignon, medium-rare."

"Six ounce or ten ounce?"

Doris said, "Ten."

"For him?"

"Yes. He wants the ten. Medium-rare."

The waitress wrote. "How would you like that cooked, sir?"

I said, "Rare."

Doris said, "I want a whiskey sour."

"Yes, ma'am. With your appetizer?"

I said, "Now."

"Yes, sir. One for you, too, sir?"

I shook my head.

"Tossed or Caesar?"

"Tossed."

"We have blue cheese, ranch . . ."

I omit the rest, George. Doubtless you are ready to kill if you've read this far. For myself, I can only say I had two antique pistols which I would at that moment gladly have traded for a sawed-off shotgun.

"You must be hungry," Doris said when the waitress had left us at last.

"I wasn't before that began. Now I'm famished. It's ten o'clock—"

"Ten fifteen."

"I stand corrected."

"You like that case, don't you? You've been caressing it."

"I do. When my fingers glide along the leather, it tells me oh so softly that Charles Dickens has not yet been born."

"He wrote that thing about Scrooge, didn't he?"

"Yes. *A Christmas Carol.* He wrote it in eighteen forty-three. He'd have been thirty-one or thereabout."

"There are ghosts, aren't there, Bax?"

I nodded. "More than I've ever seen in the Black House. The Victorians loved ghosts." I glanced at the plump young woman coming toward our booth. "Can we do something for you?"

"I certainly hope so!" She was blond, and a large pimple was ripening on her right cheek. "That's a nice bruise you've got."

Rising, I said, "I fell. I'm Baxter Dunn, and this lady is Doris Griffin."

"I thought so!" The blonde was producing a business card. "She called you Bax and then you mentioned the Black House."

Doris said, "While you eavesdropped."

"I couldn't help it. It's gotten very quiet in here." The blonde turned back to me. "I spoke to you on the phone, remember? I'm Cathy Ruth. I'm on the *Sentinel*, and I'm a friend of Martha Murrey's. Remember?"

Doris said, "She writes restaurant reviews."

"And lots of other things. Do you want to tell me about the Black House?"

I said, "There's really nothing to tell. It is a quiet, comfortable house not far from the river. I like it, and I've been furnishing it with antiques. I'll let you come in and look them over when I'm finished. You probably write that sort of article, too."

Cathy shook her head.

"That's a shame. Perhaps you will by the time I'm finished, but meanwhile your food's getting cold."

"Cold food . . ." Doris pantomimed writing a note.

"Oh, I'm not reviewing this place. We're just having dinner."

"In which case, your dinner companions—"

"What's in that box?"

Doris snapped, "None of your business!"

Cathy laid a plump hand on my shoulder. "I've been nice, Mr. Dunn. Very, very nice. You've got the Black House, and you've given me next to nothing. I could print rumors. Heck, I could make up my own rumors. Confidential sources in the Department of Public Safety tell us . . . All that stuff. We do it all the time, and I'll bet you know that already."

"Yes. I do."

"All I'm asking is a little cooperation. A tiny li'l bitty bit, see? Believe me, it would be smart to give it to me. I've done the other thing, Mr. Dunn. I know how to do it, and I know what happens when I do."

"You could be sued," Doris said.

Cathy smiled. "I work for the paper, Ms. Griffin. You'd be suing the paper. It has lawyers on retainer, and it has the First Amendment. There isn't a politician in the state—and that includes the judges in the state courts—who wants to get the *Sentinel* mad at him. Use your head."

I said, "I've used mine. In return for a favor, I'll open up totally. Give you everything. It's a simple favor and I'll describe it in detail. Give it to me, and I'll be your confidential source in the Black House."

"I couldn't quote you by name."

"Correct."

"Will you deny the stuff you gave me?"

"Rarely if ever. Only when I must, in other words. In the vast majority of cases, and perhaps in all, I will simply decline to comment if questioned."

Doris told her, "He's good at that."

"I'll bet. Tell me what the favor is, and I'll think it over."

"Be careful, Bax."

Smiling, I ignored it. "In a nutshell, my brother George has been arrested for assaulting a police officer. I'm asking you to keep his name out of the paper. If it's printed, it will destroy his career. I want to spare him that if I can."

"He hit a cop?"

I nodded. "With his fist. He had no weapon. I could give details, but you will want to get them from her."

Cathy's eyes went wide.

"You may, of course, use everything you learn except my brother's name. His name is George Dunn. I don't want you to print that."

"I give you my word, and you'll empty the bag?"

"Exactly."

Doris's drink and fish chowder came. I offered to buy Cathy a drink, which she declined.

When the waitress had gone, Cathy said, "We have a deal. It's good until you hold back on me. Hold out and it's off."

"Naturally. I won't."

She grinned and offered her hand. I shook it solemnly without bothering to count my mental reservations.

"Now open that box."

I did.

"Hey, wow! I thought it was going to be pictures. Or love letters. Maybe both."

"They are dueling pistols," I explained. "A legacy from an old friend."

"Cool! Do you know how they work?"

I nodded. "I could load and fire them for you, but I certainly will not do that here."

"What's in the little boxes?"

"I haven't opened them, but one is probably patches and the other bullets. This big brass flask is for powder, and the little one's for priming powder. This is a ramrod. There's only one for the two pistols because they were sold as a set."

Cathy pointed. "What's that?"

"A bullet mold. You heated lead in a crucible—you'd have to buy those separately—and poured it into this. It is smaller than many." I took it out and opened it. "Only two bullets, enough for a single exchange of fire. In most cases, that's all there was to a duel. The duelists stood twenty paces apart, aimed, and fired. Quite often, both missed. They shook hands and retired with honor intact."

Doris said, "How do you know all this, Bax?"

"There are a great many duels in Victorian literature. To understand them properly, and what the author is saying about them, I familiarized myself with the real duels with which the author would have been familiar. The famous duel in which Aaron Burr ended the life of Alexander Hamilton, for example."

Cathy pointed again. "What's this little brass hammer for?"

"To start the bullet. A patched bullet fits tightly in the bore. You didn't really require a brass hammer, of course. Many shooters tapped their bullets in with the handles of their knives. But the hammer's a nice touch."

Doris had picked up one of the boxes and opened it. "These are flints."

189

I shrugged.

Cathy had the other box. "These are the bullets. Pretty, too! Hey, there's a note in here. . . ." She pulled it out.

I tried to take it from her, but she drew it back. "I found it and I get to read it." She paused. "Hey, listen to this. 'The werewolf will claim my son. Spare her if you can. His mother may help. These bullets are silver.' There's no signature."

Doris said, "Bax, you slipped that note in there."

I shook my head.

Cathy had picked up a bullet. "I think these really are silver. I'm going to show this one to my boyfriend's father. He's a jeweler."

"You can't take it," Doris told her.

"Right over there." Cathy gestured. "I'm having dinner with my boyfriend and his parents." She was gone before Doris could protest again.

The jeweler rose as she returned to the table, and after a moment or two followed her back to ours. "You probably don't remember me, Mr. Dunn. I'm Dick Quist."

"I certainly do."

"Have you noticed his ring, Cathy? That's a star sapphire, the best I've ever seen."

"You know I have!" Cathy gave her future father-in-law a quick smile before turning to me. "Poppa Quist says they're silver, Mr. Dunn."

"Coin silver, probably." He returned the bullet Cathy had taken to the box. "They're a bit tarnished, of course. But silver."

Cathy nudged him. "Somebody thinks Mr. Dunn might have to shoot a werewolf."

Dick Quist chuckled.

Doris said, "Somebody does, and I think I know who. Not who it is, but who it was."

"An eccentric, I'm sure."

"I wish I could be. Did you know Alexander Skotos, Mr. Quist? He died three years ago."

"I've got to get back to Louisa. She'll be mad if I'm gone too long."

He left, and Doris said, "He knew Alexander Skotos."

Cathy shook her head. "He's a family man, that's all. You two wouldn't make trouble for me with Robert's folks, would you?"

I said, "I certainly would not."

"I won't," Doris told her, "provided you go back there right now."

My steak and Doris's salmon arrived. I closed the pistol case hastily and laid it on the seat beside me.

When the waitress had gone, Doris said, "That bitch kept your note."

I was grinding pepper. "It doesn't matter."

"She'll put it in the paper."

"Perhaps. What if she does?"

"Don't you care, Bax?"

"I would rather she put it in there, accurately, than that she attempted to reproduce it from memory. She might write, 'The werewolf widely known as the Hound of Horror,' for example."

"You believe in werewolves."

I nodded. "I've seen and spoken to a woman I believe to be a werewolf. No, whom I believe to be *the* werewolf—the one who killed Martha Murrey's neighbor. You need not credit me."

"I believe you saw someone."

"Correct, I did—the woman by the river who gave me your keys. I'll introduce you at the first opportunity."

"You're looking terribly thoughtful. What is it?"

"Well, well, well . . ." I fear I sighed. "I've always wanted to play the Great Detective. We read a great many mysteries in prison."

"You were in prison?"

"I was. I was trying to tell you in the car, but I lost my nerve and never finished. I defrauded my brother, Doris. After that, I defrauded several of his friends. I was caught, of course. I was caught, and I begged them not to prosecute. I swore that if they would only give me a few years, I would repay every cent."

"I can see how this hurts you, Bax. Why don't we drop it right here?"

"They wouldn't. It took me a long time to understand why, but eventually I did. May I please explain? This is the Great Detective, too."

She nodded.

"The amounts were trivial. Not to me, but to them. What mattered was the insult to their pride. They thought themselves sophisticated businessmen. They thought me a poor, unworldly scholar—which was true enough. Now the poor, unworldly scholar had sold them three lost mines, a swamp, and half the town hall of El Dorado. He wasn't going to get away with it, by George! So they prosecuted, led by my brother."

"I understand. You believed those lost mines—or whatever they really were—yourself, didn't you, Bax?"

I shook my head. "No, I didn't. I was lying, and I knew it."

"Your steak is getting cold."

Dutifully, I sliced off a small piece, chewed, and swallowed. "Back in the attorney's office, you heard my brother say I had defrauded him. It was true, and perhaps you wondered why I haven't repaid him. I have not, because my offer to repay was spurned. I spent three years and some odd months in prison. That was the payment he wanted, and he has had it. He will get no more from me."

"You promised to tell that girl anything she wanted to know to keep your brother's name out of the paper."

I cut off another bite. "I'd like to think he would do the same for me. He wouldn't, but I like to think it."

"Great Detectives always have weaknesses."

"I've noticed. Mine is wandering from the subject. There's a mystery in that note. Surely you caught it."

"I don't even remember what it said."

"I believe I can quote it verbatim. 'The werewolf will claim my son. Spare her if you can. His mother may help. These bullets are silver.'"

"All right, I'll try. Why would he want the werewolf spared?"

I shook my head. "There could be a thousand reasons for that."

"I've got it!" Doris snapped her fingers. "Alexander Skotos wrote that note. Why didn't he leave his property to his son?"

I smiled. "That isn't what's puzzling me, but let's leave it there. As you said, I ought to be eating."

"Me, too. You know, I felt sure you were going to say Trelawny could've written it. How's your steak?"

I chewed another piece, swallowed, and tried to imitate a gourmet. "Excellent without quite reaching superb. Did the Salmon Rangoon live up to its star billing? My potato is good, by the way. Good, but not great."

"No comment on Trelawny?"

"Only this. His secretary might have written it, too. So might Mr. Hardaway. Not to mention Cathy Ruth. Did you see the note before you saw it in her hands? Are you sure? I did not."

"You're being silly. Two women."

"How do we know the note's telling the truth? You think there's no werewolf. What if there's no son? Either woman could be conning us. It's entirely possible they're working together, and no more unlikely than Trelawny."

"I was going to eliminate that. I don't believe he did it."

"We could explain to each other why he's exceedingly improbable. Shall we do it?"

Doris shook her head. "It would be a waste of time."

"I agree. Nor will I play the Great Detective, which would be another. Here's a real question, by which I mean one that I can't answer. Why was Dick Quist so reluctant to talk about Alexander Skotos? We agree that he clearly knew him."

"Yes. You know, Bax, a good many people must've known him, not just Mr. Hardaway and that lawyer. If we could find some of them and get them to talk about him, we might learn a lot."

"You're right." I pushed aside my plate and took out my telephone. "Have you ever listened to your date trying to date another woman while he was with you? I realize that it cannot have happened often."

Doris shook her head. "You're up to something."

"I certainly am." I switched on the phone, dialed Directory Assistance, and specified this state and town. "I'm trying to locate a policewoman named Kate Finn. Her address is eight eleven Walnut."

. . .

Doris whispered, "Isn't that the one your brother socked?"

I nodded.

"Well, is there a Finn at eight eleven Walnut?" A gesture silenced Doris.

. . .

"That will be a relative, I'm sure," I said. "Would you give me the number, please?"

"Give it to me and I'll write it down."

I covered the speaker. "They're ringing it now."

. . .

"This is Baxter Dunn, Officer Finn. I'm calling for two reasons. The first is that I want to say how sorry I am about what happened tonight. On behalf of my brother George and our family, I apologize most humbly."

. . .

"That's very good of you, officer. I hope you'll find it in your heart to forgive my brother someday. He is a good-hearted man with a bad temper. There's a great deal of stress associated with his work."

. . .

"I realize that, believe me. The second reason is that I need to talk to you. I'd be delighted to buy you lunch or dinner tomorrow. Your choice. Will you join me?"

. . .

"Here's the thing that worries me, officer. If it goes to trial, I'll certainly be called as a witness for one side or the other. I'll tell the truth, of course. But I'd like to tell it in a way that does no harm at all to you and Officer Perrotta. George was beaten quite severely, as I'm sure you realize. He's sure to allege police brutality, and quite frankly I don't feel he deserves to get away with that."

. . .

"No, we're not at all close. And of course he struck me, too. I'm sure you remember."

. . .

"Wonderful! I'd love a home-cooked lunch. Tomorrow about noon? I'll be there." I hung up.

"You didn't say anything about Alexander Skotos," Doris observed.

"Certainly not. That will come later."

"I see." Doris looked thoughtful. "The waitress took your plate. There was a little steak left and half your potato. She took mine, too. Do we want dessert?" When I said nothing, she added, "This is on me, you know. On my expense account."

I shook my head.

"What about a drink?"

"No. But go ahead if you'd like one yourself."

"You're driving."

"I'm driving, and I don't drink. I used to—used to drink too much, to tell you the truth. I've given it up."

"I'll skip the drink if you'll answer three or four questions."

"I'll try, and if I don't know something I'll say so." When I put the case of dueling pistols back on the table, Doris's face betrayed an unasked question. I said, "I want to put in flints and load them."

"Why?"

"Because I think we may need them on the return trip." There were rectangles of soft leather in the box of flints. I folded one over the back of a flint, put it in the jaws of the cock, and tightened them.

"Is this because of the white horse?"

I put down the pistol and stared at her. "Are you asking whether I intend to shoot it? Absolutely not."

"It didn't look like a regular horse to me."

"Nor to me." I got out the powder flask.

"Could that thing go off?"

I shrugged. "I have it on half-cock, but yes. That's always possible."

Doris ordered a whiskey sour.

"No more questions?"

"Do you love me?"

I sighed. "I don't say it often, because anyone can say anything. Words really mean very little. Men can be defrauded with words and women can be seduced with words, and it really comes to about the same thing. I'm not a fighter, Doris."

"I never thought you were."

"You were right. But if there is danger tonight I'll be out in front of you, fighting." I poured a measured charge of black powder down the barrel of the first pistol. "I want to have something to fight with, and these are all I have."

That brought the smile I love so much.

"You're worried about the white horse, because you think you saw something you didn't understand."

She nodded.

"So did I, and since I got closer to it I probably saw more. I saw something else as well—something you didn't see. I saw that absurd car stopped beside the road. I saw you in the front seat, and I saw myself standing alongside it with these pistols thrust into my belt."

"Bax, have you gone crazy?"

Here I must close, George. There is no more paper. I will buy some tomorrow, and begin a fresh letter as soon as I can find time.

———————————

Yours sincerely,
Bax

Hey, Prof!

You probably are wondering why I am writing you so fast, and have I heard anything about the Greek. Okay, I have, but it is not much. And I am writing you real fast because of what you said about chicks. Having two can be a lot a fun. I have been there and I know. Only if one finds out she will rat you out in a New York minute. You know what she might sing better than me, but I know there has got to be stuff she might tell.

Listen up. You never trust a prosecuting attorney, a automatic, or a chick. Never!

Okay, here is the rest. I run into a guy they call Iron Mike. He had been out and come back about six months ago. He is a cat burglar, and they say pretty good. He said yeah I talked to the Greek only I did not rat out the Prof or anybody.

Here is what he said. He was flat and wondering how he could buy a few tools when his ex phoned him. She said a guy had talked to her that wanted to talk to him, maybe, and if he had something the guy could use he would pay. She said Iron Mike should meet him in a diner. That did not sound too bad so he went.

The Greek came all right and had a long skinny torpedo with him. He says the skinny guy never said a word, just grinned the whole time. Mike says he took one look and knew he better not go anyplace with these guys only they never tried to get him to go anyway. The Greek said he would like something to eat, that Mike would. I guess he looked hungry. So Mike said he would and ordered a burger and fries and pie to go with his coffee. The Greek ordered two coffees, only the skinny guy never touched his.

The Greek said you were in quite a while. Mike said yes. Well, maybe you knew Baxter Dunn. Mike said, yes, we were like that. You are lying, the Greek said. Do not lie to me or you get nothing. Right, Mike said, I knew him but we were not real close. Who was? Mike says he did not know.

You lie, says the Greek and the skinny guy gets out a piece of clothesline and starts running it through his fingers. Mike said he had funny fingers. I said funny how but he would not talk about it. So Mike fingers a couple guys you were close with, one being me. How is he doing, the Greek says? He is doing swell, he is maintenance crew now and a cinch for parole, Mike tells him. He said people could push you around some but only so far and some other stuff and the Greek gives him a hundred and splits.

That is all I got, Bax, but I will keep my ears open.

Sheldon Hawes

Number 25

THE HITCHHIKER

Dear Mrs. Pogach:

Let me first thank you for your extreme kindness in visiting me psychically. For me, it was a new experience; and I mishandled it badly, I know. I apologize. I should never have left you as I did. From the bottom of my heart, I am most terribly sorry.

There has been a fresh development with which I ought to acquaint you. It is that the paranormal activity I had previously associated with my house exclusively appears to extend to an antique limousine I discovered in my garage. My friend Doris Griffin and I used this limousine to visit a restaurant some distance south of Medicine Man yesterday. There were oddities—to say the least—on our drive out. Still more on our return trip. Indeed, these were, if anything, more marked and peculiar, perhaps because the hour was later.

I will describe one now. If you accede to my request, I shall be more than happy to detail the other. You may wish to quiz Doris as well; if you do, I will do my utmost to secure her cooperation.

When we left the restaurant, everything seemed quite normal. The familiar road carried only a little traffic, but that was to be expected as the hour was late. We had not gone far when we saw a young woman in a white gown standing on the shoulder of the road. We stopped and asked whether she required assistance.

"A ride. Only a ride." Her voice was thin and sad. "May I ride with you?"

"Certainly," I said. "Just get in back. Where are you going?"

"Where you are going."

That seemed a bit odd, but I supposed she meant that she was returning to Medicine Man. A window permitting passengers to communicate with the driver stood open. Looking through it, Doris Griffin introduced herself and asked the hitchhiker's name.

"Mary King."

Doris began another question, then screamed. I braked so hard and so suddenly that I stalled the engine.

"She's gone! Bax, she disappeared! I was looking at her!"

I got out and opened all four doors of the passenger compartment. There was no one in there. Some distance away from the road, I could just make out what appeared to be a ruinous church and a cemetery. Here I should explain that though the moon was full, it was often obscured by clouds.

I started toward the church and its tottering grave markers, but Doris called me back; she was terrified, and kept repeating that the hitchhiker had vanished while she (Doris) had been looking at her.

There were also, as I have indicated, other incidents.

Thus I ask your assistance. Please come. I will of course pay all reasonable travel expenses, and will gladly and promptly pay your fee if you succeed. (As per your letter.)

Yours sincerely,
Baxter Dunn

Dear Millie:

Have I told you that I have had a letter from your adviser, Madame Orizia? I have, and a most remarkable psychic visit as well. Now I have written her requesting her assistance.

In the meantime, I have begun to assist myself. Allow me to tell you about it.

Two incidents determined me. The first occurred last night, as Doris and I were driving back from a restaurant on the shore of Brompton Lake. Our car was surrounded by huge wolves. I could not be sure how many there were, but there were certainly half a dozen and there may well have been more. I have read that wolves do not normally attack human beings, but these did not seem to be normal wolves.

The road was narrow and rutted, and I was driving very slowly. Doris urged me to more speed, and upon my request contrived to squeeze through the window communicating with the passenger compartment to lock its doors from inside and secure all its windows. Is it a lie to conceal one's good motives?

If it is, I lied to Doris. I indicated to her that I feared the wolves would enter the passenger compartment; the truth was that I feared they would invade the driver's. Although the driver's seat is somewhat higher than his passengers', his compartment is open on both sides and thus much more accessible.

That is in fact what occurred. If it had not been for one of the antique pistols I had pushed through my belt, I would certainly have been badly bitten and might well have been killed. As it was, I thrust its long barrel into the brute's mouth and fired.

The second determining incident occurred this morning after my return home. Emlyn introduced me to a young woman he clearly admired; she was Lupine, the psychotic I had met beside the river.

I have lived in this house for weeks now, but in all that time I have done little more than observe. This morning I resolved to do much more. I shall investigate. I am determined to make myself the master of this house in fact as well as in name. I began by reviewing my earliest experiences here. I have a scholar's memory, Millie. That can be a curse, but it can be a blessing as well.

Very quickly I hit upon Jake. I had asked Doris about Mr. Black's first name, and she had indicated that "Jake" had known it. I telephoned her and asked whether it would be possible for me to speak with Jake.

It was soon arranged. Jake would be most happy to buy Doris and the owner of the Skotos Strip dinner that night. It reminded me that I had promised to join Officer Finn and her mother for lunch. I was washing and shaving when my cell telephone chimed.

"Mr. Dunn? It's Cathy Ruth. I'm in the neighborhood and I have something that belongs to you. Can I drop by and return it?"

"As it happens," I told her, "I must join someone for lunch at noon. Could you give me a ride over? I was planning to walk, but not looking forward to it. A house on Walnut."

"Why, I'd be delighted to, Mr. Dunn. I'll be there right away."

I had supposed that right away would be twenty minutes or more, but apparently the fine old phrase has a different meaning for reporters. She was knocking at my front door in less than half that, was escorted into the living room by old Nick and his little terrier, and was left to cool her heels while I finished dressing.

Dressed, I welcomed her and received the possession I had expected—a note presumably written by the late owner of my antique pistols, Alexander Skotos.

"This gives me a perfectly grand chance to ask you about ghosts and strange happenings, Mr. Dunn. What can you tell me?"

"Very little I'm afraid. There have been no strange happenings in the house lately, but there are a couple of areas I want to look into. One is the trunk strapped to the car. I found an old car in the garage, you see, and I have a locksmith coming."

"Let me know what was in there if you find anything, okay?"

I nodded. "I certainly will. The other area is the cellar."

"O-o-o!" Her eyes went wide.

"I've been thinking of doing that. Midnight would be the best time, wouldn't you say?"

"Midnight tonight?" She was clearly eager.

"Yes, tonight, assuming that you can make it tonight."

"You're serious, Mr. Dunn?"

"Entirely. You'd better wear old clothes—I would imagine there will be a good deal of dust." I was careful not to mention to her (although I will tell *you*, Millie) that Nick had already been down there, knew about the furnace, and had gotten a washer and dryer installed there.

"I'll be here. Say eleven thirty or so?"

"Sounds good. I'm going out to dinner, but I should be home by then. Bring a large flashlight. Even if there are lights down there—which I doubt—we'll have to find the switches."

Cathy agreed, and drove me to eight eleven Walnut for my luncheon date with Kate Finn.

The Finn house was a modest bungalow, which was what I had expected, but homelike, neat, and clean. A smiling, gray-haired woman opened the door for me. "Mr. Dunn? I'm Biddy Finn." Seeing my surprise, she added, "It's really Bridget, but everybody calls me Biddy and I hope you will, too."

"I'm George J. Dunn's brother, Biddy, and he's the only Mr. Dunn as far as the family's concerned. Please call me Bax."

"I will. Oh, I will! Please come in. I see your face is still a little swollen."

"And my jaw's still a bit sore, but neither is really troublesome. Doris Griffin—she was there as well—got an ice pack for me at some drugstore, and I was able to keep it on my face now and then. How's your daughter?"

"A little worse, I'm afraid. She's in the kitchen making donuts. Do you care for homemade donuts?"

I smiled. "You know, I don't think I've ever had any."

"You will. They're Kate's specialty." For a moment Biddy looked stricken. "Mine's lobster salad. You don't object to lobster, I hope? So many people are allergic to shellfish."

"I love shellfish. Lobster particularly."

"That's wonderful! Please sit down. Kate will be here in a moment. It will be a very simple lunch. But good, I hope. Soup, sandwiches, salad, and Kate's donuts."

"My mouth's watering already."

"Well, it won't be gourmet food, but—"

Kate had come in. "Hi, Bax! How are you feeling?" The bruises on her face were very apparent, and for the first time since he had struck her I was truly angry with George.

I rose. "Much better than you do, Kate, I'm sure."

"I know how hideous I look. You've got to make allowances."

"You look like a most attractive young woman who's been brutally assaulted. If George were here, I'd be tempted to kick him."

Biddy asked, "Does he beat his wife?"

It was something I had never even considered and took me aback. "To the best of my knowledge, no. No, I—well I'm sure he doesn't. Millie would have told me."

"Half the time, wives don't."

"I'd never even considered the possibility. George isn't—or I never thought he was . . ."

Kate said, "My donuts are cooling, and everything else is ready. What do you say we go in?"

I had expected vegetable; but the soup was oxtail, with sherry stirred into it just before serving. I could have made a meal of that and I told them so.

"It's was Ray's favorite." Biddy smiled, happy to be reminded of better times. "Ray was my husband."

"I think I saw his picture in the living room."

"He was a sergeant, two years from retirement when he passed on, Mr. Dunn. We were going to take a cruise. I'd never been on one. You're not married, Mr. Dunn?"

"No woman has ever been foolish enough, Biddy, and I thought we'd agreed upon Bax."

Kate giggled. I had never heard a police officer giggle before, Millie, but I heard one then.

Biddy said, "Only if you promise that you'll always call me Biddy."

"I will, Biddy." I raised my right hand.

"In that case, Bax, I know you'll tell me the truth. Why would woman be a fool to marry you?"

"I will, but not all of it. I'm afraid you'll have to be satisfied with one good reason. I'm closemouthed. No woman wants a closemouthed man."

"The more fools they. Do you drink, Bax?"

I had been expecting that and shook my head. "I used to. I've given it up."

"How long has it been?"

I considered. "Three years and ten months now. Almost eleven."

"That sounds rather permanent, and you have to call me Biddy."

"It is, Biddy."

"What about gambling? Cards? Dice?"

"Horses. And the answer's the same. I used to, but I gave it up. In that case, I gave it up because I had to. I ran out of money. Later when I'd gotten more, I realized that if I began again I'd lose it—that in the long term, my chance of coming out ahead was zero. So I stopped."

"Roulette?" Kate asked. "Did you go to casinos?"

"No. Only to racetracks."

"Kate," Biddy said firmly, "has no bad habits."

"Oh, Mom!"

"Well, you don't, Katie."

"I do so! I squeeze the toothpaste in the middle. The floor of my room's paved with magazines. I put things off. I—well, lots more. "

Curious, I asked whether curiosity was a bad habit.

"Not in a cop, Bax."

"Then perhaps I ought to become one. I'm curious about my house, you see. You and I talked about it a bit when you gave me a lift home. I realize that Mr. Black, who used to own it, has been gone for some time. But I'm not at all sure how long that time has been. Do either of you have any idea?"

"Since I was a little kid," Kate said.

"That cannot have been very long, surely."

"Well, I'm twenty-four, and I'm pretty sure the Black House was already empty when I was ten."

Biddy made a small sound that might have been a cough. "I've seen him since then, Kate. I know I did."

At that moment, Millie, I knew how a hound must feel when it catches the scent. I said, "You've seen him? Why this is delightful! Do you know, Biddy, you're the first person I've found who has? What did he look like?"

"You sound as if you think he's dead, Mr. Dunn." She snapped her fingers. "Oh, there I go! Bax, I mean."

"I suppose I must. It's just that everyone talks as if he's dead. You don't believe he is?"

"I saw him in some store just a few years ago. He was alive and looked well."

Kate fidgeted. "I think you must've mistaken somebody else for him, Mom."

"Well, I don't. I told Mr. Dunn—"

I interrupted. "Please call me Bax, Biddy, and tell me what he looked like."

"Well, he's small, not a whole lot taller than I am, and has a big nose. One of those noses that look like you could split firewood with it. Do you know what I mean?"

"I believe I do."

"Wavy hair—towhead going gray—and rather a pale complexion, I believe. Snapping black eyes."

Kate said, "Blonds almost never have dark eyes, Mom."

"Well, he might bleach it. I see brown-eyed blonds all the time."

I said, "I've seen blond men with dark eyes, I feel sure. Not many, but a few. How did you know the man you were seeing was Mr. Black?"

"Because I remembered him from when he lived in the Black House, that's all. People use to point him out."

"Have you ever spoken to him? Did he ever speak to you?"

Biddy shook her head. "No, I just saw him in this store. There was a woman with him, and they were buying something. I've seen her around town, but I don't know her name."

"I see. I wish I knew where he is now. I'd like very much to talk with him."

Biddy hesitated. "I could call you if I ever see him again."

Kate said, "Have you seen the woman since then? Can you describe her? I think that's what Bax is getting at."

"I think so. Wait a minute. She was wearing a charcoal-gray dress, I'm sure. High heels. I remember those because I noticed she looked a little bit taller than he did and looked at her shoes. She'd have been about his height in flats."

"She's probably changed her dress by this time."

"Don't be sarcastic, Kate. I was trying to remember how she looked, and the first thing I remembered was that dress. Charcoal-gray and very plain, but it looked like good wool. Brown hair a little shorter than mine. Too much lipstick."

"Oh, Mom!"

"Well, it was. She was quite an attractive woman, though. Stylish. She had a good figure. I'm a bit too stout, and I know it. She wasn't."

I said, "Please try to guess her age. It doesn't have to be exact."

"Younger than I am, but older than Kate. About your age, Mr. Dunn, or a little older than that. Younger than Mr. Black, though. How old are you?"

"Forty-one. How old would you say he was?"

"I really don't know, but at least fifty. He could be older. He's one of those small, active men. They . . ." She snapped her fingers.

Kate said, "What is it?"

"I just remembered where I saw him. What store they were in. It was in that store where they sell footballs and helmets. All Sorts, or something like that?"

I asked, "Could it be All Sports?"

Kate nodded, and Biddy said, "That's it. Kate had run out of gun-cleaner. She's got to go to the range twice a year. Ray used to do it, too."

"We put forty rounds through our Glocks," Kate told me. "Slow fire, rapid fire, one-handed right and one-handed left, ten rounds each way. That's how we qualify. A bull's-eye is ten, and your score has to be three hundred or better."

"She had asked me to pick her up some, so I was in there waiting for the man to wait on me. He was busy with Mr. Black. Could they make a special gunpowder for him?"

I shook my head. "I doubt it very much."

"Well, they kept talking about Black powder."

The pistols Alexander Skotos left me use black powder, Millie; and when I heard that, I felt sure that Skotos was Mr. Black, something that I have suspected almost from the beginning. I felt—I still feel—like Sherlock Holmes. I have bought a little notebook, and another pen as well. When I got home I made notes on my conversation with Kate and Biddy.

And now I must do this and that, and prepare for dinner with Doris and Jake.

Forever your loving friend,
Bax

Dear Shell:

Thank you for your information. Believe me, it has been helpful to me. I believe the Greek was the man I mentioned in my earlier letter. That seems just about certain. It is the identity of the tall man with him that puzzles me. At this point I have no idea who he was; but I have been snooping here and snooping there, and I think that I am getting close.

Please keep asking around, and let me have anything you find out. Anybody who is with the Greek or seems to be working for him is of great interest to me.

I have made up a package for you. I am going to put it into the mail today. There are cigarettes, cigars, gum, and candy in there. Things you will want and things you may be able to trade. (Here I am telling you, when you were the friend who wised me up to begin with.) I have also signed you up for some magazine subscriptions, ones I think you may like. Your first issues should be arriving soon. Let me know what you think of them, and whether there are others you would like to get. I will see to it.

Should I send some money to your wife? Let me know. I do not want to do that without your imprimatur.

Remember the dueling pistols I told you about? I have done a little shooting with one now. I hit the animal, but it was just about on top of me and I could hardly miss. Any tips on loading and firing pistols like mine will be greatly appreciated.

Yours sincerely,
Bax

Dear George:

I trust that Millie has found you a lawyer by now, or that you have found one for yourself. You may recall that I volunteered to engage one on your behalf in an earlier missive. Receiving no response, I have not acted.

Even so, I have done what I could. The policewoman you struck—three times, I believe? Or was it four? This policewoman will clearly be the most important witness against you. I have spoken to her and endeavored to soften her opinion. I cannot help but remark that the accusations of brutality you have leveled against her partner were less than helpful in this regard, although they may have been tactically shrewd.

Enough of that. You are no doubt better informed regarding your own case than I am.

You believe I am deranged. I resent it, George, yet I shall allow it. Possibly you will laugh at my ravings, but there can be little merriment in your present situation. I welcome your hilarity; if you are wise, you will treasure all that I provide.

Furthermore, I must point out that it is you, the sane twin, who is confined at present. I am entirely sincere in wishing your confinement short, and I will do my utmost to amuse you until your release.

I had expected the locksmith yesterday afternoon. There is a trunk strapped to the back of the limousine I discovered in my garage. I think I may have mentioned it. Although Joe (I cannot recall his surname) had said it was light, I was eager to examine its contents. The locksmith, Les Nilsen, was to open it for me. He telephoned shortly before I was ready to go out to dinner and warned me that he would be late, although he would come. I told him that the limousine was parked in my driveway and the trunk was readily accessible. He might call upon the butler whose existence so greatly offended you if he required help.

I was to dine (I do not believe I have mentioned this to you previously) with Doris Griffin and Jake Jacobs, a salesman from her office. Jake and Doris had settled on a Chinese restaurant, the Garden of Happiness.

"It's only Chinese," Doris told me when she picked me up, "and I know you must've eaten Chinese a thousand times. Everybody has. But Medicine Man's not what you would call big on exotic cuisines, the Garden of Happiness is clean and quiet, and the food's really very good."

"Are the portions plentiful?" I asked.

Doris grinned. "Absolutely. Guaranteed."

"In that case I assent most readily. I had a good lunch, but we ate early and now that seems a long, long time ago. Let's go!"

Jake is short and stocky and white-haired. I would think that he must be close to retirement. He shook my hand (of course), thanked me with apparent sincerity for joining him, and invited us to sit down.

"Doris said you wanted to ask me about old Black, the previous owner of your house. I don't believe I ever met him, even though I heard a lot about him." Jake chuckled. "There were stories. And I mean what I say—stories. I doubt that there was a word of truth in any of them."

Doris was looking at the menu. "The dim sum's good here."

"If we order that," I told her, "we'll be interrupted every few minutes. Wouldn't it be better just to order dinner?"

She nodded. "Good thinking."

As you know, George, I am far too familiar with prison food; it would be cruel for me to torment you with details in my description of our dinner. I shall pass in silence over the three appetizers we shared. As Doris implied earlier, we have all dined in Chinese restaurants. Let it suffice to say that Doris and I ordered the specialty of the house, Stuffed Duck With Eight Precious Ingredients, and that Jake chose the Chinese Barbecued Pork.

"I wish you had met Mr. Black," I told Jake when our waitress had gone. "I have yet to speak with anyone who did."

Jake looked thoughtful. "There must be quite a few around town."

"I hope so. Do you know anything about the house? Anything concerning its history, I mean."

"It was one of the first in this area. I know that. Might be older than the town. Maybe you've had a look at the foundation?"

It had never occurred to me to do so; I shook my head.

"Well, I'd do it if I were you. It's most apt to be stone. That's how they built 'em then. Thick stone walls to hold up the house and a dirt floor in the basement. It would be concrete now, with a concrete floor."

Recalling a promise, I told him I would look that night.

My remark made Doris drop her chopsticks. "Are you really planning to go down into the cellar tonight, Bax? After dinner? You're not kidding?"

You may recall, George, that I had promised to be Cathy Ruth's source in the Black House—you may, that is, if you bothered to read my earlier letter. Now I explained that I had promised her a tour of the cellar. "I'm relying on her to keep George's name out of her paper," I told Doris, "so I had to toss her a bone. The trunk—which didn't interest her—and the cellar were all I could think of."

"I'm coming with you."

213

"That's very good of you, but if—"

"No buts. You're going to need somebody to keep her in line, something you're much too much of a gentleman to do. That's me. We'll have a nice dinner here, Jake will pay and go home, and I'll drive you home and come along. It's all settled. Would you want to walk home at ten o'clock at night?"

Smiling, I confessed that I would not.

"So you need me. You'll need me tonight down in that cellar of yours, too."

Jake grinned at us. "Let me know if there's wine."

I must have looked surprised. "You know, it's entirely possible. In that house anything is possible."

Doris said, "I thought you didn't drink."

"I don't, but I may entertain, send gifts, and so forth. Besides, it would be interesting."

Our soups arrived, hot-and-sour for Jake and me, and egg drop for Doris. While we sipped it (it seemed close to boiling), I asked Jake whether he recalled Mr. Black's first name.

"Sure do. Can I let you in on a little sales secret, Mr. Dunn? I've been selling houses and lots for thirty years now."

I said, "I'd like to hear it."

"A salesman wants a name that's easy to remember but short and not hard to spell. Easy to remember means the client doesn't know other folks with the same name, or pretty much the same, so he gets them mixed up. Like I'm Jake Jacobs. You know anybody else with that name?"

I stirred my soup and shook my head.

"You don't, but it's easy to remember and anybody that can spell at all can spell it. So I'm interested in names. I notice the names of people in my business and watch how they make out. Take Doris. The name's short and easy, but you probably don't know any other Doris."

"A nice smile helps, too," Doris put in.

Jake grinned again. "Glad you said it, Doris, 'cause I wouldn't." He turned back to me. "Last name? Griffin. Sort of like a dragon. There aren't any, but everybody's got a picture of one in their head."

"You're right," I said. "What about Mr. Black?"

"I'm getting to it. He had an easy last name, and a first name that jumped out at you. It even gave him an initial not many have. Suppose you were looking for him in the phone book. There'd be a lot of Blacks, but only one Z. Black, right at the end."

At that moment, George, I felt that my twenty-to-one shot was pounding around the final turn with a lead of four lengths.

Doris said it for me, "What did the *Z* stand for?"

"Zwart." Jake spelled it for us. "You know anybody with that name? I don't."

Doris ignored his question. "What is it, Bax? Something just jerked your chain."

"I think I may have met one of Mr. Zwart Black's sons, that's all. A young man told me his father's name was Zwart, and as Jake says there aren't a lot of people named Zwart. As a name, it's unique in my experience."

"Mr. Black's son?"

I nodded and sipped my soup, my thoughts whirling.

Doris said, "Do you know, it had never even crossed my mind that Mr. Black might have had children. But I suppose he might have. People do."

Jake said, "He was married. I know that for a fact."

"You do?" Doris seemed almost as excited as I felt.

"Sure do. They split up somehow. Divorced, or else he died. Something like that. Anyway, you're too young to remember the old A&I agency, but she went to work—"

My cell telephone rang. Trying to catch my breath, I motioned Jake to silence and answered it.

"Mr. Baxter Dunn?"

I said it was.

"This is Toby, your footman, Mr. Dunn."

A footman? For some preposterous reason, I found myself picturing the footmen in *Alice*. I managed to say, "I didn't know I had a footman."

Toby coughed, a short bark that sounded a trifle embarrassed. "I was engaged at—" He coughed again, not quite so loudly. "You engaged me when you engaged your butler, Mr. Dunn, sir."

"Oh, yes. Yes, of course. Toby."

"The locksmith is here, sir. He has solved the lock of the trunk you desired him to open."

"Good. Please ask him to leave his bill. I'll take care of it."

"He has a question, sir. As do I, sir. We wish to know whether you desire us to open the trunk? We can leave it undisturbed to await your return, sir, should you prefer it. There are clasps, sir. You will recall those, I'm sure. A bit rusty, sir. There are big straps, too. And an odd sort of odor about everything, sir, if I may be so bold."

"Leave it alone, please. Let's open it by daylight."

"That's wise I'm sure, sir." From his voice, Toby might have been wagging his tail. "There's quite an odor, sir. I'm sensitive to odors."

"So you said. I understand."

"Little scratchy sounds, too, sir. It could be rats. I'm a fine ratter, sir. I hate them."

"I certainly approve of that, Toby. Tell Les to leave his bill, please, and you and I will open the trunk in the morning."

I hung up and switched off my telephone, apologizing to Doris and Jake. "I'm sorry about that. I've turned it off, so it won't interrupt our dinner again."

Doris said, "Do you have a footman, Bax? I thought I heard that."

"So it would appear. There are footmen who are fish, and there are footmen who are frogs. Mine happens to be a dog."

Shaking her head, Doris turned to Jake. "Ever had a client with two Ph.D.'s? This is what it's like."

He grinned. "Better you than me."

I said, "I'd like to return to the subject, if I may. You never met Zwart Black?"

Jake shook his head. "Just heard about him."

"You must have met Alexander Skotos, however. He died only three years ago, if I remember what I've been told correctly. Did he ever come to the Country Hill office?"

Jake nodded. "I took care of a few little things for him when Jim wasn't around. He wasn't a friendly kind of guy, but he knew what he wanted and why he wanted it, and he didn't waste my time. I'll say that for him."

"I'll try not to waste any more of ours. I'm going to try to describe him. Please tell me if anything that I say sounds wrong. He was shorter than I am?"

Jake nodded. "Three or four inches shorter, I'd say."

"Would you call him a brisk, energetic little man with a big, sharp nose, dark eyes, and yellow hair?"

Jake looked thoughtful "Sort of a yellowish brown, I'd say. About the same color as yours. Say it like that, and you've got him."

Doris muttered, "I'm beginning to think you must have known him under another name, Bax."

I shrugged. "I can't be held accountable for your thoughts."

Our dinners arrived, bringing with them enough appetizing odors to fill a lecture hall. You will have dined in Chinese restaurants I feel sure, George. Perhaps you have even dined in one nearly as good as the Garden of Happiness. I shall merely tell you that there were side dishes in plenty, including Country-Style Rice, Chicken Fried Rice (yes!), and my favorite, the delicious Mandarin Rice. I know all those names, you see, because we asked the waitress about them. Doris and I amused ourselves by trying to identify the eight precious ingredients. The easy ones were oysters and shrimp. A third was either octopus or squid, although neither of us could be quite sure which. The remaining five provided us with a good deal of amused conversation.

Before that, however, I had a final question for Jake. "This is a catchall, I admit. Tell me anything that pops into your mind. What was peculiar about Skotos? Did you notice any mannerisms? Was there something eccentric or unusual in the way he dressed? Anything of that kind?"

"Just one." Jake was looking thoughtful. "He had this stick. Sort of like a cane. It came about shoulder high and had a V on top. Jim said he had some big antique pistols, and when he shot them at the range he'd lay the barrel in the V to steady it. I never saw that."

Doris said, "But you saw this walking stick of his?"

Jake nodded. "There was something funny about it, but I can't put my finger on it. He told me once that it was an antique and it sure looked old, but why did he carry it around with him all the time? He didn't need it to walk with."

"I should have asked this before. I'm sure the lawyer would have known, and Mr. Hardaway probably would've known as well. What was Skotos's cause of death? Do you know?"

Jake shook his head. "He died out of town, I know that. Off on a trip somewhere. They flew the body back here."

Doris asked, "In Port Saint Jude? Something like that?"

"Huh uh. Out of the country. Haiti? I think it was down there in Central America somewhere."

I asked, "Is there anything else can you tell us?"

"Nothing much. I didn't go to the funeral. Jim did, though. Jim Hardaway. He said it was closed-casket, and there were only three people, counting him."

Doris touched my arm. "I don't suppose you were one of them, Bax?"

Wishing I had been, I shook my head.

"What about your brother George?"

"It's possible, but I don't know. Whether Jake does is the question. Do you, Jake? Who were the other two?"

"I've got no idea. Ask Jim."

"I'll do it," Doris told me. "I'll catch him first thing in the morning and phone you."

"I want to play a game," I told her. "It's cocky of me, and it may be stupid, too. But I think I can name one of them." I got out my little notebook.

"Name one, but not the other?"

"Correct." I wrote a name, tore out the page, and folded it twice. "Don't read this until you've talked to Mr. Hardaway."

"I won't. Girl Scout's honor."

I handed the paper to her. "Call me after you read it and you can tell me what a fool I was."

"I will, but speaking of calls . . ." Doris pointed. "Somebody seems to have called one of us."

218

Our waitress was approaching, cordless telephone in hand. I sipped my tea and waited.

"Mr. Dunn, he here?"

I raised my hand.

"You sec'tary on phone." The waitress smiled and bobbed her head. "She Chinese! Is velly nice lady!"

As I took the telephone, Doris muttered, "Now you've got a secretary?"

I shrugged and said hello.

"Is this Bax?"

"Yes, it is. Hello, Winker. What is it?"

"A lady came and asked for you. I let her in. She's gone, Bax. We can't find her!"

"Really?"

"Yes! Toby and I went looking for her. I didn't find her, and Toby's gone, too."

"Thank you for calling, Winker. Young? A plump lady with yellow hair?"

"By plump you mean fat?"

"That's right, fat."

"Then she's the one."

"I see. Please find her if you can, and call me if you do. I'll—"

"Your phone's off!"

"I'll turn it back on as soon as we're through, I promise."

"All right, I'll call."

"Wait—do you speak Chinese?"

Winkle giggled. "Riddle bit speak."

"I . . . see. Please call me if you find her." I hung up and returned the instrument to our waitress.

Doris said, "Now there's a missing woman. Is this another girlfriend, Bax?"

"Hardly. It's Cathy Ruth. She came early and seems to have decided to investigate on her own. Toby's looking for her."

"I see. You know, I never knew just what a footman does. What if he doesn't find her?"

I sipped tea. "In that case, you and I will look for her tonight."

"I was hoping you'd say that." Doris glanced at her watch. "It's getting late. Does your secretary live with you?"

"To be honest," I said, "I really don't know, although I suspect she may. To tell you the truth, I don't know where she lives. It's a big house."

Jake laughed. "Doris told me what happened when you got socked. I wish I could have listened in when the cops questioned you."

"You would have been entirely welcome. It gave me a wonderful opportunity to tell them what a truly fine man my brother George is."

Doris gave the thumbs-down sign.

"You two had better stop talking and eat," Jake told us. "I'm almost through."

"Excellent advice." I picked up my chopsticks and ate.

Doris said, "I've got a question for you."

I chewed and swallowed. "I have half a dozen."

"Well, I don't have answers. Only questions. Could the Ruth girl get hurt in that weird house of yours?"

Recalling the beating I had received from Ieuan Black, I nodded.

But now, George, I must cease to write. I began this letter because, exhausted though I am, I could not get to sleep. Now I feel that I may sleep for a week.

Yours sincerely,
Bax

Number 29
HELP IS ON THE WAY

Mr. Dunn:
———————

Thank you for your letter. I will certainly be in transit by the time you receive this, and may well have landed. I have reserved a room at the Medicine Man Hilton. You may contact me there, should you desire to. Otherwise I will contact you, probably by telephone.

Before I do, it would be well for you to review all recent manifestations. I would suggest that you give each one a short name, such as "Gray Figure in the Garden" or "Piano Played at Midnight." Be as specific as possible regarding times and places. Also, *persons present*. It is a key element. I will question you as to other details. For example: Just what was seen, if anything? Just what was heard, if anything? Was there an odor? A sensation of cold? Please search your memory for such details.

Your sister-in-law has told me you were attacked by wolves of more than natural size, and mentioned, as you did in your letter, that you feel that your car, as well as your home, is a site of supernormal activity. Such may be the case, but I think it unlikely. More plausibly, it is *you yourself.* We must examine this possibility.

Yours truly,
Mrs. O. Pogach
"Madame Orizia"

PS: Mrs. Dunn thinks the wolves may have been werewolves. She also said you shot and killed one. That is unlikely, as only silver bullets would have been effective.

Number 30
FREEDOM!

Dear Bax,

Glorious news! George has been released from Jail. He just telephoned me from his hotel. I said, "Does this mean you're coming home, dear?"

He said no because he cannot leave town. He would be arrested again. But he said Ben had found him a bail man. I do not know who Ben is, perhaps you do and will tell me. Please ask Ben and the bail man, too, to let him come home.

It is not that I love George, Bax, but I know you do. You will say he married me for my money, and I know you are right.

Also he calls me stupid. If he were smart himself, like you, he would not do that.

But his office keeps phoning with Questions. I cannot answer them, but they just think up more. I have not told them George was in jail, but I have not told them he was not, either. It is not a lie not to tell people things. Especially if they do not ask me.

Also George has the keys to the good car, which will be parked way out at the airport. I only have the old one, which is very hard to start. Besides, everyone knows it is old.

So if you see him, Bax, please let him know to call his office. Also mail me the keys. I would take a cab out and drive the car back. Then when he came home he could take a cab. I think you will see that is fair.

I like Miss Finn and her mother, too. Thank you for telling me about them. I have told Madame Orizia about the werewolves, but she did not believe me. She said she did, but I know she did not. This was the only time I have ever said anything and had her not believe it. Don't you think that is sad? I do.

But you told me and I believe you. Please be careful. Do not feed them or try to pet them.

Please tell George that I said that if you ever want to visit us you would be most welcome here. There is a big spare bedroom, and you could stay as long as you like. It would mean I would have somebody to talk to when George was at his office. When he was here, too. He will not talk to me mostly except to call names.

Fondly,
Millie

Dear Millie:

If memory serves, I told you in my last that I had promised a reporter (Cathy Ruth) that I would investigate the cellar in her company. A friend called while I was at dinner to tell me that she had arrived and was wandering through my house. I reacted to that as I suppose you or George or anyone else would; I might very well have given her permission to wander through my house, but I had given no such permission. Toby, a friend of my manservant's, was trying to find and expel her. All this resulted, I am very sorry to say, in our losing your husband. Let me explain.

Concerned by Cathy's disappearance, Doris Griffin returned to my home with me. The friend who had called me was not to be found.

Nor was Toby. Nor was Cathy. After talking it over, Doris and I agreed that the most likely explanation was that Cathy had set out to explore the cellar on her own, and that Toby had tracked her there.

The cellar doors at the back of the house stood wide, which we took as confirming our conclusion. I changed into rough clothes, and loaned Doris an old shirt and a pair of Dockers. She had worn high heels to dinner, but there was nothing either of us could do about that; my shoes would have been far too large. After loading both my pistols, I offered her one. She declined, so I thrust them both into my belt.

Not long after Doris and I had changed, we encountered my manservant and apprised him of the situation. He was greatly perturbed and wished to accompany us, although he is lame and limps along with a crutch. I ordered him to remain upstairs near the telephone instead. I would have my cellular telephone and would call the house's landline number should we require assistance.

"Oh, Bax!" you will say. "Can't you see that these elaborate precautions were absurd?"

If I were there with you, Millie—and I have often wished I were—I would talk in just the same way. I am here, instead; and I have been dealing with this wonderful (often frightening) house for weeks. My precautions were not excessive, as you shall see. They were insufficient.

Our flashlights soon found the washer and dryer my manservant had caused to be installed in the cellar. They are in a small room near the door.

There was a wall behind us and another to our left; otherwise that cellar seemed a vast cavern. Here and there stood tables and shelves, some empty or nearly so, others heaped with all sorts of objects veiled in dust.

There were cobwebs everywhere, and most were filthy with dust. I will try not to write too much about them, but they were a constant irritant to which we never grew accustomed. They got onto our faces and into our hair. They clung to our clothes and our hands. From time to time, our flashlights revealed hairy spiders as large as saucers; they fled the light.

Far ahead (indeed it sounded impossibly far) I heard the excited yapping of a small dog. Once something held my jeans near the ankle and tried to pull me back.

Doris screamed and dropped her flashlight. I turned mine on her. A rat that looked larger than her head was clutching her hair. I clubbed it with my own flashlight, and it dropped to the floor and scuttled away.

She clung to me and wept. I embraced her and did everything I could think of to comfort her. I know that you do not care for Doris, Millie, and know, too, that she is no paragon. Yet I do not believe I have ever pitied anyone except myself quite as much as I pitied her then.

When at last she was a little calmer, she said, "Get me out, Bax. Please! Just get me out of here."

I tried. Or as I ought to say, we tried, for Doris picked up her fallen flashlight and helped me look for the long flight of wooden steps by which we had descended into that fearful cellar.

At last, she thought she had found it. I knew that she had not. I re-called the wall behind those we had come down, and I saw that there was no wall there; but they led up, plainly back to the ground floor, and that seemed to me all that we could hope for and more. To confess the truth, I scarcely noticed that the frantic yapping of the small dog seemed nearer as we mounted the high, uneven steps. (I must explain here, Mil-lie, that I supposed the dog we heard to be my manservant's little terrier, which proved to be the case.)

We had nearly reached the top when I heard a woman scream; it was not Doris, but someone on the other side of the door at the top of the stairs.

"That's her, Bax!" Doris shouted. "It's got to be!"

She was at once wrong and right.

The door was locked. I shook the knob, tried to kick it open, and flung myself against it with all my strength; it gave not a hair's width.

"Shoot it!" Doris urged me. "Shoot the (expletive deleted) lock!"

I told her that shooting locks worked on television and in films, but nowhere else unless the shooter had a powerful shotgun.

"Try, damn it! Try!"

I did, and the echoes that my shot woke in that cellar are something I shall never forget.

"Push it! Push hard!"

The bullet had shattered the wood near the lock. I threw myself against the door once more, and it gave.

In the candlelit room beyond the doorway, a muscular dwarf of surpassing ugliness grappled a half-naked woman larger, darker, and substantially heavier than Cathy Ruth. I drew my other pistol and shouted for him to stop.

He dropped her, planted one foot upon her, kicked at the frantically barking dog, and grinned at Doris. He had the largest mouth, and the largest teeth, I have ever seen; below the waist, I shall not describe him. "Welcome, my lovely lady. Oh, you are *so* welcome. Come here."

She shrank back, clinging to me.

"Quorn will break you. Quorn will teach you to answer the lightest touch of his whip. You'll like it, too. Yes, you will! You'll kiss the lash, I promise. You'll see."

I wanted to say, "I believe your name was Quilp when last I heard of you," but I did not. Instead, I pointed toward his collar. "That's steel from the look of it, and there's still a bit of chain hanging from it. Haven't I seen you before?"

"You see the maggots in your own eyes, fool."

"I don't think so. Not long ago, you were chained to Ieuan's door."

He cursed Ieuan roundly, ending with: "He's the only son of snot I've ever seen filthier than you are."

"You're quite correct." I leveled my other pistol. "I am filthy. So is Doris, but we'll bathe and change clothes and be clean. Your filth is within you. If it were gone, you'd collapse."

Behind him, a woman gasped, "Please, Mr. Dunn! Oh, please!"

"Think I'm afeared of your popgun, fool?"

I pulled back the cock. "You had better be."

"They call me Ironskin." He advanced, still grinning, and I pulled the trigger. The priming powder flared in the pan, but the pistol did not fire.

The fat woman on the floor shrieked, "Shoot! Shoot!" and the dwarf stopped to laugh.

It enraged me, Millie, as few things in my life ever have. I dropped the useless pistol into my pocket, and pointed both index fingers at him as though I held modern revolvers. I intended to shout, but perhaps I screamed—I cannot be sure. *"Get out of here, you devil! This is my house! Out! I don't want you here!"* With much, much more in the same vein.

The blood drained from his face, leaving it a dirty gray. He backed away. "Sorry, sir! I meaned no harm! No harm at all!" He took a few more steps backward, knuckling his forehead, and fled. I ought to have been amazed, but I was raging and there was no room for it.

Behind me, Doris gasped, " Bax! What the hell . . . ?"

We helped the fat woman to rise. I expected tears, but she looked every bit as warlike as I felt. "Do you know me, Mr. Dunn?"

I shook my head. "I haven't had the pleasure."

"We've met, Mr. Dunn, but it was in the spirit world. I am Madame Orizia."

"Of course! I apologize. I should have known you at once."

"You saved me from that beast, Mr. Dunn. I could not be angry even if you deserved it. To prove my gratitude, I will charge no fee. None! I must ask you to compensate my travel costs, however. My straitened circumstances require it."

"They're not refundable," I said.

"Precisely." She was asking my indulgence.

Doris said, "I'm Doris Griffin," and the two women shook hands.

Madame Orizia managed a rather savage smile. "Let us hope we meet again under more pleasing circumstances."

"I'm in real estate, and I've been told over and over that this house is haunted. I never believed it." Doris turned to me. "Could we have the boy next time, Bax? The one who drops things? I think I'd like him better."

"I'm sure you would." I sighed. "I'd rather have his brother. His brother had that fellow chained up, though he seems to have broken his chain." I was shaking, and tried to relax.

We found Cathy Ruth at the back of the room, securely bound with scraps of rope and strips of rag. The big camp knife I had bought as I would have bought cuff links proved its worth again; I might have used it earlier to threaten the dwarf, but that thought had never crossed my mind.

Cathy whispered to Doris, and Doris said, "He raped her. We've got to get her to a hospital."

I agreed. An unbroken door promised an exit from the room. I was leading the three women toward it when it was thrown wide by Winker. Cathy screamed, Doris cursed, and Madame Orizia grunted.

Winker knelt, bowed her head, and held out a pillow of scarlet silk upon which rested an ancient sword. "This is for you."

Madame Orizia gasped and gripped my arm. "Is that a spirit?"

I was too unsettled to be polite. "Of course not!"

Winker looked up. "It is a blade of spirit, Bax-san. It's the Fox Sword. I present it to you. Accept it, please."

I did and she rose, tucking the pillow beneath her arm. "This is a new reign. There's a new emperor now."

"What emperor?" I wanted to draw the sword and examine it, but good manners prevented me.

Winker ignored my question. "Once in each reign we present the Fox Sword to a hero-friend."

It made me stammer, Millie. I will not write all the stammering, but stammer I did. "I'm your friend, Winker—God knows I'm your friend, but—"

Doris told me loudly, "And a hero!"

Madame Orizia whispered, "You may not refuse the gift. Who is this geisha?"

Winker's eyes twinkled. "This was the weapon of the Great Fox when the Kami were young. The weapon of many a hero."

Cathy said, "Oh, God! He got my camera."

I put the other pistol into another pocket, and Winker helped me position the long Japanese sword we put through my belt, edge up.

We might readily have become lost in the house if Winker had not hurried us back to the familiar butler's pantry, and from there to the living room and out through the reception room and across the porch onto the dark front lawn.

Doris said, "I'm going to drive Cathy to the hospital. Okay?"

I nodded and thanked her.

"Then I'm going home for a stiff drink." She paused. "A shower. And bed. I'll phone you in the morning."

Madame Orizia pointed. "That is my car, which I have rented at the airport. If you could kindly lend me—lend m-m-me . . ."

I put my arm around her shaking shoulders. I was filthy and she was naked, and we must have looked like fools, which is what the dwarf had called me; but it did not feel foolish at the time.

The old man appeared, seemingly out of nowhere. "We must procure some covering for the lady, sir."

I nodded, and he called, "Toby!"

It brought my footman, who proved to be short, wiry, and very erect. I said, "Thank you, Toby. I appreciate your help, and I'm sure Madame Orizia here does, too."

A fresh car pulled into the driveway, blocking Doris, who had just bundled Cathy into hers. She yelled, "What the (expletive deleted) is this?"

"It's George," I told her. "It's my brother George." I had recognized him, thanks to the interior lights that came on in his car when he got out. I tried to hug him, which he would not permit.

"Who the hell are all these women, Bax?"

Doris yelled, "We've met already and I'd rather not do it again. Move your goddam car so I can take this girl to the emergency room." When he ignored her, she backed up until her bumper banged his and made a U-turn on my front lawn, driving over it to Riverpath Road.

Tightly buttoned into one of my shirts, Madame Orizia would clearly have liked to present George with her card. "You are the husband of Mrs. Dunn. I am her psychic. You may require a psychic, George Dunn."

He stared at her, then looked around at the dark lawn and darker house. "There was a Jap girl here, too. What happened to her?"

"I am staying at the Hilton," Madame Orizia told him. "You, also, are staying at the Hilton. Should you desire to consult me, you can ask the hotel operator to connect us. Should I be gone—"

"Balls! Why the hell should I need a psychic?"

"Because you are this man's brother. Because you stand here, before this house of his."

I said I would ask George to move his car so she could get out.

"You need not trouble. To me this is of professional interest, I think."

If I had been wearing a hat, I would have removed it. "You are a formidable woman, Madame Orizia."

"My profession requires it, Mr. Dunn."

"What in the hell's going on here?" George wanted to know.

"Madame Orizia ventured into the house alone and was nearly raped by a dwarf," I explained. "It was a harrowing experience, I'm sure."

"I came," Madame Orizia said. "This servant let me in. I set out in search of psychic vibrations. You know the rest."

The old man cleared his throat. "I told her, sir, that you were in another part of the house. I seated her in our parlor, sir, and went into our kitchen to prepare tea. When I returned with it, she had gone." He coughed politely. "I attempted to communicate the occurrence via telephone, sir, but—"

"But mine was out of service. Switched off. You're right, it was."

George was examining the back of the limousine. He tapped the trunk. "What's in this thing, Bax?"

I said, "I have no idea. I intend to open it tomorrow morning."

"Why tomorrow? Why not now?"

"Because I believe it wiser to open it when we have daylight."

"You've got something alive in there. I can hear it moving around."

Here I made a mistake, Millie, and it proved to be a bad one. I said, "I have nothing in there, and this is not your car."

George unbuckled the big straps and threw open the rusty clasps faster than I would have believed possible.

Madame Orizia gasped. "Ahhh . . ." For a moment, that was the only sound—or at least, the only sound that I remember.

An instant later the trunk flew open, and a man like a tall skeleton in rusty black jumped out. The skin was so tightly stretched over his face that it seemed it must tear; only his eyes were alive.

No. His eyes were more than alive. Will you grasp what I am saying, Millie, if I say they flamed?

He bowed to us as a marionette might bow. His voice was iron on iron. "I am Nicholas, the butler." Awaiting no reply, he marched into the house.

I heard someone whisper, "Good God . . . ," and only later did I realize that the whisperer had been me.

George grabbed a handful of my filthy shirt. "You set this up, you bastard!"

I shook my head.

"You know it and I know it." His face was within half an inch of mine. I felt his spittle. "You and your crazy stories!"

The old man laid a hand on his arm. "Please contain yourself, sir."

George pushed him aside. "I'm going to catch that bastard and get the truth out of him." He sprinted into the house, and it was only then that I realized I had begun to draw the sword Winker had presented to me.

Toby and I searched for George for hours, Millie, but we did not find him; and at last I bathed and went to bed so utterly exhausted that I could scarcely stand.

Now it is morning, and I am still in bed. Thanks to old Nick, I have breakfasted on soft-boiled eggs, toast, and three cups of very good coffee; and I have been writing to you for half the morning. The old man brought me paper and this pen, and I brace the empty tray upon my knees.

George is gone, and only God knows where. I must find him, and I will. I am still tired, but I have lingered too long in bed already.

Ever your loving friend,
Bax

Number 32
A REQUEST

Hey, Prof!

Got your letter and all the stuff. I owe you, man. Anything you want, ever. I gave Vicki your address and told her to get in touch if she needs some money.

Could you send me some pencils and paper with lines on it? Writing stuff is tough to get here.

Nothing new about the Greek. I have feelers out, but nothing so far.

You asked about guns. I do not know one thing about the kind you have. I seen them in movies, but movies hardly ever get stuff right.

But a gun is a gun. Hold it tight. The tighter you can hold without your hand shaking, the better. You have got to be fast but not fumble. Take your time, but do not waste any time doing it. It is grip, front sight, and trigger when you shoot. Get all three right, and there is not a lot of people who will beat you. Hold it tight, put your front sight on him, and pull back the trigger fast without jerking it. Practice can be good or bad. It is good if you do it right, bad if you do not. A lot will burn up three boxes of ammo and think they have learned, but in a fight it is the first shot that counts. Do not miss. Do not stall around. Shoot smooth and fast. Where did it go?

Sheldon Hawes

Number 33

ON THE HOME FRONT

Dear Bax,

Your last letter got me very, very upset. You started by saying that George was gone, then told me all those other things about you and the dwarf. When I read the end I understood that you were telling me that George might be in a lot of danger.

You were still tired when you wrote all of that, so I understand. But you are worrying way too much. George can take care of himself. In fact, he can talk his way out of just about anything. I ought to know.

It is you I worry about, Bax. Not about the dwarf or any of that, but about all those women. You are not used to dealing with women. How could you be? We women say that men are only interested in one thing and what we mean is you know what. But a lot of single women are interested in just one thing too. Only it is not the same thing.

You must keep that in mind, Bax. For my sake. Think of me. I am enclosing my picture so that you can. I am not a good talker or a good letter writer either, I know. So I am going to let my picture talk for me.

Do you like it? I hope so.

I think a bathing suit should cover up a person more than that one does. I like a one-piece suit with a cute little skirt. But George made me take that one so he could show me off. I am his trophy wife. That is what he said.

Well, I do have a nice figure even if it is a little bit too big in certain places. That is what Brenda says. (She sews my dresses.) A lot of the girls did not like me at Mount Holyoke and made jokes about blondes. As if I would not know that I had to buy a ticket.

But my grades were bad, and that helped. Except for Prof. Foley, who gave me good ones in Women's Studies. She was really down on all men and wanted to hold my hand so I let her.

Then my father told me to marry a rising executive in a growing industry, so I married George. I felt I could not go against my father after he left me so much.

Now I am here in this big house, all alone and lonesome except for Fluffy Cat and my maid. (Her name is really Maria Josefa, but I just call her Maria.) So when you look at my picture, Bax, please remember how much I would like to talk to you. If you wanted to hold my hand, I would not pull away. But do not tell George that.

·   ·   ·   ·   ·

The skip up here means I stopped writing because lunch was ready and Madame Orizia phoned. She has never phoned me before and I do not know how she got my number. She told me a lot, especially about George. I do not think she really likes him but she would not say that. I explained that I do not, either, but she still would not say it. She had seen him in the lobby. She had seen you in a trance, so she thought

George was you! When she saw George, she wondered what you were so mad about!

She thinks that house is dangerous and you ought to move out right away. So do I.

Fondly,
Millie

Dear Millie:

"How did you know?" That was Doris on the telephone, and it was (as you will soon see) the question that roused me from my lethargy.

At the time I could only ask her, "Know what?"

"Who one of the mourners at Skotos's funeral was. I—I'm going to be honest about this. I peeked, Bax. Okay, I know I promised I wouldn't, but I got so damn curious. Now you get to say you'll never trust me again."

"All right, I'll never trust you again. Do I have to mean it?"

"No. Anyway, after I'd read the name I thought no way, he's really lost it this time. So I grabbed the next chance I had to talk to Jim—his door is always open and all that crap—and asked him about the funeral. He said, 'The other two besides me? I can't be sure. It's been three years.'

"So I said, 'everybody in the company marvels at your memory, sir,' and laid it on really thick. Finally he said, 'I've got them now. One was a man I didn't know.'

"I asked if it was the lawyer, but he said no. 'Just a little guy I'd never seen before, Doris. I don't believe I've seen him since, either.' Now you're going to tell me who that was."

I said, "No. I could tell you who I think it was, but I could be wrong and it would be pointless. So I won't. I take it that Mr. Hardaway named someone eventually?"

"That's right. He said the other one was a woman he knew, somebody in the business, but he couldn't think of her name. When he said that, I felt like kissing you. And kicking you afterward, too, for not telling me last night."

I said, "I did tell you. I wrote it—"

"Okay, I peeked. He couldn't think of her name, he said, but she had a little one-woman shop now. So I said, 'And she attended Alexander Skotos's funeral, sir? Is she involved with the will?' He said no, and he had no idea why she showed up for the funeral, but her name was Martha something."

When I heard that I was no longer tired, Millie.

Doris continued. "I couldn't hold it in any longer and there was really no reason to, so I said, 'Would that be Martha Murrey, sir?' and he snapped his fingers and said that was it. Now who was the third one, the short man?"

I said, "I hope to be able to tell you today. Not a guess, but a certainty."

. . . . .

Here I was interrupted by old Nick, Millie. You will get our conversation in its proper place.

After having my suspicion confirmed by Doris, I bathed again, shaved and dressed, called a cab, and visited the public library and the county courthouse, where a twenty-dollar bill convinced a clerk that I was in serious need of her assistance.

Then, in an unaccustomed burst of genius, I revisited the elderly woman who had loaned me her mower and given me dinner. "I hope you can help me, Mrs. Naber," I said after a few preliminaries. "You told me once that you'd lived here all your life."

She nodded. "I have. I've lived here ever since I was born."

"There was a lady named Murrey—that's Murrey with an *E*—who used to live in my house. I've found something that belongs to her. It's valuable, and I'd like to return it. Have you ever known anyone with that name?"

She laughed. It is always pleasant to hear an old person laugh when there is real humor in it; or at least I have found it so. "Have I known anybody of that name? Why, at first I thought you meant *me*, Mr. Dunn. Murray was my name, but with an *A*." She spelled it. "I'm perfectly sure that there's never been a family here who spelled it the other way. I'd have known about them. Would you like to see a picture of my family?"

Of course I said I would, and five minutes later I was blessing the wonderful mother who had adopted George and me and taught me to be polite. The Murrays stood before me in black-and-white, preserved through so many decades in their sturdy silver frame: the parents stiffly erect but smiling, their twin daughters relaxed and giggling despite starched white dresses. It did not seem possible, but as I studied their faces I grew increasingly confident. "You were a twin! An identical twin? I'm one myself."

"An identical twin? Are you really, Mr. Dunn?"

"I certainly am, Mrs. Naber. I am the evil twin, and my brother George is the good twin. I am harebrained and poetic, you see, while George is solid and reliable."

She smiled, God bless her. "Harebrained, poetic, and kind. Yes, we were twins, Mr. Dunn. Perfect likenesses. Martha and Thelma. I'm Thelma."

It took very little urging to get Mrs. Naber to show me her wedding pictures. Though blond, the blushing bride might easily have been a somewhat younger Martha Murrey. While longing with all my heart to hug Thelma Naber, I said as casually as I could, "I couldn't help noticing that your sister wasn't one of your bridesmaids. I hope nothing happened to her."

The tears that filled Mrs. Naber's faded blue eyes made me wish I had held my tongue. "Did something happen to her? Yes, I'm afraid something did, Mr. Dunn. She . . ."

"She isn't dead, I hope?"

"Dead? I've no way of knowing. She eloped, Mr. Dunn. I found her packing one evening. We shared a bedroom."

I nodded. "I understand."

"She said Mamma and Papa would never approve of the man, but she was going to marry him just the same. I watched out the window hoping to see him, but I never did. After that I kept thinking she'd write, or phone if they lived close. But there was never a word from her. I have just one hope. You're a twin, too? It's what you said."

"I am. George and I are identical twins."

"When one twin dies, the other one dies, too. Not at the exact same time, but not long after. Sometimes there's a medical cause or else an accident, and sometimes there isn't. I suppose you know about it."

"I've read about it, yes. It doesn't always happen, but it's not uncommon."

Mrs. Naber nodded, I would guess mostly to herself. "You've read it, so you know. Well, I'm not dead, am I? I'm getting close to ninety, Mr. Dunn. There aren't but a few people my age left, but I'm still here. So I think most likely Martha is, too. Not here in Medicine Man, but somewhere."

"I think so, too," I told her. Out of honesty I had to add, "Perhaps she's even here in town."

After that I got another cab and called on Martha Murrey.

Her smile faded when she saw my face, but she asked me to come in. "It's much too late for breakfast, I'm afraid, and I just finished lunch. I could fix something for you, if you want it."

I shook my head. "I want something you offered me when you gave me breakfast. You offered to show me the instructions Mr. Black had left with you. May I have a look at them now, please?"

She got them without a word, a single handwritten sheet. I glanced at it and handed it back.

"You were so hungry that morning. I knew you couldn't have been eating regularly."

"You're right," I said.

"I thought you'd return soon—that you'd come back and I'd get to fix you another meal. Only the next time your face was all bruised. Remember?"

"I do. I've been grateful ever since."

"I saw the ring then, so that was when I knew with certainty. You know, too, don't you?"

Her reference to my ring confused me, Millie. For a moment I supposed she meant the gold band that Doris had given me, Ted's old wedding ring.

"You must know," Martha repeated. "Why don't you say so?"

"I know very little, Martha. Mostly, that one of your sons needs your help."

She started to speak but did not, and I said, "Yes?"

There was a long silence before she said, "I want some coffee. Would you like some?"

"Your coffee was superb. If it's even half as good as it was the last time, I'd love some."

She hurried into the kitchen and returned with a tray. This coffee was fully as good.

"I made it about a quarter of an hour ago, and I'd just finished a nice big cup when you came. This is all there is, I'm afraid."

"That's a great pity."

"Coffee lasts half an hour or so. That's all. After that, you've got to throw it out and make fresh. I could make a fresh carafe, I suppose, if you want more."

"You're very kind," I said.

"I try. Won't you tell me which son it is?"

At that I relaxed. "It's Emlyn."

"Really? I—oh, never mind. You're going to say . . ."

"To say what?" I waited, but she only shrugged.

At last I said, "Will you help him?"

"I will if I can. How did you know?"

Sipping coffee, I collected my thoughts. "People must grow old more slowly there."

"They don't grow old at all, Bax. No one does. You don't mind my calling you Bax?"

"Of course not. Your sister Thelma's still alive."

"I know." Martha nodded.

I said, "Could you telephone her? Just once? Or write her a note? It would mean the world to her."

"If I promise, will you tell me how you knew? My promise is good, believe me." Martha sighed. "I'm a bad woman, I know. But I keep my promises."

It felt good to smile then. "Substitute 'man' for 'woman,' and I could have said that. I try to keep mine, too, which is all any of us can do."

She nodded gratefully.

"You said you would promise. Do you?"

"Yes, I do. I can swear by river and tree, grass, wind, and hill if you want."

"It won't be necessary, but I want you to promise something more. Promise that you'll tell me what I don't know, what I missed. If you'll do that, I'll help you save Emlyn. I'll do everything I can."

"I won't ask if that's a promise," Martha said. "I can see you'd do it anyway."

I shrugged, knowing she was right.

"We have an agreement, but you have to speak first. Now tell me, Bax, and you can ask me whatever you want to afterward."

"There is one question I want to ask first, because the answer may save me a great deal of talking. I think that Zwart Black and Alexander Skotos are the same person. Am I correct? If I'm wrong, then I don't know anything."

Martha nodded. "You aren't wrong. How did you know?"

"I guessed, that's all. I came here, and you told me a mysterious Mr. Black wanted me to have his house. It wasn't true. You gave me the house, and I thank you for it. But until very recently I believed you."

"I understand. You don't know why I did it?"

"No. Nor do I know why you said that Mr. Black was my benefactor."

"I think I'm going to tell you, Bax. But not now."

"Then I learned that Alexander Skotos had made me his heir. I asked some questions, and it seemed that Skotos had appeared about the same time that Black had vanished. I've studied Greek and knew that 'skotos' means *darkness*. I found Greek coins—valuable coins—in an old escritoire in the attic of the house that had been Black's. Clearly he had been interested in the Greeks, and had been rich enough to drop those coins into a drawer and forget them." I made some futile gesture. "It didn't prove anything, I know. But it seemed likely the two were the same."

"They were. Go on."

"I tried to get descriptions of both. Skotos was easy because a man named Jim Hardaway had known him well. Then I came across a woman who'd seen Black several times and told me about the last. He was with a woman who sounded very much like you. The description she gave me of Black checked reasonably well with Jim Hardaway's description of Skotos."

"You said that I was the one who gave you the house." Martha sounded thoughtful. "That was right, too. How did you know?"

"This morning I did something I ought to have done a long time ago—I looked into GEAS, the company that had owned the house before I did. It had been incorporated in this state, and I found a list of its officers on one of the computers at the library without much trouble. Vice president, Z. Black. Secretary and treasurer, Alexander Skotos. President and CEO, Martha Murrey."

"I see." It was a whisper.

"Alexander Skotos left me a cased set of dueling pistols. You didn't know about them?"

She shook her head.

"I can see it bothers you."

She waved my remark aside. "Go on."

"There was a note from him in the bullet box. I've done time— been imprisoned. That doesn't surprise you?"

"No. I knew it."

"Then you know I'm telling the truth. It's hard to make friends in prison, because most of us are people we wouldn't want for friends. I made two, however, and one is a forger. He knows a lot about handwriting and taught me a good deal. The note you showed me was signed by Zwart Black, but the writing was nothing like Skotos's. To me it looked feminine, confirming what I had concluded when I saw that you were the CEO of GEAS. You were my benefactor, and I'll always be grateful."

"I wish I could believe that," Martha said.

"No doubt you know more than I." I paused, waiting for her to speak again. "I've told you what I guessed and how I guessed it, and I'd appreciate some information from you. Was the man you eloped with Zwart Black?"

She only nodded.

"He took you, his bride, to the other place. To the place where he lives."

"To faerie. Yes, he did."

"Is that really what they call it?"

Martha shook her head. "That is what I call it."

I sipped my coffee. It had cooled a little, but it was still very good. "Just out of curiosity, what do they call it?"

"The real world. Reality."

"Of course they do—it was a foolish question. Emlyn and his brother are your sons?"

She nodded and smiled. "Twins run in my family, Mr. Dunn, and—"

I cut her off. "Go back to calling me Bax, please."

"I will, if we're still friends."

"We are," I said. "Friends and allies—or so I hope. I apologize for interrupting you."

"You did me a great favor. I need to tell you a good deal more before I say what I was about to say. Faerie's a terrible place, Bax. You haven't been there?"

"I have been, but only once and only briefly. A few hours."

"It's beautiful. Its rivers run clear and the wind never stinks. There are wonderful mountains and sweeping plains. Mighty forests. Those are what most visitors remember above all, those forests. There are strange and wonderful animals, some of them very beautiful. Nothing ever grows old there." She sighed. "People, animals, and plants—none of them ever grow old there. Never. Do you understand why I fell in love with it?"

I did, and I said so.

"I loved it, and I loved him. I suppose I still love him, though I always loved him much more than he loved me."

I said, "Yet you left him, or he sent you away. Which was it?"

"He tried to get me to stay, but I wouldn't. He's been trying to get me to come back ever since. That was one of the reasons he's spent so much time here."

"But you won't?"

She shook her head. "Faerie is lovely and wonderful, I've probably said that. It's cruel, too, and very, very dangerous. Wouldn't you think that a place where people never age would be overrun with them? That it would have a dense population?"

"Yes, I certainly would."

"There's almost no one there. A few people, here and there. Scattered villages, each smaller than the last. Lonely mansions like the one I lived in. Sorcerers who war with sorcerers. Sorcerers who war with witches. Warlocks who war with everyone."

"No fairies?" I asked. "You called it faerie."

"They *are* the fairies, Bax. They are the gnomes and trolls and elves, the satyrs, nymphs, and fauns, and the godlings of a dozen faiths. They are a great many other things, too."

"Werewolves? I know one. What about werefoxes?"

"Yes, to both. They kill one another, and from time to time they kill us. There are predatory animals, too. Some of the animals are much more intelligent, and much stronger, than anything in Africa. The more you learn about faerie, the more frightened you become."

"You ran away?"

"He wouldn't let me. I wanted to go home and take my babies with me." Martha sighed. "Twins run in my family, Bax, and I had given him twin sons."

"Emlyn and Ieuan? I've met them both."

She shook her head. "Finally he said that I could go home, or our sons could. But not both. I know he thought I wouldn't be separated from my babies."

By that time, Millie, I had understood something that I ought to have understood much sooner. It was hard to speak but I said, "That was what he thought, Mother. But he was wrong."

"Exactly. I took you both to an orphanage here. I left you there and went back. Can you forgive me?"

You cannot possibly know how I felt at that moment. I will not try to explain it, knowing that I would be certain to fail. I assured her— assured my birth mother—that there was nothing to forgive, and we embraced and wept.

That is really all I want to write at present. There is more, but you will get it in another letter. More about my birth mother, and something about the old man.

Here are the main points, the summary I feel compelled to provide before I close this letter. Martha is George's birth mother, as well as mine. She is your mother-in-law, in other words.

Emlyn and Ieuan are our brothers, and are as much your brothers-in-law as I am. I hope you can meet them someday, and Martha, too.

Ever your loving friend,
Bax

Dear Shell:

You asked me for paper and pencils, etc., and I have been kicking myself for not having thought of them. Lord knows I wanted them myself in there. So here you are: lots of envelopes, five lined tablets, a box of #2's, a minisharpener, and a book of stamps. If you need anything else that will get by Charlie, just tell me.

I know they won't let Lou have anything like this; but if he has something to say to me, I feel sure you will pass it along. Please let him know I have not forgotten him, or the talks we used to have in the metal shop.

Now I need some advice. I told you about the old guns and shooting the wolf. I shot at a door with one, too. After that I wanted to shoot at a rat. He was a great big bastard and I thought I could not miss, but my pistol would not fire. Since then I have been shooting at bottles in the river. And missing them, for the most part. You used to say, 'Close only counts pitching horseshoes.' I learned how right you were when I was shooting at those floating bottles. I will say this, however. Both pistols fired every time.

That is because of what I learned when I could not shoot the rat. After I got home I checked my pistol over, and the touchhole (I believe that is what it is called) was clogged with burned powder. There is a pick to clear it screwed into the butt of each gun; they have had work to do from that time until this.

. . . . .

Continuing today. There is a range outside town. A man I know is a member, and he and I are going out there so I can practice shooting targets with those guns.

I checked with my brother's lawyer first, and it is all legal. I cannot legally buy or own a gun because of my felony conviction; but the law applies only to modern guns, which means those less than a hundred years old. Antiques are not restricted.

Come to think of it, I do not think I told you about my brother. He is charged with resisting arrest. (He punched out a nice copchick I know.) He made bail, but now he has disappeared. I do not believe he skipped; it would not be like him. Something has happened to him, Shell, and I wish to God I knew what it was.

My brother and I do not get along well. I know I have told you much more about that than you ever wanted to know. Now a woman who knew the man who gave me the pistols thinks he did it so my brother and I would use them on each other—that he wanted one of us to kill the other.

I do not want to believe that, but I am afraid she is correct. I am afraid my brother George may want to fight. He has beaten me so often, and in so many ways, that he is bound to be quite confident. I can refuse, of course; but if I do (and I probably will) I will have to fight anyway, with fists, and feet, and furniture.

When I shot the door and tried to shoot the rat, I did my best to keep what you told me in mind. I focused on my front sight, gripped the gun tightly, and tried to take my time fast. Any further advice will be welcomed, believe me. I have not the least desire to kill George, although he has never treated me like a brother; but if I must kill George to keep him from killing me I will.

You will be up for parole in less than a year. There is a woman here who heads a little company, GEAS Inc. If you think a job offer on that letterhead would help, just let me know.

Yours sincerely,
Bax

Dear George:

You believe I have lost my mind, and perhaps I have. Perhaps writing you when I have no idea where you are is more evidence of it.

Still, madness has its privileges. I need to unburden myself to you, so I will do it and send it to your dear and loyal Millie, who will keep it for you. Have you ever realized how fortunate you are to have a wife so beautiful and so devoted?

I have searched for you, believe me, finding rooms I did not know existed and even venturing into faerie. I have Winkle and Toby, who are far more familiar with its dangers than I am, searching there for you now.

When I gave up my personal search, I had a long talk with the old man. I will try to give you the significant parts. Please read this carefully.

"I need to quiz you at length," I told him. "Let me say before we start that I'm not a hostile questioner. I like you and you've done a wonderful job, but there are things you know or may know that I need to know, too."

"No fear, sir. I quite understand."

"Let me begin with names. You told me once that your name was Nick. Was it the truth?"

"I did not, sir. I told you only that people called me so, which is the truth."

"I see. It's not your name?"

He shook his head. "No, sir. It is not, although I am called that."

"May I ask your true name, Nick?"

"You may indeed ask, sir, but I cannot answer. I have none."

I thought about that, and at last I said, "What is a true name, Nick? What do you understand by 'true name'?"

"It is the name given at birth, sir." This was said very firmly.

"If that is the case, I don't know mine, either."

His voice softened. "You have my sympathy, sir."

"Thank you. It is one thing not to know one's true name, Nick. It's another to have none. Will you explain?"

He hesitated. "It will infallibly cause you to think less of me, sir."

"I think so much of you now, Nick, that you could lose a great deal of my regard and still stand very high."

"Believe me, sir, I am deeply appreciative. I have no true name because I was never born, sir. I am a thing, if you will allow the word. A thing rather less fine than your sword, sir." He paused. "Only a thing, like your sword, that strives to serve you."

When I heard that, George, my first thought was that he was mad; an instant later I recalled that you think me mad. I am not, and had to consider the possibility that the old man was not, either. "May I ask that you serve my brother George as well?"

"You need not ask, sir. He is your brother, and I am aware of it. I shall assist him to the best of my ability, provided that his interests do not conflict with your own."

I nodded. "That is all I can ask, Nick. You have no appellation other than Nick?"

"None, sir."

"I see. You'll recall that when we released the man—if it was a man—who had been locked in the trunk, he said that he was Nicholas, the butler."

"I do, sir."

"You yourself are a butler, one—"

"Your butler, sir."

"Yes, indeed! I was about to say, Nick, that your appellation is very like his."

"It is, sir. May I explain? I fear my explanation will be lengthy, sir. My explanation and your questions."

"I see. It will be lengthy, you are old, and I am keeping you standing. Let's go into the kitchen, Nick. You can make coffee for us, sit down, and join me in a cup."

"You are too kind, sir."

The truth, George, is twofold. I felt sorry for the old man, thing or human, and I wanted some time in which to think over what he had told me already.

I got precious little. He set out cups and saucers, and cream and sugar, while the water was heating. His coffeemaker was a stainless device wholly new to me. He ground coffee beans in an electric mill in a trice, loaded his stainless machine, and poured in the boiling water. There was a startling hiss and a puff of steam, and coffee cascaded into the carafe.

"Martha Murrey makes coffee nearly as good as yours," I told him, "but it takes her three times as long."

"She may learn, sir. Would you like a bite to eat, sir? A poached egg, perhaps?"

"No, thank you. This wonderful coffee will be all I need. Do you drink coffee, Nick?"

"I do, sir." He smiled. "You fear I may be a mere mechanical device. I drink coffee, sir. Or water. I eat even as you do, sir. I sleep as well, and I should bleed if cut."

"Then please pour yourself a cup and sit down." When he had done both, I asked, "Why Nick and Nicholas?"

"In proper order, sir, it would be Nicholas and Nick. He was made first, and I subsequently. We were grown in the same trough, sir."

"Grown by . . . ?"

"You know young Ieuan, sir. Perhaps you know his brother Emlyn as well?"

I nodded.

"Our creator was their father, sir. Zwart is, or was, his common name."

"You think he may be dead?"

The old man cleared his throat. "You, um, sir. Or the boys, sir. Emlyn, I would think. Or both, sir."

"I did not kill him, Nick. I have never killed anyone . . ."

"Sir?"

"I shot a wolf. It was attacking me. I shot him, and he—well, he was a man when he fell off our car."

"A silver bullet, sir?"

I nodded.

"They are said to be effectual, sir. I have never seen it."

"I have. We left a naked man writhing in agony behind us. I—I had fired into the wolf's open mouth." I needed a moment to collect myself. "We were talking about Zwart. He lived here in Medicine Man for ten years or more—or so I believe—after he had quit this house. At that time, he called himself Alexander Skotos. You must have known about it."

"No, sir. I did not."

"Alexander Skotos died, supposedly. Three persons attended his funeral. One was a friend we needn't concern ourselves with. One was Martha Murrey. I believe I've mentioned her already."

"You have, sir."

"Do you know who she is?"

"My old master's former wife, I believe, sir. The mother of Ieuan and Emlyn. I was to obey her, sir, until the—ah—former relationship dissolved, sir. I did so."

"All correct. The third was Zwart, once more calling himself Zwart Black. I had guessed that earlier. Martha tells me I was correct. That was three years ago."

"I understand, sir. It has been far longer than that since I have seen him."

"He abandoned you?"

"No, sir. He assigned me to this house, sir. I am to serve its owner. As I do, sir." The old man paused. "You inquired concerning Nicholas, I believe. The similarity of his name to my own, sir?"

I nodded.

"He came before me, but his conduct—ah—failed to satisfy. I am not personally acquainted with the details of his conduct, sir, although I have heard rumors I would not care to repeat."

"So have I."

"Finding him less than satisfactory, my old master discharged him and, um, brought me into being, giving me the cognomen I bear."

"One more question, Nick. Did you know that Nicholas was locked in that trunk?"

"Absolutely not, sir. Had I known, I should have informed you."

"He did not tarry with us, Nick. He went straight into the house."

"He did, sir."

"With my brother on his heels."

"Precisely so. I observed it, sir."

"Do you think he'll harm him?"

The old man looked embarrassed. "I, er, really cannot say. Nicholas is reputed to drink blood, sir. I cannot testify to the truth of the accusation."

Toby returned, having failed to find you or any trace of you. I slept, after having taken various precautions to secure my bedroom. Nicholas, the old man had assured me, would never attack the owner of the house. I took those precautions anyway, and fell into bed exhausted.

_____

Yours sincerely,
Bax

PS: I debated long before resolving to write this, George. Not because I would not wish you to know it, but because Millie will certainly read it. After a good breakfast and a short walk I have decided to come clean (as we used to say in the place to which you condemned me). Millie has read worse already.

Winker joined me in bed. I had locked and barricaded both doors, shut and secured the dampers of the fireplaces, locked the windows, and taken various other precautions.

Yet she was there. At first I thought I might have dreamed it, but there was a painted fan on the floor on her side of the bed. That fan certainly was not there when I retired.

Later. I have resolved to enlist all the help I can in searching for you. Doris is willing to help, but only in my company.

Martha will join us, and has asked me to join her in search of her son Emlyn. I am more than willing to do so, since Emlyn and his tri-annulus may be of great service to us.

Madame Orizia is here already, and has gone off with Toby.

Bax, you cowardly bastard, I have been looking all over for you. I want that house of yours. I want it but most of all I want to be rid of you.

Forever.

I met a wonderful girl who really knows her way around that place. There is gold there and the gold is just for starters. A man could organize things. Pretty soon I will have a country of my own. President for Life in a country where nobody gets old and dies. You could never swing it, Bax, but I could. I can. *I will.*

But I need that house. I need to own it, so I can come and go. And I am going to own it.

Here is what I propose. You have those damn pistols. I mean the ones that lawyer pointed at me. Fine. You had taken them but I got your butler to show me the case with the powder flasks and all the little tools.

You and I will fight it out with those. Back in those big woods nobody will ever find the body. You know the woods I mean.

But first we make wills. You leave all your property to me. I leave all mine to you. That's nearly a million, plus my house, my cabin on the lake, that damned beach cottage Millie likes so much, the cars, the SUV, and my boat.

So do we fight? It will be fair and all that. Just like a game. Do we settle things once and for all? Or are you scared?

George

Dear Millie:

Wonderful news! Let me tell you how it happened. I went into my bedroom, and there was Winker looking as sly as ever, with the Japanese sword she had given me on her lap. "You sleep good, Bax?"

"So did you," I told her.

"Oh, no! No-no!" She giggled and snapped open her fan. "No sleep at all. Busy-busy! I looked for George."

"Have you found him?"

"Almost." She grinned. "I found someone who'll teach you how to find him."

"Really?"

"Yes! Really!" She jumped up and handed me the sword. "Put this on. Manjushri's very wise. He knows, you look!"

I have mentioned the Oriental screen that conceals one of the bedroom fireplaces? Winker swung back the center panel of that screen like a door. It was pitch-black in there, but we went in.

"It's night," she said. "Night without moon or stars. That's ignorance, see?"

As I told her, I could not see a thing.

"You need a light. I'll find one for you."

We walked on, I would guess a mile or more. At last Winker halted and knocked on a door I could not see.

I heard the hinges creak, and she spoke rapidly to someone inside, saying that I was a seeker of wisdom, that she was my guide, and that we required a light.

An old woman emerged carrying a paper lantern. By its watery light I saw that Winker and I had been walking down a road bordered by flooded fields thick with grain.

We walked on, the old woman hurrying before us, taking many short steps very quickly and rocking from side to side as she walked. Our road grew less level and less straight.

Three young men with swords blocked our path, shouting that we must halt. "You are no samurai!" exclaimed the first.

"Yet you bear a sword!" shouted the second.

"You must fight us!" the third declared.

Winker bowed low. "My master is no samurai, as you say. Any samurai will defeat him easily. Therefore, let not the most renown among you engage him, rather let the least renown and least skillful."

They quarreled among themselves as to whom the least renown and least skilled might be, and we slipped past them. When darkness had closed behind us and I could no longer see them, I heard the whistling stroke of a long blade and an agonized cry.

Gray light filled the sky, and I found that we walked among rugged hills dotted with wind-twisted pines. Winker dismissed our lantern-bearer, giving her a string of small coins. At the summit of the ridge we climbed stood a lone man, not large, with two swords.

"I am Miyamoto Musashi," he told us when we had come nearer. "I am the greatest samurai. To reach the shrine, you must pass me."

I bowed. "I am no samurai, only a humble man seeking wisdom; but if I must fight you to find my brother, I will fight you."

"You I fear," Miyamoto Musashi said, and stepped aside.

I bowed again, Winker bowed, and we walked past him. When we were within sight of the shrine, I said, "Why would he fear me?"

"For two reasons," Winkle told me. "First, you know nothing about the sword and might do the unexpected."

"I see."

"Also he would win no glory if he killed you, but would lose face if you win."

As I nodded, a booming voice echoed from the rocks, seeming to come from everywhere: *"The third. The Eternal Presence would favor such a one."*

I looked around. Winker and I were alone on the road.

"Enter the gate and pray. Within, all is holy."

I cannot say what got into me. Perhaps I ought to say that something came out that I had never known I contained. A wrong note had been struck in what I had just heard—let us leave it at that. It woke a new thought, and I said, "I see nothing here that is not holy."

Hands grasped my shoulders, hands far larger than mine and much stronger. They shook me ever so slightly, and released me; it was as though someone had slapped my back. "Ask." The voice was behind me now.

I turned. The being who stood behind me was a head taller than I and muscled like an athlete. Although his hands had been on my shoulders only a moment before, one held a book and the other a naked sword.

His head was the head of a lion.

Winker nudged me.

"I am looking for my brother George," I said. "How can I find him?"

"Tell me."

And so I told the lion-headed man a great deal about George and a great deal, too, about myself, ending with the note I had found that day.

"Read it, so that I may hear it."

I did.

"Read it more slowly, so that you may hear it."

I read it a second time, read it as if I were trying to memorize it. Which I was, Millie.

"Your brother struck you, and struck the woman."

I said, "Yes."

"You will find him when you and the woman he struck join forces. Not before."

We went home after that. The thing that I remember most about our walk back is the sun rising veiled in mist, a dull crimson disk coming out of the sea into a white sky.

I telephoned Kate Finn as soon as we returned. I had not said much when she suggested that we meet for lunch, saying she wanted to talk to me face to face. Since it was nearly noon by then I agreed, suggesting the Medicine Man Diner, only a short walk from my house.

We got a booth in a quiet corner, exchanged the usual pleasantries, and ordered.

"Now then," Kate said. "Let me get this straight. You want to hire me while I'm on leave?"

"Correct. Police officers often earn extra money by working while they're off duty. Security at rock concerts. All that sort of thing. You must be aware of it."

She nodded.

"I want you to help me find my brother. There can't be anything illegal about that, surely. I believe he's somewhere in my house. It's a big house, and I want you to help me search it."

"Hiding in your house."

"He may be hiding. Or he may not. I don't know."

"He came to live with you when he got out?"

I shook my head. "He went back to the Hilton. He'd taken a room there."

"He's not back there now?"

I shook my head again. "I telephoned them. He's checked out."

"He's probably gone back home."

I did not want to mention the note I had read to the lion-headed man, so I simply said that I did not think so. "He's supposed to stay in town."

"Right. In the jurisdiction. You know that, and I know that, and he knows that. But that doesn't mean he did it. Maybe he figures he can go home, get a lawyer, and fight extradition."

"In that case we won't find him—"

"No. In that case we will, because I'm going to get somebody at headquarters to ask your department to check on him for us. He could be back in jail, too. Did you think of that?"

"I should have. But no, I didn't."

She got out her cell phone while the waitress brought our sandwiches and French fries.

When she hung up, she said, "They haven't got him."

I said I was not surprised.

"I hate to let this get cold, but I'm calling headquarters."

When she had gotten through to a Sergeant Eastman she said, "There's a guy named George Dunn. We booked him for assault and resisting arrest. He got out on bail Tuesday?"

She had looked her question at me. I nodded.

"Yeah, Tuesday, and he seems to have skipped. Have a look around."

She put away her cell phone, and I said, "You didn't tell him to find out whether George had gone home."

"I didn't have to. He knows what to do. You're talking to me because this Japanese guy told you to?"

"That's correct. I have a Japanese friend. I told her what had happened, and she said that I ought to talk to this man. I did, and he said that the way to find George was to get you to help me search. I saw the wisdom of it and called you when I got home. I'll pay you two hundred dollars a day, starting today." I got out my wallet and laid four fifty-dollar bills on the table.

She picked them up, folded them over once, and put them into her purse. "Tell me again about the last time you saw him. The old car. You talked about it on the phone."

"There was an antique car in the garage when I got the house.

I don't have a title, but I assume it's mine—that it goes with the house."

"Sure. You can get one."

"I had an expert refurbish it. AAAA Autos of the World?"

Kate nodded. "I know them. Seems like a good outfit."

"They did a fine job, but they couldn't get into the trunk. I called a locksmith who promised to come over and open it without damaging it. As it happened, I was away from home when he came, but my houseman showed him the car. He picked the lock, but did not open the trunk. I suppose he was afraid I would accuse him of taking something from it. You look thoughtful."

"I am. You're an ex-con."

"Correct. I didn't know you knew."

"I checked up on you." Kate smiled. "Mom wants me to marry you."

"Really?"

"She keeps talking about how nice you are. And you are nice, but you're an ex-con and I tell her that to shut her up. You're an ex-con, first conviction, fraud. You've been out less than six months, and you've got a houseman."

"Yes. I do."

"Want to tell me about it?"

"No. You would begin investigating me. You would find nothing illegal, nor would you find George."

She laughed. "I'm not trying to snap the cuffs on you, Bax. What would Mom say? Let's hear more about the trunk."

"I returned home. George came. I think he had gone to his hotel room after he was released. Then he came to my house."

"Sure. Shower and clean clothes."

"We were standing outside when he heard something in the trunk— something moving around, he said. He opened it, and a man stepped out of it, a very tall, very thin man dressed in black. He said he was Nicholas, the butler, and went into my house. George pursued him. I haven't seen him since."

"This was at night?"

I nodded.

"Was the house well lit?"

"No. There were a few lights. Not many."

"Had you ever seen the man who got out of your trunk before? Don't answer straight off. Think."

"Absolutely not."

"Nowhere? Never? Describe his face."

"It was horrible, almost like a skull. Sunken cheeks. Big teeth showing through thin lips. White, as white as bone."

"Could it have been a mask? It sounds like one."

I considered. "Yes, it could have been. I don't believe it was."

"Uh-huh. Nicholas the Butler is a local legend. It sounds to me like somebody got dressed up as him and hid in your trunk after the locksmith opened it, then made noise so you'd let him out. Let's forget about that and worry about finding George. You think he's still in your house?"

"Yes. I do."

"Then we'll find him."

We searched, Millie, but we did not find George. Nor did we find Nicholas the Butler. We found a great many rooms, with and without furniture. There was a studio, a conservatory, a study, a workshop, a sunroom, two dressing rooms, a rather startling laboratory, and many more, most of which we could not identify.

But no George.

In the attic, I showed Kate (a Kate who was already stunned) Goldwurm's Spire. She said there was no such tower, and seemed to think the window glass a television or something of the sort. Together we opened the window. (It had been painted shut and took a good deal of effort.) The spire remained.

"I never saw anything like this," she said, "and I never expected to."

"There is a young man named Ieuan who used to go around breaking windows in this house," I told her. "He knew the windows would be boarded up, you see, and he didn't want anyone to see what these windows sometimes reveal."

"I think he was right," Kate told me. "If this gets out, somebody will burn down the house."

"You know, I hadn't thought of that."

"I won't tell anybody. Not even if you ask me to."

"It's bad luck to see the sea serpent," I said.

"I don't get that. In the river?"

"No, just a nineteenth-century saying. A captain who noted the sea serpent in his log had a hard time getting another command."

"Yeah." She nodded. "The old guys tell me every cop sees things he'd better not report. Same deal. Who's Goldwurm?"

"A warlock. It seems to mean a criminal sorcerer, one whose word cannot be trusted."

"I don't think I'd trust any of them."

"Nor would I. Emlyn—he's Ieuan's brother—told me that Gold-wurm murdered his old master, a sorcerer called Ambrosius. I seem to have his ring." I showed it to her.

"That's a nice stone."

"Thank you. It frightened my mother at first. She had known Ambrosius, and I think she must have liked him. He was a business rival of my father's when she and my father lived in this house. A friendly rival apparently."

We shut the window and went back downstairs. I showed Kate my car, and we had a look inside the trunk that had held Nicholas the Butler. After that, she called police headquarters.

"They've got him!" She gave me a broad grin. "Picked him up on the street. How about if I use some of your two hundred to buy you dinner?"

So you see, Millie, Winker was right to take me to the lion-headed man, and the lion-headed man himself was right when he counseled me to combine forces with Kate. George has been found and is safe in jail.

Which means that I myself am safe. Or at least safer. For the time being.

Forever your loving friend,
Bax

Hey, Prof!

I think you are worrying way too much about this duel thing. It is not coming off. That is my guess. To start with, I do not believe your brother is going to challenge you. In the second place, you can call the cops if he does. I would not do that with my record, but you could get away with it.

And in the third place, you can tell him to go to hell.

None of that makes you feel any better if I know you, and if I do not who does? Answer that one.

So okay. He challenges you, and you figure you had better fight because he's going to off you if you do not. You are doing the right thing by practicing. Here is three things you have got to take seriously in a nice list.

1. Your gun has got to say bang every time you pull the trigger. You know about that already, but I said it again anyway and what if his does not? Suppose there was a little dirt in the hole? You would not have to kill him, just shoot him in the leg or something. Why not?

2. Just about every gunfight is ten yards or under. So that is what you need to practice. Can you shoot fast and hit one of those targets with some guy's picture on it? That is what you need to do. Hold your gun tight, lay that front sight on him, and squeeze the trigger fast. If your trigger pull is pulling your sight off him, you are doing it wrong. Straight back, Bax, and a fast squeeze not a jerk. There is already a jerk on the other end. Two is too many.

3. Bad light. You go out to the range, and usually it is bright sunlight. Nobody can do it with no light at all. If it is pitch dark you got to have a flash, but he will shoot at it, so do not hold it in front of you. Mostly you can see but not very good. Practice like that. If the front sight does not show up, use the end of the barrel.

So fine. Now here is more. Cheat.

Hell, I cheat at Ping-Pong every chance I get. This is *your life*. He gets his gun and you get yours? He's going to shoot you, so shoot back first.

Only I do not think any of it will really come off. Take it easy. Be cool.

———————————

Sheldon Hawes

Dear Bax,
_____

This is very hard to write. I like you and I hope we will always be friends.

There was a time when I thought you might be my new partner for life, and yes, I wanted the money. Who would not?

Yes, I was hoping you would propose. It must have showed.

You were not particularly good in bed, but you were getting better but all this is just too crazy. You are crazy, your house is crazy, and when I am with you I am crazy too. I have the feeling that I am going to end up like poor Kiki, a crazy old woman living in a shack in the woods.

Besides, you were in prison.

So this is good-bye. I have quit my job at Country Hill. My brother lives in Minneapolis, and I am moving there. He will help me get settled.

———————

Good-bye,
Doris

PS: Please keep Ted's ring until I send you my new address. Then you can mail it to me.

Dear George:

I have remarkable news. You may not consider it good news, although it is in fact wonderful news; but you are bound to agree that it is remarkable.

It began with a telephone call from our mother. Come to think of it, I do not believe I have told you that Martha Murrey is our (biological) mother, but she is. The name "Mother," with the capital *M*, is one I will always reserve for Mama, our adoptive mother. I have always loved her and when I was released I would have starved if she had not accorded me an allowance.

Before going further, perhaps I should explain that Martha's last name was originally Murray. When she returned from faerie she wished to resume her maiden name, but changed one letter in order that her original family would not inquire about her background; she was, both in appearance and physiologically, much younger than her twin.

She telephoned me, as I said, and asked whether I had read the *Sentinel* that morning. I had not, and I said so. She then read an article to me. I do not have a copy, and I certainly do not remember the article word for word. I believe the headline was HELL-HOUND STRIKES AGAIN. The gist of it was that four high-school boys had been attacked by what they described as a huge wolf. They had fought it off and escaped in a van, but not before two had been badly bitten.

"That," Martha said, "was Emlyn's girlfriend. Emlyn is my son and your brother. We've got to do something."

"I agree," I said, "but what can we do?"

"Find him, find her, or find them both. If we find him, we'll take him to the hospital to see those kids. If we find her, kill her."

"And if we find them both? What if they're together?"

Martha sighed. "We'll have to play it by ear. Are you good at that?"

"Not particularly."

"I would've said you were. Now listen. This one's on page three."

The headline was AN OLD PROBLEM RESURFACES. Two poor families who shared a single house two miles down the river had complained that a tall man dressed in black was sucking their children's blood. I believe I can quote one of the closing paragraphs exactly.

> After interviewing adults (as well as two victims) of both families and studying the police report, your reporter inquired as to thefts of clotheslines and wash. There have been two such reports. All this is strongly reminiscent of stories concerning our local boogeyman, Nicholas the Butler, of forty years ago.

"What do you think, Bax? Is this the man George chased?"

"Yes." I sighed. "Absolutely. I just wish George had caught him. George is back in jail. Did you know?"

"I had no idea."

"He is, though I doubt that they'll keep him long. Have I told you I don't believe that our biological father meant for the two of us to duel? I know you think that."

"You're right, I do. You don't know him, Bax."

"Know Zwart? You're right, I don't. I'd like to."

"He has this thing about twins. I didn't leave him until Emlyn and Ieuan were old enough to run and argue, and he always wanted me to let them settle things between themselves."

I said (mildly, I hope), "He goes away and leaves them alone in my house—absents himself for protracted periods, I mean. Emlyn told me."

"That sounds like him. Why do you say he didn't want you and George to fight?"

"Because he put silver bullets in the bullet box. They couldn't have been easy to make; I think he must have gotten a jeweler to turn them on a lathe. You must shoot werewolves with silver bullets. Isn't that correct?"

"There are other ways to kill them, but silver bullets are one of the most practical."

"Lead bullets would be ineffective?"

"That's what I've been told."

"George isn't a werewolf, and neither am I. Possibly I ought to say here that I've fired each of those pistols several times for practice, but I didn't waste the silver bullets. Jim Hardaway gave me lead ones."

"I know him. Watch out."

"I will. I tried my best to search this house when I was looking for George."

"I believe you."

"Despite all my effort, I never even glimpsed him. I never saw Emlyn or Ieuan, either. I think they're probably here, but I never saw either of them."

"I think that's very likely."

"You told me once that you'd never been inside. That had to be a lie."

"It was. I—May I explain?"

"You don't have to, and I should have said falsehood or something of that sort."

"I didn't want you to know who I was. That I was your mother. You've been much kinder, much more forgiving, than I expected. Anyway, I lied. About that, and about other things. But I always tried to help you. I gave you the house, and hoped—hoped . . ."

"That I would learn about faerie and come to suspect the truth?"

"Yes."

"You lived in this house."

"Yes, when I was Zwart's wife. It was—it is—his castle. His tower. Whatever he wants it to be. It grows when people live in it, and shrinks when they don't."

"Very convenient."

"Very confusing, really, and we always needed more furniture. What are you getting at, Bax?"

"Could you have found George? Would you have been a better searcher than I was?"

"Probably not. What are you getting at?"

"Do you want to come here and search for Emlyn?"

Martha sighed so heavily that I could hear her even over the telephone. "Yes. That's why I called. It—it's probably hopeless, Bax, and I won't ask you to help. But yes, I do. It's why I called."

"I have a better idea, and I'd like you to help me with it. If it fails—and it may—I'll help you search the house for Emlyn. Doris Griffin and I went out to the Skotos Strip once. Do you know Doris?"

"Vaguely. She works for Jim Hardaway."

"She quit, but she was working for him at the time. We went there, and I found Lupine there. Lupine is the werewolf, the one—"

"I know."

"I want to go back there. Frankly, I doubt that we can achieve anything by talking to Emlyn. I've done that, and I failed. Talking to Lupine might work."

"Threatening her if necessary. Threats backed by silver bullets."

"Correct."

To my utter astonishment, Martha laughed. "You may be right, and it's certainly worth trying. I'm no witch, but you're a sorcerer—"

"No, I'm not."

"Yes, you are. You just don't know it. A sorcerer who doesn't know much magic, but a sorcerer just the same. Your father is a sorcerer, Bax, and talents are like twins. They run in families. Shall we take my car?"

I said I thought we'd have a better chance if we took mine.

After that, I put on the clothes I had bought before I went there with Doris. The pistols presented a problem—they were too big for any of my pockets. I loaded them and put them back in their case for the time being, called in the old man, and told him where I was going and why. "I'll leave my cell phone on this time," I promised, "so you can call me if anything comes up. Try to stay close to our own telephone, so I can call you if I need to."

"I shall, sir. May I send Toby with you?"

I hesitated.

"You go to hunt a wolf, sir. A good dog can be most helpful in hunting wolves."

"All right. Thank you."

"Will you take your sword, sir?"

"I hadn't intended to."

"I advise it, sir. I am, um, unfamiliar with swords. Even so, I know that when gentlemen used such pistols as you have, pistols that could be fired but once, they wore swords as well. It was thought prudent."

"You're right, of course. I'll do it."

"I wish you the best of luck, sir. I hope to see you return triumphant."

I put the cased pistols under the seat, and put the Fox Sword in the compartment intended for golf clubs. By the time I had closed and latched it, Toby arrived to perch on the seat next to mine, a dog notably small and scruffy.

The engine sprang to life at the first touch of the starter button, which seemed a good omen; we were about to pull out of the drive when he was joined by Winkle. "Do you know where we're going?" I asked her.

"Thee Martha."

"To pick her up. After that, we'll be looking for Lupine. Lupine chased you once."

"Yeth."

"You don't have to come."

"Neither do you, Bakth."

We found Lupine near the river, as I had anticipated—or rather, Toby did. ("We" meaning my middle-aged mother, a sharp-eyed little footman, a very pretty Japanese girl in a silk kimono and high, wooden getas, and your long-suffering twin with a remarkably heavy sword in his belt and a pistol in each hand.) She laughed at us.

"Those guns," Martha told her, "are loaded with silver bullets. If he were to shoot me with them, I might live. For you they will be certain death."

"They will not be," Lupine told her, "because he will not shoot me. Look upon me, Bax. Am I not young? And beautiful?"

I nodded.

"You could not shoot such a one. You have dreamed of one like me far too often."

"Try me," I said.

"As you wish." She rose from the log upon which she had been lying, and let the shaggy hide she wore slip until one breast was bare. "Here I am!" She spread her arms. "Shoot! Prove your manhood."

I did not.

"You see? Let us have no more threats."

"This is not a threat," I told her. "It is a remark. I spent three years in the penitentiary. I don't think you know what you're dealing with."

Martha said, "My son is telling the truth. As for me, I spent about forty years here as a sorcerer's wife. You are underestimating me as well."

"There's the facefox, too." Lupine grinned. "And a cute little doggy. I could not underestimate the four of you. No estimate could be low enough."

I made a mistake then, George, and a bad one. I gave my pistols to Martha and my sword to Winker before I rushed Lupine, and she was ready. Ready, and much stronger than I had supposed. She broke my grip and knocked me down, then sprang at Winker.

No doubt her intention was to close with Winker before she had time to draw the Fox Sword, but Winker only dropped it and met her with her bare hands. A moment later, Lupine was flying over Winker's hip to land heavily and head down in the underbrush.

I landed there, too—intentionally, and on top of Lupine. I got her by the hair and pulled her head back. With my right knee between her shoulders, she could not rise.

"The skin!" Martha shrieked. "Get the skin, Bax! Pull it off!"

I was much too busy holding Lupine down to do that, but Toby and Winker got it. They got it; and when they did, Lupine howled. It froze my blood; but I jerked her head again back, then shoved it forward as hard as I could to make her stop.

Martha shouted, "We have to burn this!"

She shouted it, I believe; but I scarcely heard her. I was drawing my big camp knife.

"Wolf lady," Winkle whispered. "Will it work?"

"I don't know," I told her. "Let's see." I tried its edge on Lupine's hair, and Lupine screamed.

"It cuts lovely!"

The edge was still quite sharp, and it did cut with a little muscle behind it, sawing through black hairs that seemed as hard as wires. Leather and fur reek when burned almost as much as feathers. A whiff of their smoke reached me and I began to cough.

That was when the first wolf came bounding out of the trees. I remember the boom of Martha's shot, but almost nothing else. As though by magic, I had the Fox Sword. It cut the wolves like weeds, but the blood that spurted from those cuts was scarlet and hot as fever.

"Hold, friends!" That was Lupine, naked and with half her hair shorn but even so seeming more wolf than woman. "We have them! Ring them!"

We were not exactly surrounded, but our backs were to the water and we were hemmed by the wolves on three sides. Martha held two empty pistols, I the Fox Sword, Toby the camp knife I had dropped, and Winker nothing.

"If we charge them," Lupine told her wolves, "a few more of us will die before we kill the one with the sword. I shall save those lives. Watch!"

Something—a human head—rolled out of the water and came to rest at her feet. "You," Lupine told me, "have seen this already. The rest have not. Want to tell them?" Two rotting arms (one a man's and the other, I believe, a woman's) dragged a torso across the mud toward the head.

Martha said, "You don't have to, my son. I've heard enough about these things to guess the rest." It was the first time she had called me that; I was quite touched.

"I'll soon have half a dozen." Lupine grinned. "Would you like to hear my terms of surrender?"

My cell phone rang as she spoke. I asked her to excuse me and answered it.

"Mr. Baxter Dunn?"

"Speaking," I said.

"This is Nicholas, sir. Your butler."

"Nicholas?"

"The same. I am unable to serve you at present, sir, as I have returned to my trunk."

"I—see . . ."

"Most gratifying, sir. I was, ahhh . . ."

"Yes?"

"Thus confined by my old master, sir. By Mr. Zwart. He, ahhh . . ."

I said, "Please, Nicholas. I'm really quite busy."

"Was assisted by your brother George, sir, and by two ladies. It is galling, sir, to find oneself hemmed by mere women."

"No doubt it is." I was watching Lupine as I spoke; a second walking corpse was assembling itself, no doubt under her direction. I said, "May I ask how you come to have a telephone, Nicholas?" Gray and black werewolves paced to-and-fro, their scarlet tongues lolling, their yellow eyes fixed on us.

"My captivity was a matter of negotiation, sir."

"I see."

"Your brother had a stake, sir. A stake, and an ahh . . ."

"Yes?"

"A sledge, sir. Though for a moment I thought that it might have been an ax. Either will serve, sir. One drives the stake with the back of the ax."

"I'll keep it in mind."

"The pain is excruciating, sir. Quite excruciating, and it endures until the stake rots away. I declared my intention to resist, sir. To resist, and to exact revenge should I be released."

"Admirable."

"Thank you, sir. I agreed to return to my trunk, provided that I was accorded a telephone with which I might communicate with you, sir, stating my case as it were. One of the ladies proffered hers. Thus the matter was settled without undue acrimony. Since then, however, I have received numerous calls from persons wishing to learn whether there have been offers on their homes."

Martha tapped my shoulder and I said, "I really must go now, Nicholas. Call again tomorrow, if you wish."

"Your brother wishes to kill you as well, sir. Be warned."

"Magic," Martha whispered breathlessly, "is diplomacy. It isn't just saying the words. It's who says them, how he says them, and when he says them."

I nodded.

Lupine shouted, "Give us the woman, the fox, and the dog, and we'll spare you."

I shook my head.

Martha whispered, "Raise both arms. Point that sword at the sun. Repeat what I say loudly and with authority."

Lifting my arms, I nodded.

"*Hewwo tohgodt'keyah wokpah wechoshtah.*"

"HewWO! TohGODt'keyah! WokPAH! WeCHOSHtah!" I would have said that I was almost shouting, George, until the final word; but *wechoshtah* emerged as something far greater than a shout. You will not believe me, but a lion might have spoken as I spoke then.

Lupine looked stunned, and one of her wolves howled. I heard the howl before the drum, but I suspect the wolf had heard it before me. Its thudding note was deep and dull, but loud and near.

We had our backs to the river, as I said. Thus we were looking toward the wooded slope. Lupine stood with her back to the slope, and so did not see a broad, hairy face peer through the leaves. And another.

And another.

One snarled, displaying frightful fangs. Another must have stepped forward at the same time. I did not see it until the wolf it held by one hind leg struck the ground.

It struck it, was raised again, and slammed down as if the huge hairy man who held it were beating the ground with a club. At the second blow, all the wolf-likeness fell away, leaving only a middle-aged man, half conscious and trying (I think) to shield his head.

After that the battle was joined. I remember seeing Winker kick and strike Lupine while Toby buried his teeth in her heel. I remember Martha with a wolf at her throat, and the blue fire of the Fox Sword.

But very little beyond that.

Suddenly, it was over. The dead limbs were only dead limbs. Half a dozen dead men and dead women lay scattered among them, and the remaining wolves had fled. Two of the hairy giants faded back into the forest. The third looked at me, touched his forehead, and followed them.

They are as muscular as gorillas, George, but stand erect, like men. Their height cannot be less than eight feet.

"You have seen the Riverman," Martha told me. "Not many can say that."

I was looking at Lupine. Her nose was streaming blood, and one arm had clearly been broken. Dirty and bruised and naked, she struggled to sit up and would not have been able to sit up if I had not helped her.

"I should have done that," Emlyn said. He had been hiding in the scrub next to the water. He knelt beside Lupine and put his arm around her shoulders.

"Here." It was a second Emlyn, an Emlyn naked to the waist offering his shirt and a stick. "We'd better splint that arm."

"They're not such bad boys, are they?"

I whirled at the sound of a familiar voice. The old man was coming toward us, not leaning on his crutch now, but walking with it as a hiker does with a staff. Sunshine gleamed gold upon its gold head.

Martha said, "Hello, Zwart. We could have used you earlier."

"You would not have had me." He turned to me. "There comes a time when a sorcerer must triumph on his own or die. You have triumphed, son."

I tried to say that I had not, that I would have been killed but for Martha and the Rivermen.

"You used such allies as you had gained. It is what we do."

"I won because my mother helped me."

"The mother who would have died, if you had not won."

Martha nodded, and her hand slipped into mine.

"I greet you as my son, but also as a brother sorcerer. What are we going to do about George?"

The abrupt change of subject disconcerted me, but I managed to say that I saw no need to do anything about you, that you could take care of yourself.

"You have talent. I saw it early, and that's why I gave you this forest. George doesn't. You'll need to be aware of that."

Martha's voice was almost a whisper. "May I come back, darling?"

Zwart turned toward her, smiling. "I've been hoping you would for years."

"I will. Do you want my house, Bax?"

I shook my head; and Zwart laughed, saying, "He has mine already."

"I'm hoping that you'll stay here, where you grew up. At least for a while."

Perhaps I nodded. Winker pressed herself against me.

"I was so afraid of faerie, of warlocks and witches and the ghoul-bears. Of the dragons, and all the rest of it. I had a best friend. Have you ever had a best friend, Bax?"

I know I nodded then. "He's still in prison."

"Mine was Nina O'Brien. She—she's dead. The paper was full of the Horror Hound, and Nina got one paragraph in the obituaries. Just one paragraph. She was crossing the street and she was run down like a dog."

I said something inane.

"There's the Horror Hound over there, that poor girl with the broken arm and the bloody nose." Martha sighed. "You stay where you grew up until you come to understand it, Bax. Then join us in faerie."

I said I would.

Zwart had gone to speak to Lupine, and Toby had followed him. Martha and I followed him, too, after I finished hugging her.

"She pledged her soul to get that skin," Zwart was telling Emlyn. "Now she has none, and she knows it. Look into her eyes."

"I have," Emlyn said. "Lots of times."

"Many times? So you think. Are you going to try to get it back?"

"If you think I have a chance."

"You will have to do it. I won't help you. It will take a great sorcerer, learned, cunning, and bold."

"I understand, Father."

"Even a great sorcerer may lose his life. Or his soul. You understand that, too, but I felt compelled to tell you just the same. Now here is something you don't understand, although you should. When you get her soul back—I said when, not if—she may pledge it again, for another skin or for something else."

Lupine shook her head, a blood-soaked rag pressed to her nose, her right arm stiff and straight, and bound to the stick Ieuan had brought.

That is all my wonderful news, George. I found our father, who used to be the butler whose presence in my house so greatly disturbed you. I know that you did not find him, that it was as Nick, my elderly butler, that he cornered Nicholas. Cornered him, that is, with your help and that of the "two ladies."

I found our father as I had found our mother already, although I did not have an opportunity to tell you. They have been reunited—more wonderful news, is it not?

Emlyn loves Lupine and will become a sorcerer of great wisdom and power for her sake. What she may become, God only knows.

Ieuan has promised to assist Emlyn, to whom he feels inferior. (Most of his "badness" proceeds from that, I believe.) Zwart tells me he is maturing more slowly, but says, "The weeds shoot up. The acorn's child will tower above their generations."

Nicholas told me you want to kill me, and you had told me the same thing in your note. I do not believe either of you, George, although you may believe you wrote the truth. When you stand before me holding a pistol (if it comes to that), you will surely realize your mistake. Then you and I will clasp hands as brothers should.

Yours sincerely,
Bax

Number 42
A Terrible Mistake

Dearest Bax,

I have been trying to telephone you, the landline in my apt. I press your number up to the last button, then I realize I have no idea what to say.

Really I have a hundred and know I will try to say all of them at the same time and you will think I am drunk.

Well, maybe I am. I saw Ted, Bax. I was starting to pack and I went out to the kitchen to get plastic bags, and when I came back to my bedroom Ted was sitting on the bed, crying.

I jumped back and shut the door. After that I went back to the kitchen and found an old bottle of tequila and poured myself a shot that damned near knocked my head off. If there had been more in the bottle, I think I would have emptied it, but that shot had emptied it already. I ran the bottle through the garbage disposal just to have something to do while I got up the nerve to go back to the bedroom.

He was gone, but he had left something behind. I will not say what it was but it was wet and had his initials in the corner, TAG.

Did he say anything to me? No, not one word. Did he leave a note? Maybe I should say he did. It would be a good lie. Do you know what I mean?

Because I *know* why he was crying, Bax. Laugh all you want, but I know. He wanted us to be together and thought it would happen, and now everything has fallen to bits.

When I found the thing that I found I started crying, too. I still have not stopped, so that is another reason for not phoning you.

Bax, I made a terrible, terrible mistake.

I love you.

I love you, and if you never forgive me and we never have dinner again or ride in your big old car I will still love you just the same. I know I must have hurt you terribly. Please forgive me.

Phone or write or ring my doorbell. That would be the best of all. I am staying right here, and I am pretty sure I can get my old job back.

———————

Your Doris

PS: It was just you and I against the werewolves. Do you remember that? Nobody else. Your basement is just so awful, but I would go down there again if you were going.

I went to your house after I finished this letter. I could not phone but I thought that if I could just hold you and kiss you it might be all right. Your butler gave me a crucifix and a garlic necklace and got me to help him hunt Nicholas. The other hunters were your brother George (I still do not like him) and Mrs. Pogach, the fat lady the dwarf tried to rape. We cornered Nicholas and he agreed to go into the trunk (tied on the back of your car) and let us close it if we would give him a cell phone.

So I let him have mine. He wanted that one because it had both your numbers on the speed-dial feature.

He got into the trunk and George fastened the straps and catches but he could not work the lock. Your butler got it to lock somehow, tho.

After that the fat lady and I went to her hotel room and ordered room service and talked. I gave her my card. I needed to get Nicholas out of my mind, his eyes and those long arms and big hands, and talking to her helped. Now I am going to bed, but I wish I could say we.

Mr. Dunn:

I have returned home. I hope you found my note.

As others will certainly have told you, I was able to locate the center of the disturbance at your home, a vampire. I compelled him to yield, and locked him in an old trunk. These creatures, as perhaps you know, are quite difficult to kill, as they are already dead. One treats them as one treats other ghosts, compelling or persuading them to find a more suitable abode.

I would suggest that you dispose of this one by posting the trunk to a museum out of state. They will almost certainly open it. Should they return the trunk to you, do not open it. It might be best to refuse delivery.

In the course of my search for the vampire, I covered your home quite thoroughly, finding nothing amiss save he. I therefore consider your case closed, at least for the time being.

As you will recall I promised to charge you no fee. This in connection with Mr. Quorn. It is with some regret that I must ask you to refund my travel costs. An itemized list is attached. $4,387.76 will cover everything.

Should you have further need of my services, do not hesitate to contact me.

Yours truly,
Mrs. O. Pogach
"Madame Orizia"

Number 44

HOME!

My Darling Millie:
_____

I feel sure you thought you would never receive a single letter from me. Now here I sit with pen and paper. I could not resist after our telephone conversation. You could not keep track of everything, you said, and wanted me to write it down.

So I will.

The chief thing is that we will never see my brother Bax again. He is in faerie, and he will stay there.

Bax is not a bad fellow. I know that now, and know that I was often too hard on him—and too hard on you for that matter. In future I am going to take a page from his book. You will find me much easier to get along with, a more kind and much more loving George.

This one probably seems bigger to me than to you. I am going to quit my job. You and I are well off, as I am sure you must realize. We have saved and invested wisely. We do not need the money.

Besides, I have a new job now—managing Bax's properties. (I hold his power of attorney.) The Skotos Strip alone is worth millions, and there are two houses, a checking account, and large savings accounts in three banks. He will certainly remain in faerie, so I shall have him declared dead in seven years. His will (I have that, too) leaves everything to me, but that "me" means the two of us, Millie. It will be our community property under the law.

Those are the major matters. Here are the minor ones.

I will not be able to return home immediately, as I had hoped. My trial was today. I pled guilty as charged, expressed my utter remorse, and threw myself upon the mercy of the court. Kate Finn—God bless her!—said under oath that she forgave me, and urged the judge to be merciful "to this first-time offender." (I dropped my police brutality charge against her partner two days ago.)

My sentence was thirty days of community service, which will mean reading to children at the library and telling them stories. There are a great many grand old Victorian tales that will be fresh and new to children today. I plan to begin with *Mopsa the Fairy*, and I would like to work in more than a few of Charles Dickens's greatest scenes involving children. We must have Oliver Twist and the Artful Dodger, of course. Then there is *The Old Curiosity Shop*, which is simply crammed with appealing children: Little Nell, Kit Nubbles, and the Marchioness. Nor can I forget Tiny Tim. As you can tell, I am really looking forward to my month. If it were not for you, I might ask the judge to extend it.

As for telling stories, well, I have actually been in faerie myself. I doubt that Jacob and Wilhelm Grimm could say that. A few hours in faerie—but perhaps it is better not to speak of it.

Well, well! I am a convicted felon now, like my poor brother. The mills of the gods grind slowly, Millie, but they grind exceeding small. If I did not quit the company, I might very well be fired. But I will leave quietly, and not put our exalted CEO and his retinue to the trouble. I have already written my letter of resignation, which I shall mail with this. You will be seeing me again before much longer. What would you say to a cruise around the world then? The Caribbean, Central America, New Zealand, Australia, India . . . You know.

From what you said on the telephone, Bax must have mentioned the duel I proposed in one of his letters. You will certainly want to know the outcome; but I can offer only anticlimax, and not much of that. We did not fight. Neither of us really wanted to, and when the moment arrived that became very clear.

Let me see . . . What else? Have I said that I love you very, very much? Let me say it again: I adore you, Millie, and I cannot possibly say it too often. You are surely the kindest woman in the world, as well as the most beautiful.

I will be bringing home Bax's Japanese sword, by the way. He gave it to me to remember him by. It is ancient, quite lovely in its deadly way, and very valuable.

Will it upset you to learn that I may bring home an animal, too? Bax's pet fox seems to have attached herself to me. I do not confine her, you understand. She is free to roam the woods whenever she chooses. But I could not find it in my heart to abandon her. I shall take her to our summer place on the lake and leave her there, unless you have a better suggestion. You will rarely see her, and are quite certain to be pleased when you do. Someone once said that all animals are beautiful, each in its own way. I find I cannot agree, but one sleek red fox more than makes up for half a dozen hogs and a team of mules.

Europe is another possibility. We might start with Moscow, go on to Krakow, Berlin, Vienna, and Paris. You would love to shop in Paris, I know; and I would love to watch you do it. Then Rome, Florence, Venice, Barcelona, and London. And so home. You will notice that I have said nothing about Athens. That is because I see Greece and the Mediterranean as a separate trip. What do you think?

Soon—very soon—I will be in your arms.

Your adoring husband,
George

COMPILER'S NOTE

The vast majority of the letters that make up this book were loaned to me by Mrs. Millicent Kay Dunn. Some had been the property of her husband, George J. Dunn, who vanished two years ago. (Her brother-in-law, Baxter Dunn, the author of the majority of these letters, had vanished still earlier and is legally dead.) I cannot adequately express my gratitude to Mrs. Dunn.

I also wish to thank Mrs. Orizia Pogach, who turned over to me the letters she had received from Baxter Dunn.

Finally, thanks are due to Mrs. Tina Hawes Kojac, who answered one of my advertisements and very graciously agreed to sell me the letters her late father, "Shotgun" Sheldon Hawes, had received from his former cellmate.

Baxter Dunn's letters are given here almost word for word. Some of the other letters in this book have required extensive corrections as to spelling, syntax, and grammar. Footnotes indicating these would be bothersome and of small or no real value. I have tried to retain the native flavor (if it may be described in that way) of the originals, the naïveté and tenderness of Mrs. Dunn's, for example.

After a prolonged period of soul-searching, I have chosen to omit dates. Baxter Dunn dated his letters only rarely, and at least half the dates he provided were clearly incorrect. Sheldon Hawes never dated his. In short, I have disregarded such dates as I had, and have tried to arrange these letters in a (not *the*) logical order.

I have made strenuous efforts to locate the Japanese sword mentioned by George J. Dunn, without result. To the best of Mrs. Dunn's recollection her husband kept it in a metal chest (or locker) in the basement of their summer home. There I discovered a vertical storage cabinet with a combination lock. It was, alas, quite empty. Collectors of such weapons have been unable to assist me, although I have made extensive inquiries. It would seem to have been a Japanese sword of the earliest type, a *ken*, having a straight, single-edged blade. Mr. Kisho Kurofuji, an acknowledged expert on early Japanese swords, tells me that this one (as described by Mrs. Dunn and others) can hardly date later than the twelfth century.

The Black House still stands, but it is a private residence not open to visitors. The Skotos Strip has become the suburb of Riverscene. In a few cases I have changed names to protect innocent persons.

Baxter Dunn was unquestionably a most imaginative and picturesque liar, but all that he tells us cannot be false. By some means he came into possession of Riverscene, the Black House, and the house that had been Mrs. Martha Murrey's. The back files of the *Sentinel* fairly bristle with Hound of Horror stories.

How much is true? How much fabrication? Perhaps we shall never know.

Significant Names

All persons of importance mentioned in these letters are listed here, with some of lesser significance.

Ambrosius A murdered sorcerer.
Black, Emlyn The sorcerer's son who dropped his father's triannulus.
Black, Ieuan Emlyn Black's identical twin brother.
Black, Zwart A previous owner of the Black House.
Dunn, Baxter A scholar whose career has been blighted by a conviction for fraud. He is the author of the majority of these letters.
Dunn, George J. Baxter Dunn's identical twin brother.
Dunn, Millicent Kay George J. Dunn's wife.
Finn, Biddy A police widow.
Finn, Kate A policewoman, Biddy Finn's daughter.

Goldwurm A warlock.

Griffin, Doris Rose A real-estate agent.

Griffin, Ted Doris Griffin's late husband.

Hardaway, Jim The head of the Country Hill Real-Estate Agency.

Hawes, Sheldon "Shotgun" Baxter Dunn's former cellmate.

Jacobs, Jake A real-estate agent.

Kiki An elderly woman befriended by Baxter Dunn and Doris Griffin.

King, Mary A hitchhiker.

Lupine A werewolf.

Manjushri A personification of wisdom.

Miyamoto Musashi A great samurai, the author of *A Book of Five Rings*.

Murrey, Martha The operator of a one-woman real-estate agency.
    (Murrey is a dark purple, very close to black.)

Mutazz The operator of the Riverman Motel.

Naber, Thelma Baxter Dunn's nearest neighbor.

Nick The old man who becomes Baxter Dunn's butler.

Nilsen, Les A locksmith.

Paxton, Star The first victim of the Hound of Horror.

Perrotta, Dominick A policeman, Kate Finn's partner.

Pogach, Orizia "Madame Orizia," a psychic.

Quist, Dick A jeweler.

Quorn A malevolent dwarf.

Ruth, Cathy A newspaper reporter.

Skotos, Alexander An eccentric gun collector.

Toby Nick's dog.

Trelawny, Urban The attorney for the Skotos Estate.

Winker Baxter Dunn's name for a friendly Japanese girl.

Winkle Baxter Dunn's pet fox.